TEXAS TRUE

Don't miss any of Janet Dailey's bestsellers:

Christmas in Cowboy Country
Merry Christmas, Cowboy
A Cowboy Under My Christmas Tree
Always with Love
Bannon Brothers: Honor
Bannon Brothers: Trust
American Destiny
American Dreams
Because of You
Calder Storm
Can't Say Goodbye
Close to You
Crazy in Love
Dance with Me
Everything
Forever
Green Calder Grass
Lone Calder Star
Lover Man
Masquerade
Mistletoe and Molly
Santa in a Stetson
Something More
Stealing Kisses
Tangled Vines
Texas Kiss
That Loving Feeling
To Santa with Love
When You Kiss Me
Yes, I Do
You're Still the One
Heiress
Rivals
Let's Be Jolly
Maybe This Christmas
Happy Holidays
Scrooge Wore Spurs
Eve's Christmas
Searching for Santa
Santa in Montana
Calder Promise
Shifting Calder Wind
Going My Way
It Takes Two
Happily Ever After
Try to Resist Me
Bring the Ring
Ranch Dressing
With This Kiss
Wearing White
Man of Mine

TEXAS TRUE

JANET DAILEY

KENSINGTON BOOKS
www.kensingtonbooks.com

KENSINGTON BOOKS are published by

Kensington Publishing Corp.
119 West 40th Street
New York, NY 10018

All Kensington titles, imprints, and distributed lines are available at special quantity discounts for bulk purchases for sales promotion, premiums, fund-raising, educational, or institutional use.

Special book excerpts or customized printings can also be created to fit specific needs. For details, write or phone the office of the Kensington Special Sales Manager: Attn. Special Sales Department. Kensington Publishing Corp., 119 West 40th Street, New York, NY 10018. Phone: 1-800-221-2647.

ISBN-13: 978-0-7582-9395-4
ISBN-10: 0-7582-9395-X
First Kensington Trade Edition: August 2014

eISBN-13: 978-0-7582-9394-7
eISBN-10: 0-7582-9394-1
First Kensington Electronic Edition: August 2014

10 9 8 7 6 5 4 3 2 1

Printed in the United States of America

TEXAS TRUE

PROLOGUE

When Virgil "Bull" Tyler left this life, it was said that his departing spirit roared like a norther across the yellowed spring pastureland, shrilled upward among the buttes and hoodoos of the Caprock Escarpment, and lost itself in the cry of a red-tailed hawk circling above the high Texas plain.

Later on, folks would claim they'd felt Bull's passing like a sudden chill on the March wind. But his son Will Tyler had felt nothing. Busy with morning chores, Will was unaware of his father's death until he heard the shouts of the husky male nurse who came in every morning to get the old man out of bed and into his wheelchair.

Will knew at once what had happened. By the time his long strides carried him to the rambling stone ranch house, he'd managed to brace for what he would find. All the same, the sight of that once-powerful body lying rigid under the patchwork quilt, the lifeless blue eyes staring up at the ceiling, hit him like a kick in the gut. He'd lived his whole thirty-nine years in his father's shadow. Now the old man was gone. But the shadow remained.

"Do you want me to call nine-one-one?" The young man was new to the ranch. Bull had gone through a parade of hired caregivers in the six years since a riding accident had shattered his spine, paralyzing his hips and legs.

"What for?" Will pulled the sheet over his father's face. In the movies, somebody would've closed those eyes. In real life, Will knew for a fact that it didn't work.

"We'll need to call somebody," the nurse said. "The county coroner, maybe? They'll want to know what killed him."

Alcohol and pain pills, Will surmised. But what the hell, there were protocols to be followed. "Fine, go ahead and call," he said. "I'll be outside if you need me."

Bernice Crawford, the plump, graying widow who'd been the Tylers' cook and housekeeper since Will's boyhood, met him in the hall. Tears were streaming down her apple-cheeked face. "Oh, Will! I'm so sorry!"

"I know." Will searched for words of comfort for her. "Dad thought the world of you, Bernice."

"He was a miserable old man," she said. "You know that as well as I do. But he carried the burden God gave him, and now he's free of it."

Will gave her shoulder an awkward squeeze before he turned away and strode toward the front door. He needed fresh air. And he needed time to gather his thoughts.

He made it to the wide, covered porch before the raw reality slammed home. Setting his jaw, he gripped the rail and forced himself to breathe. His father was dead. He felt the void left by Bull's passing—and the weight of responsibility for this ranch and everyone on it that was now his to shoulder alone.

The morning breeze carried the smells of spring—thawing manure, sprouting grass, and restless animals. Hammer blows rang from the hollow beyond the barn, where the hands were shoring up the calving pens for the pregnant heifers that had been bred a week ahead of the older cows. The rest of the cattle that had wintered in the canyon would soon need rounding up for the drive to spring pasture above the escarpment on the Llano Estacado, the Staked Plain, given that name by early Spaniards because the land was so flat and desolate that they had to drive stakes in the ground to keep from losing their way.

Looking down from the low rise where the house stood, Will

let his gaze sweep over the heart of the sprawling Rimrock Ranch—the vast complex of sheds, corrals, and barns, the hotel-like bunkhouse for unmarried hands, the adjoining cookhouse and commissary, and the line of neat brick bungalows for workers with families. To the east, a shallow playa lake glittered pale aquamarine in the sunlight. It made a pretty sight, but the water was no good to drink. With the summer heat it would evaporate, leaving behind an ugly white patch of alkali where nothing would grow.

Will scowled up at the cloudless sky. Last summer's drought had been a nightmare. If no rain fell, the coming summer could be even worse, with the grass turning to dust and the cattle having to be sold off early, at a pittance on the plummeting beef market.

Will had managed the ranch for the past six years and done it as competently as his father ever had. But even from his wheelchair, Bull had been the driving spirit behind Rimrock. Now that Bull was gone, Will felt the full burden of his legacy.

"Looks like we'll be planning a funeral." The dry voice startled Will before he noticed the old man seated in one of the rocking chairs with Tag, the ranch Border collie, sprawled at his feet. Jasper Platt, Bernice's older brother, had been foreman since before Will was born. Now that rheumatism kept him out of the saddle, he was semiretired. But Will still relied on him. No one understood the ranch and everything on it, including the people, the way Jasper did.

"When did you find out?" Will asked.

"About the same time you did." Jasper was whip spare and tough as an old saddle. His hair was an unruly white thatch, his skin burned dark as walnut below the pale line left by his hat. The joints of his fingers were knotted with arthritis.

"You'd best start phoning people," he said. "Some of them, like Beau, will need time to get here."

"I know." Will had already begun a mental list. His younger brother Beau was out on the East Coast and hadn't set foot on the ranch in more than a decade—not since he'd bolted to join the army after a big blowup with their father. The rest of the folks who mattered enough to call lived on neighboring ranches or fifteen miles down the state highway in Blanco Springs, the county seat. Most of them could wait until after the date and time for the funeral had been set. But Will's ex-wife, Tori, who lived in Blanco with their twelve-year-old daughter Erin, would need to know right away. Erin would take the news hard. Whatever Bull had been to others, he was her grandpa.

Neither call would be easy to make. Beau was out of the army now and working for the government in Washington, DC. He had kept them informed of his whereabouts, but an address and a couple of phone numbers was all Will knew about his brother's life out East.

As for Tori—short for Victoria—she'd left Will five years ago to practice law in town. Shared custody of their daughter had kept things civil between them. But when they spoke, the tension was like thin ice on a winter pond, still liable to crack at the slightest shift.

The nearest mortuary was in Lubbock. He'd have to call them, too. They'd most likely want to pick up the body at the coroner's. *The body.* Hell, what a cold, unfeeling process. Too bad they couldn't just wrap the old man in a blanket and stash him in the Caprock like the Indians used to do. Bull would have liked that.

As if conjured by the thought of Indians, a solitary figure stepped out of the horse barn and stood for a moment, gazing across the muddy yard. Fourteen years ago, Sky Fletcher, the part-Comanche assistant foreman, had wandered onto the ranch as a skinny teenage orphan and stayed to prove himself as a man known across the state for his skill with horses.

"Does Sky know?" Will asked Jasper.

"He knows. And he said to tell you that when you're ready, he'll crank up the backhoe and dig the grave next to your mother's."

"Sky's got better things to do."

Jasper gave him a sharp glance. "Bull was good to that boy. He wants to help. Let him."

"Fine. Tell him thanks." Will looked back toward the barn, but Sky was no longer in sight.

Squaring his shoulders, Will took a couple of deep breaths and crossed the porch to the front door. It was time to face the truth that awaited him inside the house.

His father was dead—and the void he'd left behind was as deep as the red Texas earth.

CHAPTER 1

When it came to big gatherings, there was nothing like a good old-fashioned Texas funeral.

From the doorway of the cavernous ranch house parlor, Beau Tyler sipped his bourbon and studied the Texans who'd come to mourn and swap stories about his father. Now that Bull was properly eulogized and planted in the family cemetery, the real get-together could begin.

From the pit-barbecued beef in the backyard to the salads, casseroles, and desserts the neighbors had brought along, there was plenty to eat—and to drink. Guests heaped their plates from the groaning buffet table, filled their glasses at the bar, and took advantage of the rare chance to socialize.

After eleven years away, Beau felt like a stranger. Children had grown up in his absence. Middle-aged folk had grown old, and some of the old ones had passed on. Scanning the crowd, he could spot only a few people he recognized. Every now and then he'd spot a familiar face but rarely could he link a name with it. He supposed it was to be expected.

Catching the sound of the front door closing, Beau automatically glanced in its direction, obeying the well-honed instinct to locate and assess the person coming up behind him. His gaze landed on a big, burly bear of a man, dressed in the uniform of a local law enforcement officer, in the process of removing his hat. There were more lines in his craggy face and some gray in his hair, but Beau had no trouble recognizing the county sheriff, Hoyt Axelrod.

At almost the same moment, the sheriff spotted him, briefly narrowed his sharp eyes, then nodded his head in recognition. "Beau Tyler." He walked straight toward him, a hand outstretched in greeting. "A lot of people around here were wondering if you'd come back for the funeral. Some were even placing bets on it."

"Someone got lucky, then." The handshake was firm but brief.

"I'm sure your brother appreciates having you here. Sorry I couldn't make it to the funeral, but I got tied up at the courthouse."

"Duty first," Beau responded. "Comes with the badge."

"That's right. You'd know about that, wouldn't you? You're an agent with the DEA now, aren't you?" Axelrod asked.

"I am."

"I never figured you were the kind to go into law enforcement. Growing up, you always seemed more interested in good times and partying," the sheriff remarked, while his gaze made a fresh study of him in this new light.

"People change," Beau replied, and idly swirled the bourbon in his glass.

"That they do," the sheriff agreed. "And Lord knows, there isn't a part of this country that isn't plagued by drug problems of some kind. I'm just glad we aren't any closer to the border than we are. But this isn't the time or place for shoptalk." The cell phone hooked to his belt beeped, advising the sheriff of an incoming text message. Axelrod darted an apologetic glance at Beau, checked his phone, then hooked it back on his belt. "If you're going to be around a few days, maybe you can stop by my office and we can trade some stories."

"I've got a flight out tomorrow. Maybe another time."

"I'll hold you to that," the sheriff replied, giving no sign he meant it any more than Beau did. Immediately he shifted his attention to the people milling in the parlor. "You wouldn't know where I might find your brother so I can offer him my condolences?"

"Last time I saw him, he was by the bar."

"I'll find him. It's good to see you again, Beau. I'm just sorry it had to be under these circumstances."

Beau nodded in response and watched as the sheriff began making his way through the throng of mourners toward the bar. He knew he should mingle with the guests, but he didn't feel like making small talk. He was about to turn away from the parlor when he caught sight of a face he recognized at once.

There was Tori, Will's ex-wife, in a knee-skimming black lawyer suit. Tall and slim, with sun-streaked hair, she looked classy as hell. Beau had always thought she and Will were meant for a lifetime together. Whatever had driven them apart must've been bad. But then Will was capable of being a stubborn, insensitive jackass, especially when it came to women. And Tori had never been one to quietly knuckle under.

Tori had been cornered by a neighboring rancher, Congressman Garn Prescott. Prescott had given the eulogy at the funeral, which was surprising since Bull and Prescott's late father had hated each other's guts. But a lot could change over time, and there was an election coming up this fall.

Reading Tori's body language, Beau surmised that the man was invading her personal space and all she wanted was to end their conversation. He was weighing the wisdom of going to her rescue when he felt a touch on his arm and heard a soft voice.

"Are you my uncle Beau?"

Beau turned to the young girl by his elbow. She looked about twelve, with intelligent blue eyes and a dark blond ponytail tied with black satin ribbon. For a split second he failed to recognize her. Then he recalled glimpsing her at the service, next to her mother.

"Erin? Is that really you?"

The grin that lit her face—a miniature of Tori's but with Will's blue eyes—answered his question.

"I can't believe it!" Smiling, he shook his head in mock amazement. "The last time I saw you, you were still in diapers!"

Her laugh was musical. "Not anymore. I'm almost in eighth grade. Someday I want to be a lawyer like my mom, or maybe a vet like Natalie."

Natalie. Something like an unhealed scar pulled inside him. He'd heard she was in veterinary school, and later on that she'd finished and married Slade Haskell. But nothing more. Not in years. He'd almost succeeded in forgetting her.

As if any man could forget his first time—and hers.

"My dad told me you were in a war. He said you got shot."

"I was, and I did. But I'm okay now." And he was okay. The nightmares about the action he'd seen in Iraq still plagued him sometimes, but he'd learned to deal with that. As for the bone-shattering shoulder wound that had gotten him sent stateside, it did no worse than hamper his racquetball game and stiffen up in cold weather. He'd been lucky over there. Damned lucky.

"And now you catch bad guys that sell drugs. That's what my dad says."

"Well, I used to. Now I get to boss other people who catch them."

"Can I get you a sandwich or something?" Erin asked. "I'm helping Bernice today. She said I could be her gofer."

"I'll grab something later. But thanks for the offer."

"Time for me to get gofering." She wrinkled her lightly freckled nose. "I hope we can talk some more while you're here. When I grow up, I want to see the whole world—just like you."

"I'm leaving tomorrow. If there's anything you want to talk about, we'd better make it soon."

"I'll do my best. But right now Bernice needs me to fetch more napkins." She flitted off through the crowd. Beau's gaze followed the path of her bobbing ponytail. A smile edged the corners of his mouth. The kid was a winner straight out of the gate.

At least Will and Tori had done something right.

* * *

Tori's hand cramped around her glass of iced tea. Her black stiletto pumps were killing her feet. The tightness at the back of her neck signaled an oncoming headache, and Congressman Garn Prescott, who'd backed her against a leather settee, wouldn't get out of her face.

Keep skunks and politicians at a distance. Bull's words came back to her as she fought the urge to shove the man away.

"How can I convince you, Tori?" The congressman was fifty-two, a big, handsome, graying man whose breath smelled of the Scotch he'd been drinking. "A woman like you, your talents are being wasted in a backwater town like Blanco Springs. As a member of my Washington staff, your salary would be twice what you're making here. And the connections—my dear, there's no limit to where you could go."

Does that include your bed, you lecherous old goat?

Tori scanned the room over Prescott's shoulder. She spotted Will standing near the massive stone fireplace, his broad-shouldered frame and dark brown hair a beacon in the crowd. But his back was turned toward her. And Will Tyler was the last man she would ask to ride to her rescue.

"Say the word and I'll make it happen—full benefits, your own town house, the works." Prescott gave her arm a proprietary squeeze. "It'll be the best decision you ever made."

Freezing at his touch, Tori shook her head. "I have a daughter, and she's happy here. I'm not about to haul her across the country, away from her father and this ranch. Sorry, Garn, but my answer is no."

"Dinner, then, at least. Give me one more chance to convince you."

Tori's patience had reached the fracture point, but she didn't want to make a scene. She was groping for a civil response when she felt a light touch at her elbow. Swiveling her gaze, she looked up into Beau's mischievous hazel eyes. Her lips moved in a silent *thank you*.

"Congressman." Beau's greeting was friendly but firm. "Hope you'll excuse us, but the lady is urgently needed elsewhere."

Taking Tori's arm, he steered her toward the front entry. "How about some fresh air?" he muttered.

"Yes. Please. This place is a zoo."

"And I've just rescued you from the gorilla." His grin dazzled as he opened the door and led her out onto the porch. Kicking off her pumps, Tori set her glass aside and sank onto the double swing. The dog, drowsing on the top step, raised his head, then settled back into his afternoon nap.

"This is more like it," she breathed. "Another thirty seconds with that man and I'd have slapped his smarmy face. I don't even agree with his politics, let alone want to work for him."

"Well, you can't blame him for trying." Beau settled at the other end of the swing, leaning into the corner so he could look at her. The two had been friends since first grade, and nobody had been more pleased than Beau when, after law school, she'd married his big brother.

She turned her face to the slight breeze that was blowing and drew in a deep breath. "Mmm, the air smells so good and clean after yesterday's storm," she declared, then added with a trace of wistfulness, "I just hope it means we'll get our usual spring rains and end this drought." Her gaze traveled back to him. "The storm made it tough for you, I hear. Will told me your flight was forced to divert to another airport. What time did you finally get to the ranch?"

"By the time I got a rental car and drove here, it was after midnight," Beau admitted. "By the way, I met your daughter in there. She's a gem."

"Erin's the best thing that ever happened to me. At least Will and I accomplished something good when we brought her into the world."

"I was thinking the same thing earlier." Beau kicked the swing into motion. The light, creaking sound blended with the distant calls of spring meadowlarks. "You and Will were the real deal. I lost my faith in true love when you split up."

Tori sighed. She should have known the conversation would go this way.

"What happened?" Beau asked.

"What has Will told you?"

"Nothing. You know Will."

"Do I?" Tori still wondered about that. She hadn't been much older than Erin when she'd fallen in love with Will Tyler. But he was older, and he'd paid her scant attention until years later when she'd returned home to Blanco Springs with her law degree. Their passionate whirlwind courtship had allowed them little time to get reacquainted. By the time she woke to the realization that she'd married a stranger, she'd been pregnant with their daughter.

"It's past and forgotten, Beau," she said. "Let's talk about something else—like you. Any special lady in your life?"

Beau shrugged. He'd always been the handsome brother, with a runner's long bones, light brown hair, and a roguish charm that matched his looks. Will, on the other hand, was chiseled in his father's dark, solid image, and he was just as intractable as Bull had been.

Bull Junior, Tori had called her husband during one of their arguments.

"Special ladies take time," Beau said. "And they expect things, like being told where you are, who you're with, and when you'll be home for dinner."

"Sounds like a passel of excuses to me." Tori gave him a roguish wink. "You'd make time for the right woman if you found her."

Beau's gaze traced the sun-streaked curl that trailed along her cheek. He knew better than to think Tori was flirting with him. They'd been friends most of their lives, but there was no romantic chemistry between them. And even though she was legally free, to him she would always be his brother's woman.

"Maybe I'm just not the right man," he said. "The kind of work I do can make you pretty cynical." He gave the swing another push with his foot. Sex was something he could get any time he wanted it. There were plenty of single, pretty women in Washington, most of them ambitious as hell. For them, a roll in the hay was just a way to let off stress, or maybe a leg up to the next level of wherever they were headed. Beau had long since learned to settle for that.

An easy silence had settled over the porch, warmed by the afternoon sun and broken only by the creak of the swing and the hum of foraging bees. Beau let his gaze wander over the ranch yard and the big landscape that stretched away from it. Little had changed since he'd left the ranch better than ten years ago. For a moment he let the familiarity of it all, its sights, scents, and sounds, take hold of him. Endless times in Iraq he had called this image to mind, times when the pull of home had been strong. And the pull was strong now, forcing him to admit he'd missed being here and being a part of the ranch's rhythms.

Before it could take hold of him, Beau shifted his position on the swing, angling more toward Tori. In the distance, barely visible, a white Toyota Land Cruiser had turned off the main highway and onto the long ribbon of gravel that led up to the ranch house.

"Remember back in fifth grade when Natalie put a garter snake in the teacher's desk drawer?" Tori asked.

Natalie again. Beau forced a chuckle. "How could I forget? The teacher went straight to Mr. Warner's office and quit." Natalie, he recalled, had fessed up to save the poor snake and got three weeks' detention for her crime. The little scamp had been unrepentant.

"How's Natalie doing?" he asked. "Are the two of you still best friends?"

"Solid as ever." Tori reached for her iced tea and took a sip.

"Last I heard, she was married."

"Yes, to Slade Haskell. It's been a few years now. No children. He runs a trucking business out of Blanco."

Beau had tried to imagine the petite, quicksilver girl he remembered with the hulking Slade, who'd made it to college on a football scholarship, then dropped out after blowing out his knee in the first game. Somehow the picture would never come together.

"Do you think she's happy?" he asked.

"You can ask her yourself. That's her SUV coming up the road."

Beau felt the catch in his chest. His feet dropped to the porch, stopping the swing. He was overreacting, he told himself. They weren't nineteen anymore. And Natalie was a married woman.

"I'd planned on bringing her with me today, but she called at the last minute and said she had a foal to deliver." Tori rose, stepped into her pumps, and smoothed her hair into place. "Looks like she made it after all. And now, if you'll excuse me, it's time I was checking on my daughter."

As she vanished inside, Beau rose and walked to the porch rail. No doubt Tori had left on purpose. Given the way he'd treated Natalie ten years ago, their meeting was bound to be awkward. He couldn't blame Tori for not wanting to be a part of it.

Guests had parked their vehicles along both sides of the road for a good fifty yards. The white Toyota pulled off and parked behind a rusty Ford pickup at the end of the line. Maybe he should go back inside, pretend he hadn't seen her. But that would be the coward's way. If the little spitfire still wanted a piece of his hide, he would take his punishment like a man.

He watched as the driver's door opened, and a petite figure stepped out. From a distance, at least, the girl who'd been Natalie Russo hadn't changed much. Doll-sized, with an unruly mane of black curls, she appeared to have come straight from her work. The black blazer she'd tossed on over her jeans and plaid shirt was her only nod to dressing for a funeral. But at least she'd come.

She must've known he'd be here. Had she made the effort because of him—or in spite of him?

When she froze in her tracks for an instant, Beau sensed that she'd recognized him. His feet propelled him forward, off the porch and down the road in long strides that ate up the distance. They met halfway, facing each other at arm's length.

"Hello, Natalie," he said.

Her lips trembled, forming a smile that didn't quite reach her dark eyes. "There were a lot of people who didn't think you'd come back for Bull's funeral. I'm glad you did, though. It's good to see you."

She extended her hand. He took it gently, checking the impulse to imprison it in his big palm. Her fingers were small, her skin cool and lightly callused.

"It's been a long time." Beau cleared the thickness from his voice. "I hear tell you're Mrs. Haskell now."

"Doctor Haskell, if you please." Her smile was almost real this time, deepening a dimple at the corner of her mouth—the dimple he'd once loved to taste. Beau forced that memory aside, knowing it was bound to return when he was alone.

"I stand corrected," he said. "You've done well for yourself. But I knew you would. You were always smart."

"And you always knew the right things to say." Freeing her hand, she gave him a knowing look. "I came to give my condolences to your family. But before I go inside, there's a mare I need to check. She's due to foal in the next few days. Since it's her first time, I promised Sky I'd look in on her."

"Thanks. Mind if I join you?" Beau asked, aware that this was likely the only time he would get to spend alone with her. At the same time, he knew it was wrong to let this go on.

She hesitated a split second, then shrugged. "If you want."

They cut across the muddy yard to the long barn where the broodmares were kept. Natalie's stride was strong and confident, even though the top of her head was no higher than Beau's shoulder. "Are you staying long?" she asked.

"Not much past tomorrow afternoon. Then I'll be driving my rental car to Amarillo and catching the red-eye back to D.C."

"Short visit. They must really need you back there. That, or you just don't want to stick around."

Beau scuffed a blob of mud off his boot heel. Natalie always did have a way of getting right to the heart of things. "There's nothing to keep me here." *Not even you.*

The wide door at the end of the barn stood partway open. Still in sunlight, she turned to face him. "When you left for the army, and I promised to wait for you—you never meant to come back, did you?"

Right to the heart. "At the time, I couldn't imagine not coming back for you. But when I went to Iraq, everything changed." His fingers tripped the sliding bar on the door. "I changed. Combat does that."

"Rather than tell me so, you just stopped writing."

"I tore up a lot of half-finished letters, but I just . . . couldn't put it into words. I don't blame you for being angry."

"I had just about decided you were dead, Beau!" Her voice quivered with emotion even as fury lit her eyes. "Finally I had to call Tori to see if you were still alive." She paused to regain some control. "That was when the message sank in that it was over between us." After throwing him a last glaring look, she pivoted sharply away. "I need to see about the mare."

There were thirty-two roomy stalls in the long barn, sixteen on either side. Natalie walked down the center, in and out of the light shafts that slanted through the high windows. The familiar place smelled of clean straw, fresh manure, and warm equine bodies. Horses moved and snorted in the shadows. A wheelbarrow stood partway down the line, a shovel and broom leaning against its side.

Beau's presence at Natalie's back triggered a tingling aura of awareness. When she'd married Slade six years ago, she'd closed the door on her memories. But some things never changed. If she hadn't known it before, she knew it now. The tension that arced between them was like lightning before a summer cloudburst.

She'd guessed he'd be here for his father's funeral. But she hadn't been wise enough, or strong enough, to stay away.

Had she already said too much about the past? Maybe she should have left well enough alone. But the pain had festered inside for so long. She had to let it out. She had to let him know how deeply he'd hurt her. At least he'd offered her an explanation. But his reasons had done nothing to give her peace.

Lupita, the mare Natalie had come to check on, was in stall number 6, partway down the row. A sweet-natured buckskin with champion quarter horse bloodlines, she was within days, if not hours, of delivery. Stopping outside her stall, Natalie glanced around.

"Looking for something?" Beau asked.

"For Sky. He said he'd try to be here. Did you see him in the house?"

"Not that I remember. My guess is he's finishing the grave. Will told me he'd offered."

"That sounds like something Sky would do. But never mind. If you can steady the mare for me, I won't need to bother him."

"No problem." Easing the stall door open, Beau walked softly across the straw bedding. The mare had been nibbling oats. She raised her elegant head at his approach, ears pricking forward. "Easy there, girl." He stroked the satiny neck, moving in to brace himself against her shoulder. "Time to hold still for the good doctor."

"I take it you've done this before." Natalie slipped a pair of latex gloves out of her pocket and pulled them over her hands. Approaching from the side, she switched on a small LED flashlight.

"It's been a while, but the smell of this place brings it all back—though I've got to say it. You make a better-looking vet than old Doc Humphrey ever did."

"Flattery will get you nowhere, Beau Tyler." Natalie felt the rush of heat to her face. It didn't take much to make that happen. But then, with Beau, it never had.

"I'm not sure how far I want it to get me now that you're a married lady."

Natalie shifted behind the mare and bent closer to examine the vulva with her light. It was swollen, as it should be, the opening beginning to loosen and stretch. The teats were beaded with clear, honey-colored drops of colostrum, a sign her milk was coming in.

"She's waxing. It won't be long now—tonight or tomorrow morning, I'd say. Make sure Erin knows. Lupita's her favorite mare, and if all goes well, her father's promised her the foal to raise as her own. With Vaquero as the sire, she should have herself a champion horse."

"Are you happy, Natalie?"

"What?" She'd put the flashlight down and was palpating the mare's belly to determine the foal's position. It was a guess at best, but so far, everything felt all right.

"I asked Tori if you were happy. She said I should ask you. So I'm asking."

"You mean am I happy with Slade?" She fumbled for the flashlight where she'd dropped it in the straw. "Not that it's any of your business, but yes, of course I am. He's a good man, and he loves me."

"But no children."

"That's not your business either," she said. "I've moved on, Beau. I have a career and a marriage—a life you're not part of." Easing away from the horse, she gulped back the ache in her throat. "So just take it for what it's worth. Leave me alone."

She couldn't help it. Always emotional, she felt the scalding surge of tears. They spilled over as she rose, stripped off her gloves, and walked out of the stall.

"Natalie, are you all right?" Beau came out behind her. Latching the stall gate, he turned her shoulders to face him and saw her tears. "Oh, dammit, I'm sorry." His arms pulled her close, a gesture of comfort. "I shouldn't have grilled you like that. You're right—we've both moved on. Your life is none of my business."

She stood rigid in the circle of his arms. "It's my fault. I shouldn't have come here today."

"No—I'm the one who doesn't belong here." His clasp tightened around her. "Tomorrow I'll be leaving."

Natalie closed her eyes, drawing him into her senses—the

warm tensile strength of his arms, the fresh sage smell of his skin, the steady drumming of his heart against her ear. After all these years, the connection between them was still there. But Beau was right. They'd both moved on.

His breath ruffled the hair on her forehead. Memories surged—the sweet and the bitter. Summer nights on a blanket under the stars, their urgent young bodies giving each other love the only way they knew how. And that last, parting moment, holding him with every ounce of strength, as if to mold his imprint to her and carry it away. Even then she'd known that things would never be the same between them. But until he stopped writing, she'd refused to believe it.

The urge to feel his lips on hers one last time touched an ache inside her—an ache too deep and powerful to be denied. Natalie's booted feet pushed her to her tiptoes. She tilted her face upward, feeling the catch of his breath as he bent toward her.

A clatter from one of the stalls startled them both. They sprang apart as if a gunshot had been fired between them. "Who's there?" Beau called. "Come on out. Now."

A slight male figure, dressed in jeans and a ragged T-shirt, stepped out of the empty stall next to the wheelbarrow. His stringy black hair hung to his shoulders.

"Who the devil—" Beau began.

Natalie touched his arm. "It's all right. He's one of Sky's cousins from Oklahoma. He works here."

Beau hesitated, clearly suspicious. "Then why was he hiding?"

"Maybe he was scared—or just shy. He's only a boy." Natalie gave the young man a friendly wave. "Hello, Lute. We were just checking the mare. Keep an eye on her, will you? Tell Sky if you see any change."

"Sure." Without raising his eyes, Lute picked up the shovel from beside the wheelbarrow and ambled back into the stall. The sound of scraping came from the shadows.

"We should go." Beau pressed a hand to the small of her back.

"Yes, we should." Natalie needed no urging. Their embrace

had been innocent enough, but neither of them relished the idea that they'd been observed.

The door where they'd entered earlier had swung shut. Reaching past her, Beau shoved it open. Bright afternoon sunlight spilled into the barn, dazzling her eyes. Only as her vision cleared did she see the looming shape of a man in front of her.

"I've been looking all over hell for you, Natalie," Slade growled. "Care to tell me what you two were doing in there?"

CHAPTER 2

Beau curbed the impulse to push forward and confront the man. But he damn well didn't like the way Slade Haskell was talking to his wife; still, any interference on his part would only make things worse for Natalie.

"I figured you'd be here when I got home early and didn't find you." Slade's eyes were glittering slits. Blond, with close-clipped hair; blunt, handsome features; and a thickening belly, he was dressed in jeans and a grease-stained work shirt with HASKELL TRUCKING stamped on the chest pocket. "Spotted your SUV out front, but when I went in the house, none of those folks had seen you. How the hell do you think that made me look—a man who can't keep track of his own wife?"

"That's enough, Slade." Natalie's voice was low and taut. "I planned on going into the house, but first I needed to check on a mare."

"And this hotshot government man just happened to wander in? Checking on a mare, my aunt Nelly's ass!" Reaching out, he plucked a piece of straw from Natalie's hair. His gaze burned into Beau like a red-hot poker. "She's my wife now, Tyler. You've got no business fooling around with her! I ought to knock you down and kick your damned teeth in!"

"You've got the wrong idea, friend." Beau spoke with great restraint. "Give your wife some credit. She's a good woman. I simply wanted to say hello to her and good-bye, since I'll be leaving tomorrow."

"Well you can say good-bye here and now!" Slade turned his fury on Natalie. "Back in high school, everybody knew you were doing it with him. If I find out you were messing around with him again—"

"Stop it, Slade!" Natalie exploded. "Don't be an idiot! We weren't even alone! Lute was there the whole time, cleaning out the stalls! If you don't believe me, go in and ask him."

Beau saw the big man pause, as if hesitant to call his wife's bluff. Then Slade took a firm grip on her elbow. "Come on, we're going to the house to say hello to all those fine folks together."

"Not now." She twisted away from him. "We both need some time to cool down. I'm going to my car. I'll see you at home."

"No, you don't." His big fist locked around her arm again. "They saw me arrive alone. I want them to see that you're with me now."

This time Natalie didn't argue. She walked beside her husband across the muddy yard, her back ramrod straight, her small chin thrust forward, her dark curls ruffled by the breeze as he marched her toward the ranch house.

Beau watched them, his hands crumbling a piece of straw that had clung to his jacket. He hadn't planned to stir up old memories or cause trouble between Natalie and her husband. Yet coming to the barn with her had done just that.

Turning away, Beau gazed westward, to the escarpment that rose in rusty white buttresses above the rolling bed of the canyon. A golden eagle, riding an updraft, soared above the Caprock where the high plain began. The scene was one of peace and beauty. But the tension in Beau's gut wouldn't go away. Holding Natalie in his arms had reawakened all the old emotions—emotions he no longer had the right to feel.

Inside the barn, Lute Fletcher smiled to himself and pushed the shovel under the last bit of dirty straw and manure. A man would have to be damned near deaf not to overhear every word of the confrontation that had just taken place right outside the barn door—just as he would have to be damned near blind not to see the near embrace between Beau Tyler and Slade Haskell's wife. And Lute Fletcher was far from being deaf or blind.

As he tossed the shovelful of debris onto the mound already in the wheelbarrow, he wondered if that little scene he had witnessed between Beau and Natalie might prove useful to him. Maybe he'd get himself into Haskell's good graces, because he sure as hell was tired of mucking out stalls. To emphasize his disgust with the job at hand, Lute let go of the shovel, letting it fall against the stall's wooden partition instead of propping it up. It clattered onto the cement floor about the same time he heard the creaking hinges of the barn door opening again.

Figuring it was Beau Tyler coming back in, Lute reached for the wheelbarrow handles. It wasn't Beau who walked in, but Lute's older cousin Sky Fletcher. Lute ran a skimming glance over Sky, noting the crisp white shirt he wore tucked into a pair of dark, belted jeans, a silver and turquoise bolo tie around his neck. A dressy, tan Stetson covered most of his midnight-black hair.

Sharp blue eyes briefly locked their attention on Lute. "I thought you'd be finished in here by now," Sky stated even as he angled toward the stall with the pregnant mare inside it.

"Almost." Lute couldn't keep the bitterness out of his voice over being stuck with such a menial task. "That lady vet was just here checkin' on the mare."

"I know. I spoke to her outside."

The longer he looked at Sky in his clean clothes, knowing how much his own smelled like shit and sweat, the hotter his resentment grew—until it spilled out. "Don't see why I gotta work on the day the big boss got buried."

Unfazed by the heat in Lute's voice, Sky slipped into the stall, moving to the buckskin's side. "Bull would have been the first to tell you that there's never a day off from doing chores."

"Maybe not, but it seems like I'm always the one shoveling

shit," he grumbled. "When you hired me on last month, this sure as hell wasn't the kind of work I figured I'd be doing. I figured I'd be out working cattle, learning the ranch business. Dammit, you're my cousin, Sky. You know this isn't fit work for a Comanche."

"It's how I started," Sky replied, never losing his air of calm. "Eventually I worked my way up to wrangler, and now assistant foreman."

"And how long did that take?" Lute challenged.

"Does it matter?" Sky countered.

"Hell, yes! I'm twenty-one and I don't plan on spending the next however many years it will take pushing this shovel."

"That's your job for now." Sky gave the mare a final pat on the neck and let himself out of the stall. "Don't forget to clean the stallion barn when you finish up here."

"Yeah, and after I finish that, I'll be taking a shower and headin' into town, so don't be looking for me around here," Lute shouted at Sky's back as he exited the barn.

With the closing of the barn door, Lute resumed his grip of the wheelbarrow handles and used the built-up anger inside to propel the wheelbarrow out the back of the barn, where he dumped the reeking mass into a shallow pit. For a moment he glared at the growing mound piled there, knowing that his next job was likely to be loading it up and hauling it off to be spread over the lower pastures for fertilizer while the cattle were grazing up on the caprock.

He wondered what the chances were that Slade Haskell would be at the Blue Coyote tonight. Lute had heard some talk that Haskell might be looking for drivers for his trucking company. But when he'd cornered Haskell about a job a couple weeks ago, Haskell hadn't been hiring.

Right now there was nothing that would give Lute more pleasure than to find work somewhere else and tell Sky where he could put this shovel.

By the time the last of the guests had left, the spring night had turned chilly. A blaze crackled in the parlor's great stone fireplace, casting its warmth out to the room's massive leather chairs and letting it rise to the open-beamed ceiling.

Will lounged in one of the four overstuffed chairs and let his gaze slide to the occupants of the other three—his brother Beau, the ranch's aging foreman Jasper Platt, and Sky Fletcher. He watched as his brother took a swig from the bottle of Mexican beer in his hand.

"It was a fine service, Will," Beau said with a nod, and absently used the back of his hand to wipe away the bit of foam on his upper lip. "But there's one thing I've wondered about all afternoon. Why in hell's name did you have Garn Prescott give the eulogy? Dad hated Ferguson Prescott his whole life, and I can't imagine that he felt much different about Prescott's son. I could almost picture Dad turning over in his coffin when the esteemed congressman took the pulpit."

Will fixed a steady gaze on his brother, reminding himself that Beau hadn't set foot on the ranch once in the past eleven years. It was time he learned the true situation, considering half the ranch would now be his.

"There are two answers to that question," he said. "The simpler one is that Garn phoned me with an offer to do it. Since nobody else was stepping up, I let him. I knew he'd do a decent job, and he did. So what if he was looking for a few votes in next fall's election?"

"As well as a vote from that good-lookin' ex of yours," Jasper added with a wink. "He's been sniffin' a trail around Tori ever since his wife died."

"Not that Tori's interested," Beau said. "I know for a fact she'd like him to take a walk."

"Tori can do whatever she wants," Will snapped. "This isn't about her."

"So what's your second answer?" Sky Fletcher was a man who did more listening than talking. Tall and lean, with the black hair, hawkish bones, and tawny skin of his Comanche ancestors, he studied Will with riveting cobalt eyes.

"The second answer's about survival." Leaning forward, Will set his bottle on the coffee table with a sharp *thunk*. "This isn't the Old West anymore. Most of the ranches in these parts have sold off their acreage to farmers and developers just to stay afloat. The biggest outfits, the ones that haven't broken up, have been taken over by syndicates of investors, a lot of them from back East or even places like Singapore and Dubai. More and more cattle are being raised on farms. As for big, open family ranches like ours . . ." Will shook his head.

"You're saying we're dinosaurs." Beau's remark wasn't a question.

"Something like that," Will admitted.

"What's that got to do with letting Garn Prescott deliver Bull's eulogy?" Jasper demanded.

"Just this," Will said. "We can't afford to have enemies. Bull and old Ferg may have feuded all their lives, but now that they're both dead, we have to make peace. We need allies—and it never hurts to have one in Congress, looking out for the interests of ranchers in these parts."

Jasper came close to spitting on the floor. "Bull wouldn't like that. He always said, 'If you wallow with pigs, you're bound to get dirty.' And he had the Prescotts in mind when he said it."

Will sighed. As foreman, Jasper was entitled to be here. But the old man wasn't making this discussion any easier, and given what needed to be said, his mood was bound to get worse.

"Let me paint the big picture," Will said. "The Prescott ranch has been bailed out by investors. Garn's the figurehead, but he's no longer running the operation. That's why he has time for politics. If we can't manage to stay afloat, we'll be fated to go the same way."

"Are we in trouble?" Sky asked the question.

"Not yet, but we're cutting it close. If we don't make changes now, another drought like last summer's could put us under." Will leaned back in his chair, studying the man his father had taken in when he was a scruffy, lost teenager. Bringing Sky Fletcher in as part of the ranch family had been one of the best decisions Bull ever made.

"One idea I have involves you, Sky. Our Rimrock cow ponies have always gotten top prices at auction, as much for your training as for their breeding. I'd like to expand the operation, to shore us up in case we have to sell off our beef early. What would you think about choosing some prime-quality colts to be brought in and broken here?"

Sky's expression barely flickered. "We could work it out. But training horses takes time. So does being second foreman. If you want me to focus on the horse side, we'll need some help."

"How about that young cousin of yours? Is he any good?"

"Not as good as I'd hoped. So far he does more complaining than working."

"In that case, if we get those extra colts, it might be easier to find a man who can shoulder your other duties." Will shifted his somber gaze to Jasper, bracing for what needed to be said. "I'm not telling you anything that you don't already know, Jasper, but there are some days when you're so crippled up with arthritis that it's all you can do to climb into the saddle. And those days are happening more frequently."

Jasper bristled with pride. "So what are you saying? That it's time I retired?"

"Not until you can train a new boss to take your place, teach him everything you know about this business and this ranch. You have a wealth of knowledge that we'll always need to draw on. So don't have any doubts—you have a home on this ranch for as long as you want it." Will could see that none of his words were sitting well with the old cowboy. But as much as he hated saying them, this had to be done. "Hell, Jasper, you were more a father to me and Beau than Bull ever was. You put us on our first horses, taught us how to work cattle and rope. And I need you to do the same with Erin. As things stand right now, she'll be the one to inherit the ranch. She'll need to know how to run it. No one could do a better job of teaching her that than you."

The old cowboy brightened. He had always regarded Erin as a kind of granddaughter. "It'd be a pleasure to take her in hand," he said, and meant it. He paused, a slight frown puckering his forehead. "But if you're having Sky focus on the horse side of the business, who are you figurin' on gettin' to be foreman?"

Will fixed his gaze on Beau. "I'm looking at him."

Ever since Will had turned the conversation to the ranch's future, Beau had suspected he'd get drawn into it somehow, but he hadn't foreseen this. He felt his jaw muscles tightening in instant resistance.

Beau took a quick swig of beer to try to cool his temper and managed an even response. "You're overlooking one small detail," he said. "I'm leaving in the morning to catch my flight back to D.C."

Will came right back at him without a pause.

"That's easily remedied. Just cancel the reservation."

"You know damn well that I have a job waiting for me." This time Beau couldn't keep the heat out of his voice. "You don't really expect me to walk away from it just like that."

"It wouldn't be the first time you walked away from something," Will countered, his expression one of hard challenge as he deliberately referenced the day when Beau had walked out of the ranch house, never to return until now.

The tension in the room was palpable, the air fairly crackling with it. Sky rose from his chair, unfolding his lanky frame with a movement as smooth as water. "The buckskin mare showed signs of going into labor. I need to check on her."

Will glanced up at him. "Erin's upstairs in her room. I know she wanted to be there when the foal came. Should I call her?"

"Not yet," Sky replied. "It's the mare's first foal. Let's wait until we're sure everything's all right."

"Keep me posted." Will directed the words to Sky's back as he left the room.

Before he was out of sight, Jasper planted his hands on the chair's armrests and proceeded to lever himself out of it. "Sky's got the right idea. You two need some time alone to hash this out, and I'll just leave you to it."

Beau watched the old cowboy hobble from the room, then

turned his attention back to Will, determined to end this discussion quickly and cleanly.

"I'm not the man for this job, Will," he stated flatly. "It's been years since I sat in a saddle, swung a rope, or doctored a cow. You need a foreman with experience."

"Do you know the kind of salary a man like that would command?" Will fired back. "The ranch can't afford it. This place is land-rich and cash-poor. Another bad year, we could be cash-broke. And, yeah, you might be rusty when it comes to ordinary ranch work, but you know how to manage men. You've got the organizational skills we need. And better yet, you know your way around a computer." With the last of his arguments thrown at Beau, his voice took on the thickness of repressed emotion. "If you have a drop of family loyalty in those ice-water veins of yours, brother, you'll cut your ties back East and stay here."

With the words still echoing in his mind, Beau realized this wasn't some spur-of-the-moment idea; on the contrary, his brother had clearly given it a lot of thought before proposing it. He started to tell Will that all his arguments had failed to change his mind. Then Beau met that riveting gaze and felt his brother's attempt to impose his will on him. He had always known that Will had been chiseled from the Texas Caprock in Bull's image, but the resemblance was more than a surface one. Will had a stubborn streak every bit as wide as their father's. Once he sank his teeth into an idea, he didn't let go of it.

Knowing it would likely be futile, Beau tried one last time to make his position clear. "Look, Will, I'm sorry you're going through a rough patch, but the ranch has been through them before. It'll make it through this time as well. In any case, it's your problem, not mine."

"What the hell do you mean, it's not yours?" Will's voice vibrated with temper. "Half of this damned ranch is yours now. It's time you accept the responsibility."

Responsibility. Beau felt the surge of old anger, every bit as hot and strong as it once had been. How many times had Bull

Tyler hurled that word at him, always following it with accusations that Beau was worthless, more interested in partying, chasing skirts, and pulling stupid pranks than he was in shouldering his workload. And every time it had ended in a shouting match between them.

Pushed by that old fury, Beau rose to his feet, fists clenched tightly at his sides. At the same moment Will stood to meet him. Realizing his temper was on a hair trigger, Beau swung away.

"Go to hell, Will." He pushed the words through his clenched teeth and headed for the front door.

Will called after him, "Dammit, Beau! You can at least sleep on it."

He didn't waste any breath answering him, not stopping until the front door closed behind his back and the chill of the night air washed over him. He paused and drank in a deep breath of it and wondered why he had bothered to come home for Bull's funeral.

"Fixing to run away again, are ya?" Jasper's voice came from the porch shadows on his right. Beau jerked his head around, quickly locating the old cowboy's dark shape sitting on the long bench. "Can't say I'm surprised, considering this wouldn't be the first time you did it."

"And I'm telling you the same thing I told my brother—go to hell, Jasper," Beau muttered.

Wisely, Jasper didn't immediately respond. He waited a couple beats, then released an amused sound that fell somewhere between a chuckle and a harrumph. "Sorta gives a whole new meaning to that old phrase 'When the going gets tough, the tough get going.' "

"Don't try to lay some guilt trip on me, Jasper. It won't work," Beau stated. "I don't know what Kool-Aid you two have been drinking, but the visions you're getting have no basis in reality. I've been gone too long."

"It'll come back to you quick," the old cowboy countered in an idle tone.

"So what?" he challenged. "For you and Will, this ranch is the center of your universe, but it isn't mine! I have a job, a home, and friends waiting for me back in D.C. I've made a new life for myself, and it isn't here. Why should you expect me to give it up?"

"Your brother needs you."

"Sure he does." Beau didn't try to keep the mockery out of his voice.

"You don't believe that, do you," Jasper stated. "I guess you have been away too long or you'd remember a Tyler breaks his own horse, no matter how many times he gets thrown. Nobody else does it for him. Will can't break this one by himself. That's a hard fact to swallow. So he did the most natural thing in the world—he turned to family."

For the first time, Beau had no ready comeback and fell silent, letting Jasper's calmly issued statement sink in. He shifted his attention to the night's darkness just beyond the porch. Overhead, the sky was a glory of stars—stars that, with all the light pollution, didn't show up in D.C.'s night sky.

Here on the ranch, the constellations greeted him like long-lost childhood friends. He could pick out the Big Dipper, the North Star, Orion, and the Seven Sisters. And stretching across the Texas sky in a breathtaking spill of light was the Milky Way.

Again Jasper's easy drawl invaded the silence. " 'Course, you're right. It is damned selfish of Will to think you might come to his rescue. Why should you care that we're short of hands and it's past time for spring roundup? I'm sure you've already used up all your vacation time, and your job's too vital to expect any extra leave—"

Beau cut across his words. "You've made your point, Jasper."

"It's about time." The old cowboy rolled to his feet, steadied himself, then moved stiffly to Beau's side.

"I never said I was staying," Beau warned.

"I never said you were," Jasper agreed. "At least now you'll sleep on it, like Will asked ya."

"Will's like Bull. He doesn't ask; he tells."

"And you bristle at just about anything that isn't your idea, just like you always did," he observed. "It amazes me how you ever took any orders in the army. I'll bet your tongue's scarred from all the times ya had to bite it."

Beau was too intent on the set of headlights coming up the lane at considerable speed to take any notice of Jasper's good-natured gibing. "Who would be coming to pay their respects this late in the evening?" With a nod of his head, he directed Jasper's attention to the oncoming vehicle.

By then both men could make out the shape of the big, white SUV as it swung into the ranch yard. "That looks like Natalie's ride," Jasper murmured. A second later the SUV swung into the ranch yard and took aim on the barn area. "The mare's in trouble or Sky wouldn't have called her. We'd better git over there." As quickly as his arthritic knees would allow, the cowboy started down the steps to his truck, parked in front of the house. "You comin'?"

Common sense told Beau that both he and Natalie would be better off if he stayed right where he was. But she was too close, and the pull of her was too strong for him to stay on the porch.

Calling himself every kind of fool, Beau went down the steps and straight to the pickup's passenger side, sliding onto the seat as Jasper clambered behind the wheel.

By the time they reached the barn, Natalie had already disappeared inside it. With all his senses in high anticipation, Beau forced himself to pause long enough to hold open the barn door for the slower-moving Jasper, then followed him inside.

Letting his long strides carry him past Jasper, Beau made his way down the wide alley between the stalls to the lighted one, all the familiar smells of hay and horses swirling around him. The aging Border collie, already curled in his straw bed for the night, noted Beau's passing with a lift of his head and a wag of his tail.

The gate to the stall stood open. Beau stopped a step short of it. The sweating buckskin mare was on her feet, hobbled and snubbed to a post at the rear of the stall. Sky was at her head, stroking her neck and shoulders, murmuring to her in the singsong Comanche way he had that invariably soothed the most nervous horse. But it was Natalie he focused his attention on.

Her sleeves were rolled up, long, rubber obstetrical gloves covering her bare hands and arms all the way to the shoulders. He studied her bent head, the dark sheen of her hair standing out against the mare's dun-colored coat. She looked so damned small next to the stoutly muscled quarter horse that Beau couldn't check the surge of protectiveness that swept through him.

Jasper halted next to him. "What's the problem?" he asked, directing the question to Sky.

"The foal's coming nose first." His voice maintained its crooning tone. "She's working to pull the front legs. Just pray it's not too late."

No further explanation was needed. Regardless of how long he'd been away from the ranch, Beau knew, as well as Jasper did, that once the birthing process began, there was roughly a fifteen-minute window. If the foal wasn't born within that time frame, it was a sign of trouble. Both the foal's life and the mare's could be in danger. No wonder Natalie had come roaring up the ranch lane like it was a highway, in an attempt to shorten the precious moments being lost.

Natalie offered no comment. She was too intent on working the unborn foal farther back into the birth canal so she could maneuver its front legs into the proper position.

"Got one." Her low mutter of victory quickened Beau's pulse. He held his breath as she went deeper, working to unbend the other leg and pull both feet into position. Seconds crawled past.

"Done!" She stumbled backward, catching her balance. Beau began to breathe again. "Turn her loose, Sky. Let's hope she can finish this by herself."

Working swiftly, Sky unfastened the hobbles, freed the rope, and stood back to give the mare plenty of room. Glancing to his right, Beau saw that Will had come in to watch with the others.

Horses most often gave birth on their sides, but Lupita didn't take the time to lie down. Bracing her hind legs apart, she strained once. Muscles rippled as her foal slid into the world and dropped to the soft, clean straw.

Will gave a whoosh of relief. Jasper was laughing and cheering. But Beau's eyes were on Natalie. She was staring at the foal.

"Something's wrong," she said. "It's not breathing."

In a flash she was bending over the newborn foal, extending its head and clearing the membranes from its nostrils. With a clean towel, she began rubbing the little body, almost roughly. "Come on . . . ," she murmured, tickling the foal's nose with a piece of straw. "Come on, breathe . . ."

There was a little sputter, then a cough as the baby sucked in its first breath of air and began to stir. Natalie sank back onto her heels, her head sagging, her shoulders slumping for a moment before she checked the foal again. "Congratulations, Lupita," she said, grinning. "You've got a fine boy!"

The mare had shifted toward her baby and begun licking him clean. Behind her, Sky was busy tying up the long umbilical cord. It had been severed, as it should be, when the foal dropped, but until the mare passed the placenta, the trailing end had to be kept clear of her hooves.

Alert now, the foal raised his head. With the membranes cleared away, his true color could be seen in the shadowy stall. Natalie noticed it first. "Oh . . ." she breathed. "For heaven's sake, will you look at that?"

Beau gave a low whistle as his eyes caught the gleam of a brilliant golden coat and the damp threads of a creamy mane. "Unbelievable," he murmured, and it almost was. A random mix of recessive genes from the foal's buckskin dam and chestnut sire had produced the rarest of colors. The tiny foal was a palomino, the first in memory on the ranch.

As if to make up for his rough entry into the world, the little fellow was already struggling to stand. He worked his rear up onto his impossibly long hind legs, toppled into the straw, and promptly tried again. The third time, with nuzzling encouragement from his mother, he made it. Wide-eyed and quivering, he stood for the first time, gleaming like a little piece of the sun.

Sky glanced back at Will. "Now you can get Erin."

But Will had no sooner turned to go than Erin burst into the barn. Still in her pajamas, fuzzy slippers, and flannel robe, she'd evidently seen the lights from across the yard and discovered that her father was missing from the house.

"Is it born?" She was out of breath, her long hair tangled from sleep. "Is my foal here?"

Erin pushed forward past the watchers. Natalie had stripped off her gloves and moved back to stand near Beau. Only Sky remained in the stall with the mare and foal. Straightening, he turned and gave her a rare smile. "Come on in, Erin," he said in a voice that scarcely rose above a whisper. "Quietly, now."

Erin knew how to behave around mares with new foals. She walked softly into the stall, making no sudden moves. Only when she was close enough did Sky step aside, giving her a full view of the foal. "Oh!" she gasped. "Oh, he's so beautiful!"

"Come and touch him," Sky said. "Since he's to be yours, you'll want him and his mother to know your smell." Beckoning her close, he took her hand and rubbed it along the foal's back. "That's it. Now put your arms around him. Lean over his back and give him a hug. You'll want your scent all over him. And you'll want him to know that scent means something good."

Almost sobbing with excitement, Erin did as she was told. As she embraced her foal, a quiver passed through the small body. Lupita raised her head and nickered.

Sky touched Erin's arm. "That's enough for now. I think this little fellow's ready for a meal."

Released, the foal tottered under his mother, butted instinctively for a teat, and began to suck. His creamy little tail twitched with pleasure as he drank.

Beau glanced down at Natalie. Her cheeks were wet with tears. As if sensing his eyes on her, she looked up at him.

"Sorry," she muttered. "For a vet, I'm way too emotional. It's late. Time for me to go."

"I'll walk you to your car," Beau said.

"No." Her eyes flashed him a warning look before she turned to gather up her gear. A moment later she said good night to the others and strode out of the barn.

Beau watched her leave, aware she was right not to trust being alone with him. Every time she was around, he had trouble keeping his eyes off her, let alone his hands. As much as he might wish otherwise, she wasn't his girl anymore. She was another man's wife. The sooner he accepted that, the better off both of them would be.

CHAPTER 3

It was almost 10:00 p.m. when Lute walked through the front door of the Blue Coyote. He'd hitched a ride to town with a cowboy named Ralph who had a '93 Chevy pickup and a girlfriend who worked the late shift at Burger Shack. One of these days he'd have his own car, Lute vowed as the pickup pulled away. And it wouldn't be a twenty-year-old piece of crap like Ralph drove, either.

Inside, the antiquated sound system was playing Hank Williams, which fit the retro theme of the place. There were autographed photos of old-time rodeo stars on the walls. A set of massive, mounted longhorns, wider than the span of a big man's arms, hung over the big-screen TV above the bar.

Stella, the busty, middle-aged redhead who owned the place, knew all her customers by name. Tonight she was dressed in a black silk shirt embroidered with roses and a tight denim skirt. "Howdy, Lute," she greeted him. "Have a seat and tell Nigel here what you're drinkin' tonight."

Nigel, who served as bartender and bouncer, seemed out of place in the Western-style bar. With tattooed arms, a wrestler's build, and a shaved head, he looked more like a biker than a cowboy. But he knew his job, and if anybody messed with him, they didn't do it a second time.

Lute ordered the cheapest beer on the menu, paid for it

with the last of his pocket change, and nursed it while he scanned the crowded bar. Just his damned luck, Slade Haskell wasn't here. But since Ralph wouldn't be by to pick him up for a couple of hours, he had time to kill.

Jess, the only waitress in sight, bustled past him with a tray full of drinks. Lute watched her walk away, liking the tight fit of her jeans, her black T-shirt, and the perky little pink boots on her feet. She was young and thin, with limp brown hair and a tired expression on her pretty face. Lute wouldn't have minded getting to know her. As a half-blood Comanche with scarcely a dime to his name, he had more sense than to hit on the girl. But once he had money and a car, things would be different.

He'd finished the beer and was fidgeting with the empty bottle when Slade walked in. He was wearing his work clothes and looked pissed, like maybe he'd had a fight with that hot wife of his. Lute bit at the edge of his lower lip, wondering whether this might be a bad time to approach Haskell about a job. Trouble was, he didn't know when there might be a better one, and he was tired of shoveling shit all day.

Deciding that tonight might be his only chance, Lute pushed off the bar stool and wandered over to the booth where Slade Haskell sat alone. "I heard a rumor you might have an opening for a driver," he remarked, trying to sound cool and offhand.

Glancing up, Slade looked him over. "You asked me about a job a couple weeks ago. You're the kid working out at the Tyler spread, aren't you?"

"I work there," he admitted, "until I can find something that pays better. Cleaning out stables isn't exactly something I want to do the rest of my life."

"So you were the one in there when she checked on that mare." His gaze narrowed on Lute in thoughtful study.

"That was me." He nodded, and wondered how much more he should say—and where it might get him. "Quite the reunion it was between two old . . . friends." He hesitated deliberately to stress the latter word.

"Really." The single-word response from Slade seemed to encourage Lute to say more.

"I got the feeling they were old flames," he volunteered. "But something told me the fire wasn't out as far as Beau was concerned."

"I knew it," Slade muttered, more to himself than a response to Lute's statement. Before he could add more, the waitress, Jess, stopped by the table with her order pad in hand. In the blink of an eye, Slade lost that half-angry brooding look and flashed her a grin. "Two Coronas for me and my friend here," he boomed, and gave a wink. "What time are you off tonight, girl?"

A shadow flickered across her face. "Not till closing. Then I've got plans."

"Too bad." The grin remained. "Well, maybe next time."

"Sure." She walked off to get their drinks.

Lute stared after her. "Slade, is that girl a—"

"Naw. Just a nice, friendly waitress. Best kind."

"Does she let you . . . you know?"

"Hell, boy, I'm a happily married man. Haven't you figured that out by now?" He sank into a sullen silence while Jess brought their beers and set them on the table. For the space of a quick breath, her gaze locked with Lute's. But what he read in her sad doe eyes wasn't an invitation. It was more like a warning.

Slade took a long swig of his beer. "About that work I mentioned. Still interested?"

Lute's pulse jerked. "What do you think I'm here for? Tell me more."

"Not much to it. You keep your job with the Tylers and phone me every few days about what's going on out there—stock coming and going, new equipment, new people, any trouble on the ranch, whatever. If I don't pick up, you can leave a voice message. It'll be like you're my eyes and ears. Long as you do your job, I'll pay you fifty dollars a week. You can come by and pick up the cash from Stella when you're in town."

Fifty dollars a week for doing almost nothing. It wasn't a fortune, but for now it would make the payments on a cheap car. And if he proved himself, maybe the job would lead to better things.

"Got a cell phone?" Slade asked.

"An old prepaid. Won't do much more than the basics."

"Use it. A new one would just draw attention. And when I give you my phone number, memorize it. It can't be found written down or entered on your phone. There can't be any connection between us. Understand?"

"Understand." Lute's pulse raced as Slade wrote his phone number on a piece of paper napkin. He sipped his beer, savoring the chilled taste. This was really going to happen. He would be more than just a shit shoveler. He was on his way to becoming somebody.

After the news ended, Natalie switched off the TV and stood gazing out the darkened front window. It was after 10:30 and she was dressed for bed in her nightgown and robe. But Slade wasn't back and she was too wired to go to sleep.

They'd settled their earlier quarrel outside the barn over a supper of Burger Shack pizza, spinach salad, and a bottle of Cabernet that one of Slade's clients had given them for Christmas. Just as the tension seemed to be easing, Sky had called from the Tyler ranch with word that the mare was having problems.

When she'd grabbed her keys to leave, Slade had blown his top again. She'd invited him to go with her, but when he'd refused, there was nothing she could do but race out the door, gun the engine, and go.

"Don't count on me being here when you get back!" he'd yelled after her. Well, he was true to his word. The candy-apple-red Ford pickup he kept shined to a high gloss had been missing when she'd pulled into the garage.

No need to wonder where he'd gone. He'd be at the Blue Coyote, drinking and flirting with the waitresses. Slade rarely got drunk, and she doubted that he got past first base with any of the women. He'd soon be home as usual, muttering apologies and wanting sex, which she'd give him to seal their truce.

Natalie was a woman who took her marriage vows seriously. Six years ago, when she'd promised to love and honor Slade Haskell, she'd meant every word. She'd faced the reality that Beau wouldn't be coming back for her. And Slade had been there—handsome and likeable, with roots in the community and enough ambition to take over the family business from his father. They could have a comfortable life together, she'd told herself.

Was it really Slade she'd fallen in love with, she asked herself now, or the person in those mental pictures?

But she was committed to making her marriage work. Slade wasn't a bad person. Neither was she. They deserved to be happy, or at least satisfied with each other. Surely they could find a way.

Meeting Beau again had been like pouring acid into an old wound. The memories of how she'd loved him, and how he'd hurt her, felt as fresh and hot as ever. She'd almost convinced herself that she was over him. But she was wrong. He'd made her feel like a silly little nineteen-year-old fool all over again.

The sudden glare of headlights and the growl of a big engine in the driveway pulled her thoughts back to the present. Natalie forced a mental shift as the garage door opened and closed. Her husband—a decent man who loved her in his way—was home, and they'd had enough contention for one night.

She would do her best to make peace.

The Eastern sky had just begun to pale from the slow rising of the sun when Beau wandered into the kitchen for a cup of coffee. He'd hoped for some quiet time alone, but Will was already at the table, digging into a trencherman's breakfast of fried eggs, bacon, and pancakes dripping with maple syrup.

"That looks like a recipe for instant heart attack, brother," Beau observed as he filled a mug from the electric coffeemaker.

A place had been set for him, but he didn't plan to use it. He hadn't eaten a big breakfast since he'd gotten out of the military.

"It hasn't bothered my heart yet." Will dunked a forkful of pancake in the yolk of his egg. "Tori tried to turn me into a health nut. But the granola and green tea didn't take."

"Dad used to eat like that." Beau took a seat. "Is that what killed him?"

"You didn't hear?" Will's thick, black eyebrows shot up. "The old man was living on booze and pain pills by the time he died. The coroner's report listed his death as an accidental overdose. But his heart and arteries were fine. You missed a lot, being gone."

"I'm aware of that." Beau sipped his strong, black coffee. "I was in Iraq when he had his accident. Otherwise I might've come home."

"Just as well you didn't. There wasn't much you could've done. We hired folks to help him. But he was in constant pain. God knows he wasn't easy to live with before the accident. Afterward, well, I think you can figure that out."

Bernice bustled in with a wire basket of fresh eggs from the coop. She paused at the sight of them together in the kitchen. She'd come to work at the ranch after her husband died more than thirty years ago and was as much a part of Rimrock as her older brother Jasper. "My, but it's good to have both you boys in here again. What can I fix for you, Beau? Bacon? Eggs? You like them over easy as I recollect."

"Coffee's enough for me, Bernice. And yours is the best. I can't get it this good for five bucks a shot in D.C."

"So you've decided?" Will lowered his fork to his plate. "On the basis of Bernice's coffee?" Impatient at the lightness of Beau's response, Will snapped. "Dammit, you said you'd let me know this morning, Beau. I'm waiting."

Beau could almost picture his father sitting in Will's place. He sucked in his breath, knowing that once the words were out of his mouth, they'd be binding.

"Let's say I've decided to stay for a while. My job entitles me to two weeks off for bereavement. I hadn't planned on taking it, but I'll call the office today."

"And?" Will was bristling with impatience.

"I'll stick around long enough to give this place a try. At the end of that time, I'll make a final decision. Fair enough?" It would have to be. Beau was already having doubts, wondering whether he and Will could get along over the long term.

Will sat silently, frowning as he mulled over what he'd heard. At last he shrugged. "Not quite what I'd hoped for, but I guess, for you, it makes sense. At least your timing's good. We start spring roundup today. You'll have plenty of chances to get those callus-free hands dirty."

Beau sighed, already knowing what he'd let himself in for. "Suits me. I'm wearing my old boots, but I'll need some gear—chaps, gloves, a hat, a saddle . . ."

"No problem. We've got extras in the bunkhouse. Think you can remember how to work cattle?"

"It'll come back to me." Beau remembered his teenage years on the ranch, riding herd until his butt blistered and his stomach caved in from hunger. Bull Tyler had been a hard taskmaster, even tougher on his sons than he was on his cowhands. Something told Beau that Will would be the same.

Picking up his empty plate, he held it out to the smiling cook. "Fill it up, Bernice. Looks like it'll be a long, hard day."

They were just finishing their plates when Erin came bounding in the back door. Bits of straw clung to her sweatshirt and her uncombed hair. Her cheeks were flushed, her blue eyes sparkling.

"How's your new foal?" Beau asked her.

"Fine. He's eating now." She splashed her hands at the sink and wiped them on her jeans before flinging herself into a chair at the end of the table. "Sky let me brush him. He said I need to touch him a lot and spend a lot of time with him before I go back to school on Monday. That way he'll remember me. It's called imprinting."

If imprinting was to be done right, it had to begin within forty-five minutes of a foal's birth. Beau realized that was why Sky had brought Erin into the stall so soon last night.

Will frowned. "That mare could get protective of her baby. You're not alone out there with that horse, are you?"

"Really, Daddy, I'm almost thirteen!" Erin poured herself a glass of milk and laced it with chocolate syrup.

"You won't be thirteen till next January, and I asked you a question, young lady."

"All right. Sky was there at first, but he had to go help with the remuda, so he called Jasper. Jasper was with me the whole rest of the time."

"Good. I want to know that somebody's always with you in the barn." Will rose and carried his plate to the sink. Erin was already digging into the pancakes Bernice had set in front of her.

"Have you named your foal yet?" Beau asked.

Erin grinned. "I have. His parents have Spanish names, so I'm going to call him Tesoro. In Spanish that means *treasure*."

"Why, honey, that sounds just perfect," Bernice exclaimed. "Wait till your mother sees him!"

Will shot her a half-irritated look, a shadow passing across his face, before he pinned his glance on Beau. "Are you coming, Beau? We still need to rustle you some gear from the bunkhouse."

"I'm on your six." Beau pushed his plate aside and rose from the table. As much as he would have liked another cup of coffee, it was clear Will wanted to get the day's work started.

As they strode across the yard side by side, Beau couldn't help noticing the rather grim-lipped expression his brother had.

"Is there a problem, Will?"

"Just thinking about that damned foal," he admitted in a near mutter. "I'd planned on gelding any colt that was born so he'd be gentle enough for Erin to ride."

Beau nodded in understanding. "And now you can't afford to geld him. A palomino stud can be worth his weight in gold, especially if he can pass that color on to some of his babies."

Beau knew there was no guarantee of that. Palomino was a color, not a breed of horse. And breeding golden horses was as chancy as rolling dice in Las Vegas.

"I'll just have to convince Erin that she can have the next foal born," Will concluded in that same pigheaded tone Beau had heard their father use.

"That would be a waste of your time. She's already named him," Beau reminded him. "You aren't going to change her mind now."

"I can't have her taking on a stallion as her first horse," Will replied with an emphatic nod. "You know what a handful a young stud colt can be. Unpredictable as hell, even rank sometimes. Too many blasted things can go wrong. Erin could end up getting hurt bad."

Beau shrugged off his brother's concern. "You'll just have to cross that bridge when it comes. If it comes. Right now the foal isn't even a day old. Put some trust in Sky's training. He isn't going to let Erin have the colt until he's sure she can manage him. Things will work out. You'll see."

Will gave Beau a pained look. "I can tell you've never been a father, especially to a girl. So many blasted things can go wrong. And in a few years, when she's old enough for boys, it'll be ten times worse."

"And she has her mother's looks." Beau shook his head, savoring the rare chance to needle his brother. "Given a choice, would you rather she'd been born plain as mud like you?"

"Don't ask. And I don't even want to guess what Tori's going to say about all this. She's even more protective of Erin than I am."

They walked in silence a moment before Beau spoke. "What happened between you and Tori anyway? You never said."

Will cast him a stormy look. "It's over. Dead and buried. So mind your own cattle."

In the last two centuries, little about the annual spring roundup on a cattle ranch had changed. Its purpose remained the same: to gather all the cattle that had wintered in sheltered canyon pastures in preparation for moving them to their summer graze on the plain above the Caprock. Once the gather was made, the herd would be sorted, culled, and counted. Pregnant cows and heifers would be separated from the rest, and any calves or yearlings that had been missed the previous fall would be branded, vaccinated, tagged, and, if destined to be steers, castrated. For the cowhands and bosses, that meant long days of backbreaking work, days that could stretch into two weeks, or even longer.

After only three days in the saddle, Beau was sore and bone-weary. Yet, despite the discomfort, he was secretly pleased that he remembered how to cowboy. Admittedly he was a little rusty, but the old skills were coming back—along with a level of contentment that was rare to him.

Between the clear spring days, the hard physical work, and the easy camaraderie with the cowhands, who weren't above teasing the "dude" in their midst, Beau could feel his tightly clenched nerves unwinding. It was as if his whole body had begun to breathe again; he was even sleeping the whole night through without waking up. Truthfully he couldn't remember feeling this at ease with himself in years.

He wasn't about to admit it to his brother, but Beau was enjoying this break from Washington and those long days of sitting behind a desk dealing with stacks of dreary paperwork and harried people who wanted everything yesterday. And the open country around him was a welcome change from that hellish D.C. traffic.

Open was something of a relative term, Beau acknowledged. This particular section of the ranch they were working stretched below the escarpment. It was a veritable maze of gullies, draws, and box canyons. And every inch of it needed to be searched.

In his side vision, he caught a glimpse of rusty red hide. He snapped his head around just as a pair of steers trotted out of view, heading up a brushy side canyon. Touching a spur to the horse's flank, he reined the gelding after them. Jutting rocks marked the canyon's entrance. Beau had already ridden past them in pursuit of the cattle before he recognized the distinctive formation that identified his exact location on the ranch. Abruptly he reined his horse to a plunging stop to look around, letting the half-forgotten knowledge come flooding back.

This small arroyo lay along the ranch's boundary line that butted against Prescott's land. The canyon itself was Y-shaped, dividing into two branches. He glanced up the left branch, recalling that it ended in a sheltered rock wall where he and Will had gone as boys to view the Indian petroglyphs scattered over its surface, making up their own wild stories as to the meaning of them.

But it was the second branch that claimed the whole of his attention now. Where once a clear stream of water had tumbled down from the rock and spilled to the pool on the canyon floor, now there was nothing but a dry wash, overgrown with scraggly brush and mesquite. Rusty strands of barbed wire blocked the path that had led to the stream. A crudely painted sign hung crookedly from the fence's top wire:

NO TRESPASSING

PROPERTY OF PRESCOTT RANCH

Beau glared at the board, surprised that he could still feel the anger of years ago so strongly.

"It still smarts, doesn't it?" Will's voice traveled across the stillness.

Turning, Beau discovered that his brother had ridden up to join him. "How many times did Bull pound in our heads when we were kids that no Tyler ever sold an inch of Rimrock land—that a Tyler would cut off his roping hand first. That little canyon and its water was Rimrock property." Beau jabbed a finger in its direction, his voice tight and low with barely suppressed anger. "And Bull sold it. And not just to anybody. No, he sold to Ferguson Prescott, the man Bull hated. And the purchase price was one dollar and 'other valuable considerations.' What the hell was he thinking?"

"It never made sense to me either," Will admitted.

"Didn't you ever ask him about it?" Beau challenged as his horse moved restlessly beneath him.

"Once. A few months ago, I was going through the files and ran across the original bill of sale. I figured it was time I learned the truth behind it, so I took the bill of sale in to him. The minute I showed it to him, he started swearing, telling me it was none of my damned business and I wasn't to ask him about it again."

"Swearing and shouting at people were the two things Bull did best," Beau said, easily visualizing the scene Will described. "I'll bet he threatened to kick you out if you brought it up again."

"More or less," Will admitted.

But it was the lack of any resentment in his voice that Beau couldn't understand. "That's where you and I are different. When he told me it was his way or hit the road, I told him what he could do with this ranch and his money and took the road."

"So that's how it happened," Will murmured.

"With a lot more yelling back and forth." He hadn't expected to feel all the old bitterness so strongly. "The essence was that he didn't give a damn if I was his son, that there was no way I was going to live off him."

"That's in the past. Nothing good comes out of dwelling in it," Will stated, pragmatic as always.

"Unless you can learn something." Beau let his glance wander over the dry streambed and the crudely painted sign on the barbed wire fence strung across it. "To get this land from Bull, old man Prescott must have had something on him."

"Like what?" Will sounded skeptical.

"Some secret Bull didn't want people to know. It's the only thing that makes sense," Beau declared, then voiced the question that automatically came to mind. "Wonder what it was?"

"I doubt if it was anything like that." Will dismissed the possibility with a shake of his head. "More than likely Bull lost a bet to him. You know what a sore loser he was. And losing a bet to old man Prescott would stick in his craw big-time."

"It might have been that simple," Beau conceded, then frowned, trying to remember another tidbit from the past. "Am I wrong, or is this the canyon where legend has it that lost Spanish gold is buried?"

The legend had been part of Texas for as long as anyone could remember. The story went that a band of lost Spanish explorers, pursued by Indians, had become trapped in the canyon and managed to hide the chest of gold coins they were transporting before the Indians attacked and wiped them out.

"That's the way the story goes—if you believe that stuff." The line of Will's mouth crooked in cynical derision. "There isn't an ounce of truth in it. But who knows, it could be why old man Prescott wanted it. I know for a fact he had a couple men with shovels out, digging all over the place and sifting the dirt through a box screen. I later heard they never found a damned thing."

"All that digging is probably what disrupted the spring," Beau guessed. "Remember when we used to fill our canteens from it? That water was always cold and good."

But Will had a more practical view. "And the cattle didn't have to walk so far for water when the spring was flowing."

Flashing him an amused look, Beau remarked, "You are definitely Bull's son."

There was a moment of hesitation, as if Will was debating some issue with himself. "Keep this under your hat, brother, but I'm working on a plan to get this canyon back."

"What?" The question came out, mingled with a near laugh. "Just what makes you think the syndicate would sell it? They sure as hell don't need the money."

"It just so happens that the syndicate doesn't own this particular parcel," Will informed him. "I did some checking and discovered that, for whatever reason, this land is part of the Prescott family trust. And our fine, upstanding congressman Garn Prescott is the trustee."

"So Garn would have the power to sell it back, assuming you can talk him into it." Beau swatted away a pesky horsefly buzzing around his face. "It explains why you asked him to do the eulogy at the funeral. You're trying to get all palsy with him."

"I told you before, we need allies, not enemies. And it so happens Prescott's up for reelection this fall. I'm prepared to make a hefty donation to his campaign in exchange for this worthless little canyon that's too steep for grazing."

"And you think he'll agree to that?"

Will's horse swung its nose around in an attempt to dislodge the fly that had landed on its neck. Will absently brushed off the fly. "Maybe he will. Maybe not. But there's more than one way to skin a coyote."

In his mind's eye, Beau saw again that scene at the house after the funeral when he'd observed Garn Prescott clearly making a move on Tori. It couldn't have been more obvious that Prescott wanted to get to know her a lot better.

"I'll bet Tori could talk him into it."

"Leave Tori out of this!" Will snapped.

Beau had seen his brother angry before, but not this hot. "Sorry." He wisely refrained from mentioning the way Garn had been hanging all over her, recognizing jealousy when he saw it. "Maybe I could help," he suggested instead. "I've never known a politician yet who didn't have his finger in some dirty pie. Ferreting out nasty secrets is part of what I do for a living."

Will briefly considered the offer, then shook it away with a half-irritated sigh. "As much as I would enjoy bringing that pompous jackass down, I'd rather this be an up-front deal." He gathered up his horse's reins. "We've got cattle to find. We'd better get to it."

"I spotted a couple headed up the canyon's other fork." Beau swung his horse around and brought it up level with Will's bay gelding. With curiosity nagging at him, he asked, "Did Prescott have anything to do with you and Tori splitting up?"

"Does it matter?" Will fired back, going all tight-jawed on him. "It happened. And it's over."

Beau doubted it was over as far as his brother was concerned. "You two seemed to fit together so well, like you were made for each other. There were times when I'd see you with Tori and would feel a little envious because you clearly had something special going."

"Funny you should say that," he countered. "You see, I always thought Natalie was the special one for you."

Beau recoiled slightly. The mere sound of her name was like being stabbed. It was impossible to think of her without remembering the feel of her in his arms, the warmth of her body quivering beneath him, or the welling of emotion that choked him.

When Beau failed to say anything, Will spoke. "You know Bull was always certain the ranch would pull you back here. I always thought you'd come back for Natalie."

"After I got back from Afghanistan . . ." Beau paused, searching for the right words. "Let's just say . . . things changed."

"But not the way you feel about her. I saw the way you looked at her that night in the barn when the foal was born. You didn't seem to be aware of anything—or anyone—else."

Beau didn't bother to deny it. "You're forgetting that she's married."

"And you're wishing you could forget it."

"It so happens that I've had the dubious pleasure of meeting her husband." Unwilling to discuss the subject of Natalie any further, Beau switched the focus back on his brother. "You were never exactly a saint. So, tell me, Will, who's filling your bed since the divorce? Do you have a mistress tucked away somewhere? Or are there some desperate housewives in town, willing to put out for any man who'll leave some money on the dresser to help with all their past-due bills?"

But he didn't get the expected rise from his brother. "I'm glad to hear you're giving some serious thought to staying here at the ranch."

Dumbfounded, Beau turned in his saddle to stare at his brother. "What the hell are you talking about? I never suggested any such thing."

"Of course you did. Why else would you ask about the ready availability of sex in town?" Will countered.

"I wasn't talking about myself! I was talking about you," Beau retorted, then added in a mutter, "Blanco Springs is the last place where I'd go looking for it."

The small town was a place of few secrets. There was too much chance that Natalie would find out if he happened to sleep with a woman she knew.

Before Will could offer a reply, Beau sank spurs into his mount, sending it jumping forward. A young steer burst from a mesquite thicket. And Beau took off in pursuit.

Erin knelt in the straw, stroking the foal. His golden coat was velvety to the touch. His young muscles, growing stronger every day, quivered beneath her palm. In a few weeks he'd be big enough to run and play in the paddock.

"Tesoro." His ear twitched as she whispered his name. "We're going to have so much fun together."

Sky had told her that Tesoro needed to learn his name and get used to the sound of her voice. So Erin talked to the foal the whole time she was with him. When she ran out of things to say, she sang old cowboy songs that Jasper had taught her when she was little. Songs like "Red River Valley" and "Streets of Laredo." Sometimes she sang the country and pop songs her school friends preferred. But Tesoro seemed to like the old songs best.

His silky muzzle nudged her arm. Sensing what he wanted,

she scratched behind his ears. Lupita raised her head, glanced at her baby, then went back to munching hay.

Erin dreaded tomorrow night when her mother would come to drive her back to town for school the next day. Foals grew up so fast. Tesoro would be bigger and more active when she came back next weekend. Would he still remember her?

The barn was quiet except for the soft horse sounds and the muted shovel-scrape of someone cleaning the stalls at the far end of the barn. Jasper sat on a wooden chair with the dog curled in the straw at his feet. The old man's eyes were closed, but Erin knew it wouldn't take much to snap him out of his doze. He was alert to everything around him.

As if her thoughts woke him, he opened his eyes and stirred, looking a mite uncomfortable. "Are you okay, Jasper?" she asked him.

He looked mildly embarrassed. "Fine, honey. But my rusty old plumbing's not what it used to be. I need to find a restroom."

"Go on. I'll be fine," she said.

"No, I promised your dad I wouldn't leave you alone. Come on out of the stall till I get back."

"Just let me stay here," Erin said. "My dad's an old fussbudget. I'll be fine."

"Don't ask me to break a promise, girl." Jasper pushed to his feet. "If you want to stay, I'll find somebody else. Lute," he called, opening the stall gate and stepping out. "Get on down here for a minute?"

A dark, skinny young fellow in a ragged blue T-shirt sauntered into Erin's view. "What's up, old man?"

"Not much. I need a break and Will doesn't want this young lady left alone in the stall. Could you spell me for a few minutes?"

"Sure. I could use a rest." He sank onto the chair as Jasper hobbled toward the barn door. He had sharp, black eyes like a bird's, and his worn leather gloves looked too big for his thin wrists. "Hi, I'm Lute," he said.

"I'm Erin." Her gaze sized him up. He looked old enough to be out of school, but not by much. "Do you work for my dad?"

"That's what I'm doing here, working." He spat out the last word as if he'd just bitten into a bad strawberry. "Sky gave me this so-called job. He's my cousin."

"Oh." Erin shifted to face him, interested in learning more. "Sky never talks about his family. I didn't know he had any."

"Sky's mother was my dad's sister. She died when he was little, and our family raised him. So he's almost like my big brother."

"What happened to his father?"

Lute shrugged his bony shoulders. "Who knows? He was just some white jerk who knocked her up. That's why Sky's got blue eyes. But he's mostly Comanche, like me."

"Oh." The young man did look something like Sky, Erin thought. But he was darker, his build smaller and more wiry, his features narrower.

His gaze had wandered to Tesoro. "That's a fine-looking foal," he said.

"He's going to be my horse." Erin laid a possessive hand on her foal's back. "Sky's already helping me train him. It's called imprinting. That's what I'm doing here."

"Sky's an important man on this ranch, isn't he?"

"My dad says he's the best horse trainer in Texas. That's why cow ponies raised on our ranch are worth so much money. And that's why we're getting more colts for him to train, so we can sell them."

Lute raised one jet-black eyebrow. "I hadn't heard that. Maybe Sky will give me a better job when those colts get here. I'm good with horses, too. When's it supposed to happen?"

"This spring, after the roundup, we'll be building extra pens. As soon as that's done, Sky can bring in the horses he wants and work with them over the summer."

"He's going to need some help. Maybe you can put in a good word for me." He rose, glancing back toward the barn door. "I see our old friend Jasper's coming back, so I'll get back to work. Nice talking to you, Miss Erin Tyler. Maybe we can talk again."

"Maybe so. Thanks for keeping me company, Lute."

"See you around." He opened the gate for Jasper and left. As he ambled away, Erin saw him take a cell phone out of his pocket, flip it open, and punch in a number.

CHAPTER 4

Slade Haskell slid out the back door of his red club-cab pickup. While his fingers tossed the condom and stuffed his privates back in his jeans, his eyes scanned the shadowy parking lot behind the Blue Coyote. Not that he was worried. The hour was late, the two remaining cars empty. Nobody was looking. And even if they were, what the hell. Everybody in town knew that Jess was a whore.

As his zipper closed with a satisfying *snick*, she came around the truck, pulling her little denim skirt down over her thighs. He had her usual payment ready—the small packet of white powder that he slipped out of his pocket and down the neck of her blouse. Whether she meant to resell it or snort it herself didn't matter, as long as she knew better than to tell anybody where it came from. Stella would likely guess if she saw it. But Stella wouldn't care as long as the girl kept her mouth shut.

As Jess trailed back into the bar, Slade pulled out of the parking lot, drove onto a side street, and stopped long enough to turn on the dome light and inspect the backseat for evidence. Finding none, he made a U-turn and headed for home.

He'd come back an hour early from a run to Lubbock to arrange a feed-hauling contract. Since Natalie wasn't expecting him till later, and since he'd told her not to wait up, Slade figured he was covered. With luck, when he walked in from the garage, his wife would be deep in clueless sleep.

Damned good woman, Natalie. Her work paid the household bills and balanced the ups and downs of the trucking business, allowing him to stash what he made on the side in a Lubbock bank. She was a looker, too, and sexy as hell. Slade would castrate any male who so much as breathed on her. But he'd never been a one-woman man, and marriage hadn't changed that. As long as he came home to his wife at night, what difference did it make?

He was pulling up to the house when he remembered that he hadn't checked his cell phone messages. Letting the truck idle, he took a moment. There were two voice mails from the Indian kid at the Tylers. The first one let him know they'd be getting extra colts to break over the summer. Maybe some possibilities there, and the kid seemed eager to please. If he proved reliable, it might be worth trying him on bigger things.

The second message triggered a spasm in his gut. Evidently Beau Tyler, who'd promised to be back in Washington by now, was still at the ranch helping with the roundup.

Did Natalie know? Had he contacted her? So help him, if she'd been with that bastard again . . .

Seething, Slade punched the remote and waited for the garage door to open. If Tyler had so much as phoned her, he would punch that smug, too-handsome face of his to a bloody pulp. As for Natalie . . .

The door cranked to a stop. The truck's headlights shone into an empty garage.

Natalie's white Toyota was gone.

Natalie turned the country radio station up full blast and willed herself to stay awake for a few more miles. She should have taken the Lindfords up on the thermos of coffee they'd offered to send with her. By the time their mare had delivered twin foals, she was dead on her feet, and the fifteen-mile drive home on back roads seemed more like a hundred.

It was almost 2:00 a.m., later than she'd planned to be gone. She'd thought of calling Slade. But she'd left him a note on the kitchen table. If he was home by now, he'd be asleep. It didn't make sense to wake him.

A jackrabbit bounded across the two-lane road ahead of her. She tapped the brake, ensuring the animal a clean getaway. Even rabbits deserved a happy life, she mused groggily.

She'd resolved not to think about Beau, but she was too tired to keep her thoughts from wandering. It was even later in Washington, D.C., than it was here in Texas. Was he asleep? Was he alone? She knew little about his life back East, but she couldn't imagine Beau having any trouble getting women—smart, sophisticated, beautiful women—into his bed. Natalie had no cause to envy them, but, heaven help her, she did. She and Beau had grown up together. They had given each other the gift of their innocence. He belonged to her in a way that he would never belong to anyone else.

The same way she belonged to him.

The memory stole through her like the scent of a pressed rose in a long-forgotten book. They'd been sixteen that summer evening, riding their horses up the canyon to a spot where a spring formed a pool in the rocks. They hadn't planned on going alone, but Tori had been commandeered to babysit at the last minute, leaving them to go without her. Beau had been herding cows on the ranch all day, and Natalie had been helping her grandfather paint his barn. Both of them were sweaty and tired. The water in the canyon was too cold for a swim, but the idea of a cool evening ride sounded like heaven.

Dressed in faded T-shirts and ragged cutoff jeans, they'd tethered their horses in the trees and climbed the narrow path up the rocks to the waterfall. On a grassy spot by the pool, they'd sprawled on their backs to gaze up at the river of sky above the steep canyon walls. The dying sun had streaked the clouds with violet and indigo and sculpted purple shadows in the recesses of the vermilion cliffs. A single star glimmered in the deepening sky.

On the trail they'd chatted—commonplace, easy talk about school and friends. But now they lay still in the twilight, listening to the splash of water and the faraway call of a coyote. Natalie could hear the sound of his breathing. Her body tingled with sensations she couldn't even name.

Until now they'd shared no more than a few playful kisses. But Natalie had loved him for as long as she could remember. At night she lay burning in her bed, daring to touch herself as she imagined his strong, golden body and the forbidden things that body could do. In spite of every well-meant warning she'd ever heard, she'd known that if Beau reached out for her, she would be his in a heartbeat.

That night, with scarcely a word, it had simply happened. They'd been lying a hand's breadth apart, their awareness of each other deepening to an ache. Natalie had turned on her side to find him looking at her, his eyes wells of raw need.

Lifting her hand, she'd stroked a fingertip down his cheek and along the edge of his lower lip. He'd moaned, taking her finger into his mouth and brushing it with his tongue. The urges that simple contact awakened had been too powerful to resist. Even as his arms reached out to pull her close, she'd understood what was going to happen, and she'd wanted it.

Softening her hips against his pelvis, she'd felt the long bulge of his erection like a solid log through his jeans. He'd been ready for her before she ever touched him, she realized. Knowing that he'd wanted her as much as she wanted him gave her a rush of courage. Taking his hand, she slid it under the hem of her T-shirt.

The day had been too hot for a bra. She'd felt his fingers tremble as they slid up her ribs and over her bare breast. The shimmering wave of pleasure was so intense it made her gasp. She arched her rib cage upward, her body begging for more. He stroked and caressed, growing bolder as he teased her nipples, feeling them shrink and harden at his touch. The low rasp of his breath quickened as his palm glided down her belly to the waistband of her shorts.

Was this his first time, too? She'd wanted it to be, but how could she be sure when there were girls with reputations who'd be more than willing to initiate a handsome boy like Beau?

Forcing the useless thought away, she'd reached down and managed to unsnap his jeans and slide his zipper open. There was nothing underneath but him, soft baby skin over tempered steel. Instinctively her fingers had circled his shaft. He'd groaned, his body stiffening as they tightened.

"Natalie—"

"Yes." The word had hissed between her lips. "Yes, Beau."

He was breathing hard now, muttering little curses under his breath as he fumbled with her shorts, gave up on the fastener, and simply yanked them off her hips. No experienced boy would have been so flustered. She'd loved him all the more for that.

Panting like a long-distance runner, he'd found her entrance, hesitated an instant, then shoved in. Slick as she was, she'd barely felt the brief tearing of her membranes. The pain was nothing compared to the thrill of feeling him inside her, moving, thrusting, both of them reeling in a world of new sensations.

Natalie swung the SUV onto the main highway to town. Her relationship with Beau had been over a long time ago, she reminded herself. They'd been two foolish children back then, crossing forbidden boundaries and making promises they could never keep. He had a different life now, in a different place. She had a husband, and she was on her way home to him. Nothing else was real anymore. Nothing else could be allowed to matter.

She would never see Beau Tyler again.

By the time she turned into the driveway and raised the garage door, it was all she could do to keep her eyes open. Slade's pickup was parked in its spot. Good. He'd made it safely home. With luck he'd be asleep. She could collapse onto her side of the bed and pass out till morning.

Closing the garage, she entered the house through the doorway that connected to the kitchen. The 15-watt light above the stove was on, casting the room into dim shadow. Slade was sitting at the kitchen table, a can of his favorite lager in one hand.

"It's about time you got home." His gritty voice oozed sarcasm. "Want to tell me where you've been?"

Please, not tonight. Stifling a groan, Natalie dropped her medical bag on a chair. "I was at the Lindfords. Didn't you see the note I left you?"

"Oh, I saw it, all right," he drawled. "The question is, was it true?"

"What kind of silly game are you playing, Slade?" Natalie was too tired to be patient. "I was at the Lindfords' place for hours. Their mare was having twins. It was touch and go the whole time. Now, if you'll excuse me, I'm exhausted. I'm going to bed." She spun away, heading down the hall toward the bedroom.

"Not so fast, you lying bitch."

His words stopped her like a brick wall. Slade had a nasty streak of temper, but he'd never used those words with her before. Steeling herself against the hurt, she turned slowly back to face him. She hadn't done anything to deserve this, and she didn't have to take it.

Every word she spoke felt chiseled out of ice. "Don't you ever call me that again. I'm not lying. I've been working all night."

His fist crushed the empty beer can and tossed it toward the trash. Missing the mark, it clattered across the linoleum. "You expect me to believe you haven't been with Beau Tyler?"

His question sucked the air out of her. She struggled for breath. "What's the matter with you? Beau's gone. He left for Washington three days ago."

"That's not what I heard." Slade folded his arms across his muscular chest, looking so smug that she wanted to fly at him and claw the smirk off his face. "A friend told me he stuck around to help with the roundup. Maybe he stuck around for a little bit of something else, too. What've you got to say about that?"

Natalie felt herself crumbling. Blinking away furious tears, she held herself rigidly erect. She couldn't let him see how his news had affected her.

"Even if I had known, it wouldn't have made any difference. I was at the Lindfords'. If you don't believe me, call and ask them. Make up some excuse—like maybe I lost my watch and want to know if they found it. Or maybe I'm not back yet, and you're worried. Right now I'm so tired I don't care what you do—or what you believe. If you have anything left to say, we can talk in the morning."

She turned away and headed down the hall, praying he wouldn't follow her. She didn't want to make up. She didn't even want to be touched. All she wanted was to be left alone.

"I'm going downstairs to watch wrestling," he called after her, and she almost melted with relief. "But hear this, lady. Nobody lays a hand on my wife. If that bastard Tyler comes anywhere near you, so help me, I'll kill him!"

On Sundays, when Tori came to pick up her daughter, she was expected to stay for dinner. Awkward as it sometimes felt, she tolerated the time-honored custom because it gave Erin a sense of family. It also helped Tori keep abreast of happenings on the ranch. Anything that might affect Erin was a concern to her.

Tonight the main dish was roast wild turkey, which Jasper had shot from the ATV he used to get around the ranch. The old man might not be able to ride a horse anymore, but his distance vision was still good and he could handle a gun with the best.

Over the years, the line between the Tylers and their longtime staff had faded. Jasper, as usual, had joined them at the table. Bernice, too, would take her place once the food was served. Sometimes Sky dined with them, but mostly he seemed to be busy elsewhere. Or maybe it was just that he preferred a peaceful meal in his side of the brick duplex he shared with Jasper. Conversations at the Tylers' table could get pretty dramatic.

Since it was a family occasion, they joined hands while Jasper said grace. As he rambled on, Tori caught herself peering at the circle of familiar faces from beneath her half-lowered eyelashes.

Erin's freshly scrubbed features revealed glimpses of the beautiful woman she would become one day. And her body . . . Tori felt a gnawing panic as she realized her daughter's little breasts were already budding beneath her pink T-shirt. When had that happened? It was time to shop for a training bra.

Jasper and Bernice were getting older, too. Now that Bull was gone, they were the only remaining links to the past, the keepers of memory and the keepers of secrets. More secrets, Tori sensed, than anyone in the family suspected.

Wise, cynical Beau, he was the closest thing to a brother that Tori, an only child, had ever known.

In their teen years, he'd been her confidant, her shoulder to cry on when Will ignored her. Then Natalie had come along. Tori had once believed that Natalie and Beau would live happily ever after. But sad experience had taught her that fairy-tale endings were just that—fairy tales.

Which brought her furtive gaze to Will.

A familiar ache stirred in Tori's throat as she studied him, head bowed, eyes closed. He looked tired, she thought. The creases had deepened at the corners of his eyes, and his dark hair had taken on a sheen of silver. He was only thirty-nine, but since Bull's accident, and especially now, following Bull's death, Will's duties as head of the ranch family weighed heavily on him.

Tori wasn't surprised that he was still single. He was married to the ranch; he always had been.

"Amen," Jasper rumbled.

With a murmured "Amen" and a whoosh of relief, Erin reached for the basket of Bernice's fresh, hot rolls, took one, and passed it on. Soon plates were filled with turkey, stuffing, potatoes and gravy, buttered carrots, and fresh green salad.

"Well, Tori, what do you think of Erin's new foal?" Bernice asked, making conversation.

"He's a beautiful little thing," Tori said. "But I'm aware of the gelding issue, and frankly, I'm uneasy about Erin raising a stud, especially for her first horse."

"Oh, Mom, I'll be fine!" Erin speared a second hot roll. "Sky's helping me train him. Tesoro already knows my smell and my voice. Anyway, I like the idea of having my very own stallion. It'll be cool."

"It won't be cool if he hurts you." Tori glanced across the table at Will. "There are other pregnant mares out there. Why not let her choose a different foal?"

"No, Mom!" Erin's fork clattered to her plate. "Daddy promised me Tesoro! He's already mine and I won't give him up!"

"Give it time, Tori." Beau had always been the peacemaker. "That foal has a lot of growing up to do, and so does Erin. For now they'll be fine together. Later on, if he shows signs of being hard to handle, we can decide what to do."

"Beau's right, Tori," Will said. "I know you're worried. I was, too, but I've thought it over. I did promise Erin the foal, and she's already attached to him. Nothing's going to happen while he's little."

"So now you're ganging up on me. Three against one." The look Tori gave Will expressed more than words. She'd surrendered the battle but not the war. When it came to her daughter's safety, there was no middle ground. She'd castrate that colt herself—or shoot him if she had to—before she'd let any harm come to Erin.

A strained silence fell over the table. Knowing she'd caused it, Tori smiled and deftly changed the subject. "So I've heard rumors that you'll be sticking around, Beau."

He shrugged, looking a bit uncomfortable. "Till the roundup's over, at least. But I'm only on leave from work. I haven't quit."

"You might as well hand in your notice tomorrow." Will

carved a slice off the turkey roast and laid it on his plate. "You know you'll end up staying."

"We'll see."

"What's to decide? You belong here. We need you. Enough said. Anybody else want more turkey?" He carved three more slices and left them on the platter. The silence had descended once more. Tori could feel the tension between the two brothers creeping upward like the red line on a pressure gauge. Was it about to explode?

Bernice, ever the wise one, rolled her eyes and gazed up at the brass chandelier that hung over the dining room table. Her round, rosy face was a mask of innocence. "My, hasn't it been a lovely day," she said. "Do you think it's too early to put out the tomato plants?"

Lute sat at a table in the Blue Coyote, sipping a Corona and feeling like a man. He'd been half afraid to believe the fifty-dollar payment from Slade would be there. But when he'd worked up the nerve to approach Stella, she'd given him a friendly smile and handed him a plain white envelope. Inside he'd found the cash—two twenties and a ten.

He'd planned on saving most of it for the down payment on a car. But his first paycheck from the ranch wouldn't be coming in for another week, and this was like found money. It was a real treat, just sitting here with a decent beer in his hand and cash in his pocket.

It was a quiet night, even for a Wednesday. There were no more than a half dozen customers in the place. Lute's gaze followed Jess as she wandered among the tables, keeping the patrons happy. She looked pretty tonight, he thought. Her clean, shiny hair curled around her thin shoulders, softening the sharp lines of her face. Her jeans were stylishly ripped—distressed, was that what they called it? Through the thready holes, glints of tanned skin triggered a light, pleasant buzz of arousal. And she was wearing those little pink boots he found so hot.

"Hi." She paused at his table. "Can I get you anything else?"

"Maybe." He remembered how Slade had talked to her. "What time do you get off tonight?"

Her gaze flickered. "About ten. We close early on week-nights."

Lute did a quick mental calculation. Ralph wouldn't be picking him up till midnight, so he'd have some leeway. "Want to share a pizza? If we hurry, we can get it before Burger Shack closes at ten-thirty. I can order ahead if I know what kind you like."

Her eyes lit in a surprising way. "You're asking me out on a date?"

"Just pizza. It'll be too late for a movie. We can do that another time—I mean, if you want to." Lute felt like a tongue-tied teenager. He'd never had much luck, let alone much experience, with girls, though he'd had sex once with a girl in his high school class who'd do it with anybody for twenty bucks.

But Jess was different. She was pretty and sweet in a way that made him want to do something nice for her, like take her out for pizza. Maybe when he got money and a car, she'd spend more time with him. He'd enjoy being seen with a good-looking girl. "So how about it?" he asked. "Want to go?"

"Sure." She gave him a shy smile. "And I like Hawaiian."

Jess watched the red lights fade as the rusty pickup vanished down the street. Turning away, she climbed the back stairs to her room above the Blue Coyote. It had been nice, sharing a pizza with young Lute. He reminded her of her kid brother, who'd died six years ago in a motorcycle accident. And he'd treated her like a lady, as if he didn't know what she really was. It was almost like being in high school again. But she'd come a long way since high school—mostly in the wrong direction. She was long overdue for a change.

She'd sold Slade's high-grade cocaine to a dealer she knew. Once she might have snorted it herself, but now she needed the money even more than she craved the high. She had to get out of this place, away from the people who were dragging her down.

She'd weighed the wisdom of warning Lute about Slade, then decided the risk was too great. Lute was already under the man's spell. If he went to Slade with what she'd told him, it could be all over for her.

She already knew too much.

Slade's trucking business was done on contract, with vehicles for freight, produce, livestock, hay, and feed. He employed three local drivers who, as far as Jess knew, carried legitimate cargo. But it was Slade who made the runs to Mexico, hauling baled Texas hay to a ranch two hundred miles south of Piedras Negras.

She'd already known he got the drugs through his Mexican connection. But it was by pure chance she'd discovered what was under the hay. Three nights ago, Slade had stopped by for a quickie on his way out of town. Since the bar was still open and her room was directly above the thin ceiling, they'd done their business on a blanket laid over the hay in the back of the closed truck. Jess was rearranging herself when she discovered she was missing a favorite earring. When she couldn't find it on the blanket, she reached down between the hay bales. Her groping fingers contacted cold, smooth metal in the unmistakable shape of a gun barrel. She felt another, then another.

Slade had climbed out of the truck to let her finish putting herself back together, but he suddenly appeared below the partly raised door. "What the hell do you think you're doing?" he'd growled.

His vehemence had scared her. When she'd stammered that she was looking for her earring, he'd seized her arm and yanked her roughly out of the truck. "I'll buy you more damned earrings," he'd growled. "Now get back in the bar and do your job."

His tires had spat gravel as he roared out of the parking lot. Jess hadn't seen him since, but her instincts told her Slade was dangerous.

She'd been saving money, planning to eventually leave and make a new start somewhere else. But something inside told her that she had to leave now—tonight.

There was less than a thousand dollars stashed away in her mattress. It wouldn't get her far, but Slade would be back in the next day or two. If he found out she had discovered the guns he was smuggling into Mexico, anything could happen.

Opening the door of her grubby little room, she dragged her backpack out from under the bed and began stuffing it with the few things she could carry. She could only hope somebody on the road would give her a ride out of town, to someplace where she could buy a bus ticket.

Time was running out.

CHAPTER 5

As the sun continued its climb in the morning sky, inching ever closer to its apex, Beau could feel the warmth of its rays on his back. After nearly nine days in the saddle, he had managed to work all the stiffness out of his muscles.

Slowly he walked the close-coupled roan nearer to the milling knot of steers. The minute he spotted the unmarked yearling bull that had eluded last fall's roundup, he swung the roan into the herd, intent on separating the yearling from the rest.

As if knowing it was destined to be branded, tagged, and relieved of its cojones, the young Hereford bull made a dash for a clump of nearby mesquite. The cow-savvy roan seemed to anticipate the escape attempt, simultaneously lunging forward to block its path.

After that, Beau had only to sit easy in the saddle and let the well-trained cow pony do his job. With catlike agility, the roan gelding cut off the yearling's dash to freedom and turned it back toward the herd. The young bull made a show of returning, then attempted another break. The roan thwarted it with ease.

Spider Jones, one of Rimrock's younger cowhands, joined up with Beau and together they herded the animal to the chutes. Once the gate clanged shut behind it, Beau leaned forward in the saddle to stroke the roan's damp neck, offering low praise. "If that had been a cutting contest, you would have won us some money."

Spider Jones swung his horse alongside Beau. Together they jogged their horses back to the gather. "Nice work. But that's what I like about working for Rimrock. You've got good horses here."

"That we do," Beau agreed, well aware that the bulk of the credit for them belonged to Sky and his skill in training.

"I was wondering . . . ," Spider began, then hesitated and started over, his uncertain blue eyes darting a glance at Beau. "We've probably got only a few more days of roundup before we're finished. Me and a couple of the other boys plan on going into Lubbock to celebrate. There's a club there that has a room upstairs where a fella can go to get that manly itch scratched . . . if you know what I mean. You're welcome to join us. If you like," he added, suddenly uneasy, as if he was worried that, by inviting one of the new owners, he had violated some unwritten rule.

"Sounds like the go-to place for a good time." Beau deliberately let the young cowboy believe he might accompany them. But as far as he was concerned, there was only one woman he wanted to scratch his itch, and she wasn't in Lubbock.

Although on second thought, Beau realized that the wisest course might be to go to Lubbock. Natalie was a married woman, and it was best if he kept his distance.

"You got that righ—How the hell did he get his rope tangled up like that?" Disgust and amazement mingled together in his voice. Following the direction of Spider's gaze, Beau saw Lute, his rope partially around his body and a half loop around his horse's nose. "For somebody who's supposed to be related to Sky, he sure is worthless around cattle," the young cowboy declared. "Somebody needs to take that rope away from him and put a shovel back in his hand."

"Heads-up, Beau! Two o'clock!" Will's voice barked across

the distance, directing Beau's attention to the cow and calf just breaking free of the gather.

Beau reined after them. In two jumps, the roan was at full stride. After a half dozen more, he was level with the escaping pair. The cow swung away from him and meekly trotted back to the herd, her calf trailing and bawling in confusion.

Checking the roan to a walk, Beau lifted his free hand to signal Will that the runaways were back in the fold. But Will wasn't where he had last seen him. He was galloping his tall bay toward a half dozen steers, bunched on the far side of a clearing. Intent on the strays, he didn't seem to notice that he was headed straight into a prairie dog colony. Hated by ranchers, the little rodents dug burrows that could trap and break the leg of a horse or cow.

Beau shouted a warning. Seeing the danger, Will wheeled his mount hard to the left. For a split second everything seemed fine. Then, suddenly, it wasn't.

The horse shied, shrieked, and shot straight up, twisting in midair like a rodeo bronc. In a scene that took on the slow-motion quality of a nightmare, Will flew out of the saddle. One foot caught the stirrup, then slid free of the boot as he slammed to the ground, landing flat on his back. Unharmed, the terrified bay plunged through the brush, gaining distance with every bound.

By now Beau was close enough to leap off his mount and race toward his brother. Will appeared dazed but he was moving, raising his head and shifting his legs.

A dozen strides away, Beau heard Will utter a sharp grunt of pain. Twisting sideways on the ground, Will yanked out his holstered pistol and fired three low shots at something unseen on the far side of his legs. Bits of pink and gray exploded into the air.

An instant later, Beau reached Will's side. There in the dust, inches from Will's leg, lay the bullet-riddled carcass of a diamondback rattlesnake, six feet long and as thick as a man's forearm.

Will's face was tinged with gray. He slumped back onto one elbow. "Bastard got me, Beau," he muttered, pointing to his thigh. "But I got him back."

Kicking the dead snake out of the way, Beau crouched next to his brother, his heart pounding and a sick knot forming in his stomach.

He threw a shout over his shoulder for help, yanked out his pocketknife, opened it, and slashed the denim away from Will's leg. The flesh was already swelling around the two deep red puncture wounds. Beau knew a rattler that size could inject a hefty dose of venom. More than enough to kill a man without prompt treatment.

"Bad, is it?" Will cursed through clenched teeth.

"Bad enough. Don't try to talk. Just lie still."

Whipping off his bandana, he knotted it around Will's thigh a few inches above the wound. It would need to be loosened every few minutes. A too-tight tourniquet could shut off the blood flow into the leg, doing more harm than good. And the old practice of cutting the flesh and sucking out the venom had also proven to be ineffective. The best course of action was to keep Will quiet and get him to a hospital; it was the only way to save Will's leg, and maybe his life.

Sky was the first to reach them. His cool blue eyes quickly took in the situation. He tossed Beau the canteen from his saddle. "Pour this on the bite. The nearest hospital's in Lubbock. I'll call for Life Flight." He whipped out his cell phone and punched in 911.

Beau helped Will sit up to keep his heart above his leg and slow the rise of the venom. Knowing the leg would swell, he cut off the rest of the pant leg and removed the sock. Will had lost the boot when the horse bucked him off.

"Somebody better catch that damned horse." Will's jaw was clenched. He had to be in excruciating pain, but he was playing the tough guy, determined not to show it.

"The horse will be fine." Beau used the water in Sky's canteen to flush the wound. "Right now all that matters is getting you to the hospital."

Sky was still on the phone, speaking, then waiting and speaking again, his voice a low staccato.

"Make sure they have antivenin," Beau said. "He's going to need it."

Sky asked a few more questions, ended the call, and shook his head. "A helicopter can be here in twenty minutes. But they're out of antivenin. A new shipment's coming in tomorrow."

Beau swore. The antidote for rattlesnake venom was most effective if given intravenously within the first couple of hours. Tomorrow could be too late. For all he knew, Will could be dead by then. "Try Amarillo," he said. "They've got to have some."

Sky frowned. "Wait . . . Natalie should have antivenin. She keeps a supply for dogs."

"Call her," Beau said.

While Sky speed-dialed Natalie's number, Beau busied himself with adjusting the bandana around Will's thigh. The whole leg had begun to swell. Will purpled the air with curses as Beau retied the cloth. "Bad?" he asked needlessly.

"Hurts like bloody hell." Will spat in the direction of the dead reptile. "And the timing sucks. Who's going to boss the roundup?"

"The men know their jobs. And Sky can manage things fine." Beau glanced upward. "The helicopter should be here soon. Just be quiet and take it easy."

"I could use a swallow of whiskey."

"Not a good idea, brother."

Sky had ended the call. "Natalie's got antivenin. It will be fastest if she drives to Lubbock; she should get there about the same time the copter lands."

An eternity seemed to pass before they heard the drone of the red and white Life Flight helicopter. Refusing to stay quiet, Will had spent the interim giving Sky a running litany of muttered instructions, things Sky doubtless already knew. Even in his dire condition, Will couldn't let go of his duties.

By the time the paramedics loaded him in the helicopter, Will's pulse was racing at a gallop. Beau insisted on riding along. Though it wasn't usual policy, the paramedics didn't argue. Will was a powerful man and not in his right mind. If he got hard to handle in the air, they might need help calming him.

Beau clasped his brother's hand while the technician inserted an IV with a saline drip in his arm. Will was mumbling now, demanding that he be taken back to the ranch—a sign that the venom was already seeping into his system.

Although the flight to the hospital was a relatively short one, each minute in the air seemed three times as long. As the helicopter began its descent to the hospital's landing pad, Beau clasped Will's shoulder, giving it a reassuring squeeze.

"Hang in there, big brother," he ordered. "Everything's going to be fine now."

Will looked directly at him and said something back, but the roar of the engine drowned out the sound of his voice. Even so, Beau was able to ascertain the words his lips shaped.

Call Tori, Will had said.

Beau answered with a nod of promise.

As soon as the helicopter touched down, the engine was cut back, and the paramedics scrambled to unload their patient onto a waiting gurney. Will was already being whisked inside by the time Beau climbed out of the chopper.

Once inside the emergency department, Beau had a brief glimpse of Will on the gurney before the set of double doors to the trauma unit slid shut behind him. One of the paramedics motioned for Beau to join him at the admissions desk.

"They need some information on your brother."

Reluctantly Beau allowed himself to be sidetracked from following Will into the trauma unit. Other than the absolute basics of name, age, blood type, address, and next of kin, there was scant information that Beau could provide. Any allergies or medications Will might be taking, Beau had to admit he didn't know.

After that was finished, someone else handed him a bag of his brother's personal items—his watch, wallet, and cell phone—and pointed him toward the emergency department's waiting room.

It was a small area, mostly unoccupied at that hour, with soothing blue walls, black vinyl couches, and framed prints of Texas wildflowers. Timeworn copies of *People* magazine, *Golf Digest*, and *Good Housekeeping* littered the tables. A frayed-looking woman was knitting what appeared to be an orange muffler while an unshaven man was sprawled on one of the side couches, lightly snoring.

Unwilling to twiddle his thumbs on one of the couches, Beau went to find out whether the antivenin had arrived. But no one either could or would tell him.

Again he bypassed the waiting area and walked out the emergency entrance to scan the parking lot, but there was no sign of Natalie's white SUV. He glanced at his watch and knew she had to be close. He wouldn't allow himself to consider that something might have happened en route to delay her.

To keep any thoughts blocked, he retrieved Will's cell phone from the bag and used the number in his brother's contact list to call Tori. Her phone rang once, then twice more before her voice mail came on. He left a message that omitted most of the worrisome details and asked her to call him. Not sure when Tori might check it, Beau decided to try her again in a few minutes. In the meantime, he phoned the ranch house and talked to Bernice. Again, he soft-pedaled Will's condition.

"You will let us know the minute you hear anything, won't you?" the anxious housekeeper urged as a siren's wail grew steadily louder, indicating the approach of an emergency vehicle.

"I promise. Tell Jasper not to worry. Will's in good hands."

A patrol car, its siren screaming, came speeding into view and swung into the driveway to the emergency entrance. There was abrupt silence as the siren was killed. But it was the white SUV directly behind that claimed the whole of Beau's attention.

The white Land Cruiser screeched into a parking stall next to the emergency entrance. The door flew open and Natalie spilled out of the driver's seat, one hand clutching a small medical cooler. Dressed in jeans and a wrinkled khaki work shirt, she was disheveled and windblown, her face bare of makeup.

And she had never looked more beautiful, for a multitude of reasons, none of which was necessarily related to the other.

Her head came up the instant she saw him, her back straightened, and Beau had the impression she was erecting mental barriers against him.

"Thank God you made it without being pulled over," Beau said, relieved the two-hour window wouldn't be pushed to the limit.

"I probably would have if I hadn't had an escort," Natalie told him, directing a side glance to his right.

Until that moment, Beau had totally forgotten the police cruiser that had pulled into the emergency driveway ahead of her. He turned as Hoyt Axelrod came walking up, sunlight flashing on the sheriff's badge pinned to his crisp uniform.

"Sheriff." Beau wasn't sure whom he'd expected to see, but it wasn't Axelrod

"Talk about being in the right place at the right time. I had stopped by the call center when they got the word that Will had been snakebit. Few minutes later we heard that Natalie was making a mercy run to bring her supply of antivenin." He absently shifted the holstered pistol to a more comfortable position. "I figured she could make the drive quicker, with fewer incidents, if she had an official escort." A dark eyebrow shot up. "Can you imagine a hospital in Texas running out of such a thing? 'Course, it is spring, and the rattlers are coming out of their dens all cranky and hungry."

"How's Will?" Natalie inserted.

"Not good," Beau admitted.

Immediately she struck out for the automatic door to the ER. "I brought six vials. It was all I had." She tossed the information over her shoulder as the door opened ahead of her.

Beau followed her inside while the sheriff trailed both of them. In short order, they located a nurse. Natalie passed the cooler to her and dug a folded piece of paper from her pocket.

"I'll need someone to sign this, accepting the transfer of the vials," she told the nurse.

"I'll get it signed and bring it right back to you," the nurse promised after a brief scan of the unfolded paper.

"I'd like to see my brother," Beau said.

"Not yet." The nurse smiled her regret. "When we have him stabilized, somebody will come and get you."

It wasn't exactly the answer he wanted, but grudgingly Beau accepted it, holding his silence when the nurse walked away.

"He's going to be fine now, Beau," Natalie assured him.

"Thanks to you." He glanced at the woman standing at his side and experienced a prick of conscience. "Sorry, I should have said that sooner. Heaven knows you didn't have to volunteer to bring it to the hospital."

"Will is my friend," she said with quick emphasis. "You do things like this for friends."

On the surface she seemed to be using friendship to justify her actions. But Beau had the impression she was using it to keep him at a distance.

"You're right, of course," he agreed, and smiled to himself, certain there had never been anything remotely platonic about their feelings toward each other in the past. And that was still true today, no matter how much she might try to convince herself to the contrary.

"Hey, you two!" the sheriff called to them from a small alcove outside the waiting room. "I just brewed some fresh coffee. Want a cup?"

"I could definitely use a cup." Natalie was quick to accept the offer as she turned from Beau and started across the space to the alcove.

"Make that two cups."

After passing a Styrofoam cup of steaming coffee to Natalie, Hoyt Axelrod filled one for Beau. "I heard you hadn't taken the flight back to D.C. like you planned." He handed him the second cup and picked up his own.

"Will was short-handed and faced with spring roundup. Since I was entitled to two weeks' bereavement, I decided to take it and help him out."

"Turned out to be a good thing you did or you wouldn't have been on hand when he got snakebit." Axelrod hooked a thumb over his belt and leaned a husky shoulder against the wall.

"I guess you're right." Beau blew on the coffee's steaming surface and inhaled its rich aroma.

"Have you talked to Tori?" Natalie inserted.

"I called, but it went straight to voice mail. I left word for her to call me as soon as she got my message. So far, nothing."

"I keep thinking about Erin, how upset she'll be and worried about her dad," Natalie murmured.

Beau started to pull out his cell phone to try Tori again, but stopped when he saw the doctor, a sturdy, balding man in green scrubs, pushing his way through the swinging doors. He walked straight to them.

"Here's your receipt, Dr. Haskell." He handed a sheet to Natalie, showing the respect of one professional to another before turning to Beau.

"How's my brother?"

"We've got him on the antivenin, as well as some fluids and Dilaudid for the pain. There's no reason he shouldn't make a full recovery, but it won't happen overnight. He'll need to be here several days, then rest at home until the swelling goes down. That could take as long as a month."

Relief sagged through Beau, even as he recognized that Will was in for a miserable time. And he would be hell to live with until he was back on his feet.

"Is he awake?" Beau asked. "Can I see him now?"

"He's groggy, mostly because of the pain meds. But he's alert enough to know what's going on. You can see him, but no more than a minute or two," the doctor warned. "He needs to rest and let the antivenin do its work."

Stepping into the alcove, Beau set his cup of coffee on the counter. Natalie laid a delaying hand on his arm when he started past her. "Let Will know we're all thinking of him," she said.

"Will do," Beau promised, then sensed there was something she wasn't saying. "Are you leaving?"

"That new registered bull the Caulfields bought last week is running a fever. I got a call when I was halfway here," she explained. "They're keeping him isolated until I can get there and check him out."

Some inner sense alerted Beau to the close way Hoyt Axelrod was observing the two of them. As jealous as Natalie's husband seemed to be, Beau knew he needed to be circumspect and not add any fuel to the gossip mill.

"I know I've said thanks, but I mean it."

"I know." Her smile was stiff as if she, too, was aware of the sheriff's presence.

Turning, Beau followed the doctor into the ICU and down the row of small, white cubicles. Nothing could have prepared him for the sight of his brother, propped in a narrow bed with an IV and catheter tubes, oxygen lines, and beeping monitors connected to his body. His face was a stranger's, flushed and puffy. His bitten leg, swollen like a log, was covered with a sheet.

"You look like hell," Beau said, knowing that Will wouldn't want to be pitied or fussed over.

Will's purpled lips stretched in a grimace. "A damn sight better'n *you* did that time you bashed in a hornet's nest. Come here."

Beau leaned over the bed, hiding the rush of emotion he didn't want Will to see.

"Go home now." Will's voice was hoarse, his speech slurred. "You can't do a blasted thing for me here, but I need you at the ranch to see that things get looked after. Understand?"

"I do. But Sky's more competent to run the ranch than I am. He'll manage things fine."

"Sky's good at his job, but he isn't a Tyler. It's you I want runnin' the place till I'm on my feet." Will's voice had deepened to a growl. "Promise me you'll do it."

"Fine, I'll do it. But you promise me something. The more

you rest, the sooner you can come home. I need to know you're taking it easy and letting these good people take care of you."

"All right." His jaw tightened as he shifted in the bed. "Now get going before that battle-ax of a nurse throws you out of here." Will's voice had begun to strain and fade. Realizing he'd stayed long enough, Beau turned to leave. That was when he heard a commotion in the hall.

"You can't go back there, ma'am." It was the nurse Will had just mentioned. "The doctor said—"

"I don't care what he said! Get out of my way!" The door swung open and Tori burst into the room. Dressed in her black court suit with a fuchsia-pink silk blouse, she was wind-tousled and out of breath, as if she'd crossed the parking lot at a dead run in her high stilettos.

The sight of Will stopped her in her tracks. "Oh, good Lord," she breathed.

Will managed a grin. "Tori, honey," he drawled. "You look like a chocolate-dipped strawberry. Sorry I can't get up and take a nibble."

She glanced sharply at Beau. "Is he drunk?"

"It's the pain meds," Beau said.

Bunching her fists on her slender hips, she glowered at her ex-husband. "You should've been more careful, Will Tyler!" she snapped. "How could you have let this happen?"

"You could ask the snake, but he's blown to bloody . . . bits." Will grimaced, unable to keep up the pretense that he wasn't in excruciating pain.

Tori, Beau noticed, was trembling on her high heels. Glancing around the tiny room, he spotted a folding chair and set it up next to the bed. As she moved past him to sit, he glimpsed tears in her eyes.

What happened between these two people who still clearly love each other?

"Does Erin know?" Will asked.

"Only the little I was able to tell her. She's sleeping over with a friend tonight. But I know she's worried about you."

"She mustn't come. It'd only upset her. Just tell her I'm doing fine."

"*Are* you doing fine, Will?" Her hand crept across the sheet to rest on his.

Something glimmered in one swollen eye. "Don't worry your pretty head about me, girl. I'm too mean and ugly to die." His gaze shifted to Beau, who stood in the doorway. "Get going, man. I'm here with a beautiful woman, and you've got a ranch to run."

Beau headed back to the waiting room, reassured that Will was in good hands. Tori would keep an eye on him, and heaven help anybody who tried to remove her from his bedside before she was ready to leave.

To Beau's surprise, the sheriff was still there, over by the coffeepot in the alcove. "I didn't expect you to still be here, Sheriff."

"I was just getting me a cup for the road." He popped a lid onto a cup. "How's the patient?"

"Well enough to give orders. Tori's with him."

The sheriff nodded. "Yeah, I saw her come flying through and charge on back."

"I need to head back to the ranch. Any chance I can ride that far with you?"

"I don't see why not. You're a fellow man of the law," he replied with a shrug.

"I appreciate it. I'm ready if you are."

"Let's go." The sheriff headed for the exit, cup in hand.

Sky scanned the rugged canyon pastureland, his gaze lingering on the mesquite thickets where cattle might still be hiding. Most people thought cows were dumb, and maybe they were in the ways humans measured intelligence. But long ago their ancestors had been wild, and the old survival instincts were still there, buried deep in their genes. They were smart enough to hide, and to hide well.

The roundup was organized to cover one section of the ranch at a time. When the hands finished clearing the cattle out of an area, they moved, along with everything they needed, to the next site. This lower pasture, on the border of the ranch, was one of the larger sections. It was a grueling place to work cows because of the brush, which would need to be chained and burned over the summer while the cattle were gone.

Now, after three days, the work here was almost finished. One more sweep to gather any loose animals and the branding fire would be doused, the equipment loaded onto trucks, and the whole operation moved to a new spot.

It was the custom to change horses after lunch. Sky had chosen a sturdy buckskin from his string in the remuda. With the cowhands mounted once more, he directed them to spread along the outer boundaries of the pasture and work their way toward the center, driving the last of the cattle ahead of them. He and Lute would check the bog at the lowest corner. Calves had been known to wander into the morass of reeds and cattails and get mired in the sucking mud.

Motioning for Lute to follow, he nudged the horse to an easy trot. Lute had been slacking all day. Any other new hire would have been shown the gate, but Sky wanted to give the boy the same chance he'd been given. He remembered how he'd wandered onto the Rimrock Ranch years ago, young and scared and hungry, and how Bull Tyler had taken him in and given him work. This ranch could be Lute's one chance to make a decent future for himself.

Lute was family, more like a kid brother than a cousin. Sky barely remembered his own mother, who had died when he was three, and the nameless white man who'd fathered him was long gone. If his mother's brother hadn't given him a home, he'd have ended up a ward of the state.

Life in the big, unruly Fletcher clan had been far from perfect. The mother was a descendant of Comancheros, Mexicans who'd traded with the Indians for white captives to sell south of the border. Drinking, drugs, fights, and petty crimes were so commonplace in the family that Sky had come to accept these things as normal. But he'd always sensed that he was different, and he'd held himself apart.

At fifteen, after his uncle had belt-whipped his back to a mass of bloody welts, he'd run away and found a new life. The Tylers had been good to him, and Sky was loyal to the marrow of his bones. But he knew better than to think he could ever be one of them.

"I need to ask you something, Sky." Lute, who'd been trailing behind, had caught up with him. "What can you tell me about girls?"

The question almost made Sky laugh. He'd dated some attractive ladies over the years, but they'd all ended up moving on. Not that he blamed them. Much as he enjoyed a good roll in the hay, he'd never had the time to invest in a serious relationship. Maybe he never would.

"Do I look like the right man to ask about girls?" he responded to Lute's query. "How many girls have you seen flocking around me, boy?"

"You're family. There's nobody else I can ask."

Sky scanned the brush for any sign of a rusty-red coat. "So what exactly do you want me to tell you?"

"You know. How to make them like you. What to say. How you know when it's time to make a move."

"So you've met a girl, have you?"

"Her name's Jess. She's a waitress at the Blue Coyote. Wears these sexy little pink boots. Last week she let me take her out for pizza, but I'd like to . . . you know."

Sky groaned inwardly. He'd never been with Jess, but he could name a dozen men who had. Lute's naïve young heart was about to get stomped. The lesson would be bitter, but there was one only one way for him to learn it—on his own.

"Just be yourself," Sky said. "If she likes you, fine. If not, there are plenty of other girls around. The most important thing to remember is, play it cool. Don't push her. And don't act like you care too much, even if you do. Make sense?"

"I . . . guess." Lute seemed distracted. They were nearing the bog, a place Sky had never liked. It was rank with the odors of rotting vegetation and animals that had died trapped in the muck. Today the smell seemed unusually bad. Black vultures, their ugly red heads bare of feathers, flapped in and out of the reeds. A dozen of them roosted in the dead white cottonwood that stood at the edge of the swamp.

"Dammit!" Sky swore. "I'm betting we've lost a cow. But we've got to make sure. Come on, Lute. It won't be pretty, but this is part of the job."

Dismounting, they tethered their horses at a safe distance and walked down the slope toward the patch of tall brown reeds where the birds were flocking.

Lute was first to see what they were feeding on. Without a word, he doubled over and vomited in the grass.

Sky breathed an oath as he saw it, too. The body had been here for a few days, he calculated, long enough for the birds to make a mess of it. The head and torso were hidden by the reeds. Only the bare legs were clearly visible—legs that ended in a pair of waterlogged pink boots.

CHAPTER 6

Will was propped on pillows, his expression a thundercloud. "I saw the news last night," he growled with an eyebrow lifted toward the small TV above his bed. "I hope you're here to tell me what the hell's going on."

Beau took a moment to study his brother from the doorway. The antivenin was doing its work. His gaze was alert and the puffiness was gone in his face and hands. But the bitten leg remained swollen and inert beneath the sheet. According to the doctor, he was still on pain medication and would be in the hospital at least through the weekend.

"You're looking right perky this afternoon." Beau walked into the room and took a seat next to the bed. "Sounding perky, too."

Will swore. "Lord, get me out of this place! Those blasted nurses won't even let me up to piss!"

"So I see." Beau glanced at the catheter bag that hung below the hem of the sheet. The teasing banter masked his genuine concern. His brother could have died from the fall off the horse, if not from the bite.

"So what did you hear on the news?" he asked Will.

"I heard somebody found a female body in the bog. And it turned out to be that poor kid from the Blue Coyote. What the hell happened out there?"

"Nobody knows for sure. But the ranch has been a damned circus. Cops and press all over the place. If I hadn't been needed to deal with them, I'd have been here sooner." Beau rose, walked to the sink, and filled a paper cup with water. Sitting again, he took a sip. "Sky and Lute found her when they were checking for cows. She'd been there long enough for the buzzards to get at her. Evidently she was shot through the side of the head."

"You've had experience with this kind of thing. Was the girl killed on the ranch?"

"The sheriff doesn't think so. Since they didn't find any blood at the scene, I'd agree. Her body was more than likely dumped. But you're talking fifteen miles from town. Somebody went to a lot of trouble to leave her in that bog—somebody who knew exactly where to take her. When we know why, we should be able to figure out who."

Will fingered the stubble on his unshaven jaw. Beau could sense his brother's thoughts, wandering the same paths his own had traveled. Only someone local, most likely someone who'd grown up here or worked on the ranch, would know about the bog. And the way the girl was killed, coldly, almost execution style, didn't suggest an impulsive crime of passion. Somebody had wanted her dead for a reason—somebody who knew how to kill. But why leave the body where it would attract scavengers and be found?

"Any suspects?"

"Not yet. Lute was one of the last to see her alive, but he's got a solid alibi. Ralph saw the girl when he picked up Lute outside the bar. They both swear she was fine."

"Lute was with her that night?"

"Not in the way you mean. He bought her a pizza. The cashier at Burger Shack confirmed they were there. Lute's pretty broken up, but I think it was just a case of puppy love."

"What about those two birds that run the place—the woman and the biker with the tattoos?"

"They claim she was alive when they closed up and left that

night. Last they saw of her, she was headed for Burger Shack with Lute."

Will shifted in the bed to ease the pressure on his bad leg. "Damned shame. I've had a few drinks and played some pool in that bar myself. The girl was a sweet kid, for all the way she made her side money. Nobody deserves to go that way. I just hope they catch the bastard who did it." Abruptly, he changed the subject. "What about the roundup? I hope you're not about to tell me that everything's shut down for the murder investigation."

"Relax, everything's fine." Beau had been ready to counter that concern. "The operation's moved to the northwest pasture. Everything's on schedule to finish next week, and then Sky plans to start looking for colts to train. I know you wanted me to get the ranch records on the computer, so I'll be spending time in your office."

"There's still a lot to do now. Somebody's got to see to the calving. The heifers will be dropping their babies anytime now. And as soon as the herd's up on the caprock, the manure's got to be spread on the pastures, and that mesquite's got to be chained and fired."

"I know." Beau nodded. "Trust us, Will. Everything's under control. Just take it easy and let yourself heal. As soon as you get home, you can start bossing everybody around again."

"Fine." Will winced with the pain. "Now get out of here and get back to work. You've got better things to do than sit around here keeping an old grouch company."

Beau rose, pausing at the door. "Anything else?"

"Call Tori and tell her she can bring Erin to the ranch this weekend. I know Erin wants to see her foal."

"I will, but you may see Tori before I do. She said she'd be checking on you today."

Will snorted. "She's only worried for Erin's sake, that's all. Tori doesn't give a damn about me, and I can't say I blame her."

"I won't even ask." Beau wouldn't have minded knowing the full story of their breakup. But this wasn't the time to put Will through any more stress. With a quick good-bye, he exited the room and started down the hall.

One of the nurses, a husky young man, stopped him short of the swinging doors. "Mr. Tyler, the hospital wants to replace the antivenin Dr. Haskell brought in yesterday. We've packed six vials in the cooler she left. Would you be able to get them back to her?"

"No problem." Beau's answer came without hesitation. "Since she brought all she had for my brother, I know she'll appreciate getting her supply back."

Beau accepted the cooler and carried it to the pickup he'd driven from the ranch. He'd be going through Blanco Springs on the way home. It would be easy enough to drop it off at the clinic, which was built onto her house.

Once he reached Blanco Springs, he drove right to her place, an ordinary-looking redbrick rambler on the outskirts of town with no close neighbors. The clinic was built onto one end at a forward angle, like a wing. Beyond the house he could see a stable and a corral with two horses in it, probably four-legged patients of Natalie's.

If she wasn't home, he had already decided to leave the cooler with Tori. He wondered if he should do that anyway. But Natalie's Toyota was parked outside the clinic, and next to it was a vintage pink Cadillac. Evidently she had a patient. He would just leave the cooler and go.

As he parked next to Natalie's SUV, the front door of the clinic opened and a blue-haired woman in a lavender pantsuit emerged with a gray poodle in her arms. Carrying the dog to the Cadillac, she climbed in and drove off down the street.

Walking up to the door, Beau gave it a warning rap, then stepped inside. Natalie, who ran her business without hired help, was straightening up the reception area, rearranging the magazines and throwing away a candy wrapper someone had left. She was dressed for work in jeans and a white lab coat, her curls pulled back behind her childlike ears.

She looked around with a startled glance, then smiled as he held up the cooler. "I hope that isn't empty," she said.

"No, they replaced your donation. Thanks again, Natalie. Our family owes you a huge debt."

"Consider it paid." She took the wrapped vials out of the cooler and placed them in a fridge behind the reception area. "How's Will?"

"Looking better, but he's as grumpy as a grizzly bear with mange."

"That must mean he's getting better." She walked back around the counter to face him, her liquid eyes so vulnerable that it took all his restraint to remain where he stood. "I heard about the body they found on the ranch. That poor girl. Who would do that? Why? It can't be anyone from around here, can it?"

"I don't think they have any answers yet," Beau said. "When you're on a call out on those back roads, you need to keep your eyes open, and for heaven's sake, don't play Good Samaritan. If you know how to use a gun, you'd better carry one."

"I—" The rest of the sentence died on her lips at the sound of a door opening in the rear of the clinic. It took a split second for Beau to realize it was the door leading from the main part of the house.

Natalie's face paled. She took a step away from him. "I'm up front, Slade," she called.

Beau stood his ground, waiting for Slade to appear. He hadn't meant to get Natalie in trouble. But they'd done nothing wrong, and he'd be damned if he was going to turn tail and run.

"Hello, Slade," he said as the man stepped out of the hallway.

"What're you doing here, Tyler?" The tails of his work shirt hung loose over his belly, and one hand clasped an open can of beer. He looked mean enough to spit acid.

Beau kept his calm. "Your wife's antivenin saved my brother. The folks at the hospital in Lubbock asked me to bring her a new supply. I just dropped it off."

"So, if you just dropped it off, how come you're still here?"

"Show some manners, Slade!" Natalie burst out. "We were talking about the murder of that poor girl, and Beau was asking me if I had a gun. That's all."

Slade's eyes narrowed to menacing slits. "If my wife needs a gun, I'll give her one of mine. You've got no business hanging around her. You got a problem with that, feel free to take me on. I'd enjoy beating you to a bloody pulp."

Beau's gaze flickered toward Natalie. Her eyes were big and frightened. Her mouth formed the word *Go!*

Reining in the urge to drop the man to his knees with a well-placed jab, Beau took a step toward the door. "I didn't come here to cause trouble for either of you. I'll be going now. Thanks again for your help, Natalie."

Tearing his gaze away from her, he strode out the door to his truck. Climbing into the driver's seat, he backed into the street and switched on the radio. As he headed out of town, he punched in a country music station and cranked the volume up so loud that it almost hurt his ears. He'd hoped the pounding noise would drown out the thoughts in his head—wanting Natalie, worrying about her, knowing he couldn't allow her problems to become his. It didn't work. The music's blare became annoying. He switched the radio off.

Natalie faced her husband across the clinic's small reception room. "That was uncalled for, Slade," she said. "Beau's an old friend and he had a legitimate reason for coming here today. Beyond that, there's nothing going on between us."

"Nothing, my aunt Maggy's ass!" He crushed the can in his fist and flung it to the floor. "I know you went tearing off to Lubbock to be with him. Did you think that because I was on the road I wouldn't hear about that?"

"Stop it!" Natalie's fist came down on the counter, hard enough to hurt. "Will was snakebit and had to be Life Flighted to Lubbock. Beau rode along in the helicopter. The hospital was out of antivenin, so I rushed there with what I had. That's all there was to it. Call the hospital if you don't believe me! Ask anybody who was there!"

"Like I'd want people to know I was checking up on my wife!"

Seething, she drew herself up, chin thrust at a defiant angle. “I’ve been completely faithful to you, Slade. The whole time we’ve been married, I’ve never strayed once, never even come close. Can you say the same for yourself?”

The moment the last question was out of her mouth, Natalie realized what she’d just said. She saw Slade’s expression harden, saw the color deepen in his handsome, fleshy face. And suddenly, in a flash of insight, what she’d been denying for years became brutally clear.

“Good Lord, that’s what’s behind all this,” she said in a strangled voice. “That’s why you’re so suspicious of me. You’ve been cheating all along, haven’t you?”

His mouth flattened into a grim line. “You bitch!” he snarled, lunging for her. Natalie sprang away, but he caught her wrist and yanked her back toward him. “I’ll teach you to talk that way to your husband—” His hand came up, only to freeze as the front door opened.

“Oh, goodness, I’m sorry.” It was the little old lady with the blue hair and lavender pantsuit. “I didn’t mean to interrupt. “I was just looking for my glasses. I believe I may have left them on that counter.”

With an explosive breath and a muttered oath, Slade stalked past the woman and out the front door. A moment later, Natalie heard his pickup backing out of the garage and roaring down the street.

Beau arrived at the ranch to find a van from a local TV station parked in front of the house. Pulling up next to the vehicle, he turned off the engine and slid out of the driver’s seat. A perky blond reporter sat on the front porch swing, talking with Lute as a cameraman videotaped the interview. Beau could hear her as he walked closer.

“Other people have claimed the girl was a prostitute, Mr. Fletcher. What do you have to say to that?” She was actually smiling, tilting her face to get the best angle for the camera.

Lute was hunched into himself, looking wretched. His

skinny arms clutched his ribs, and he appeared to be on the verge of tears. Beau had never punched a woman, but as he strode toward the porch, the urge was there.

"She wasn't what they say," Lute mumbled. "She was a nice girl. Nice to everybody. She even let me take her out for pizza."

"I understand you were one of the last to see her alive," the blonde continued in a voice so upbeat that she might have been covering a child's birthday party. "How did you feel when you found her body?"

Lute hunched deeper, not answering.

"Mr. Fletcher, please tell us exactly how you felt. A million viewers out there are wanting to know."

Beau had reached the porch. Moving to block the camera, he glowered down at the reporter. "This interview is over," he snapped. "You and your crew have five minutes to get off this property before I have you arrested for trespassing."

"I beg your pardon!" The reporter's eyebrows shot up. Her eyes were the brilliant artificial blue of colored contact lenses. "This is a free country, and we have every right to—"

"I have every right to sue you for harassing my employee in my place of business. Lute, get back to work. You don't have to talk to these human scavengers."

As Lute scurried off, Beau was dimly aware that the cameraman had moved and was filming him from the side. He'd probably end up on the evening news, but right now he was too mad to care. As for his legal threat, he had no idea whether it had any teeth, but for now, at least, it seemed to have worked. The cameraman had gathered up his gear and was headed for the van. The reporter followed, mincing down the steps in her high-heeled sandals and tight yellow skirt. But the most satisfying sight was the rear of the van vanishing down the long graveled drive.

They'd be back, and more like them, Beau reminded himself. He was going to have his hands full. But for now he wanted to visit the bog, just in case the local law enforcement team had missed something.

Saddling a horse and strapping on a pistol, he set out cross-country for the bog. Taking the pickup would've been faster, but in a moving vehicle it would be too easy to miss things like tracks or bottle caps or cigarette butts. And the day was warm and sunny, perfect for riding. Quail scurried out of his way, calling from the underbrush. The light breeze carried the aromas of sage and cedar and the earthy smell of cattle.

A good half mile before he reached the bog, he could smell it. The girl's body was gone, of course, but the seeping earth and rotting plant matter carried a fetid odor that lingered like a miasma. As he scanned the ground, he wondered why he even bothered to look. The rusty earth was crisscrossed with tire tracks from news crews, law enforcement vehicles, and curious spectators. And before the body had been found, there'd been cattle and horses all over the countryside.

Today the place was eerily quiet, the only signs of life a pair of red-winged blackbirds flashing among the cattails and the ever-present gnats forming a cloud over the water. Beau tethered his horse and walked toward the edge of the bog. The damp ground was trampled with boot prints. There was no way to tell if any of them had belonged to the killer. Aside from the pleasant ride, this adventure had likely been a waste of time.

The tracks were thickest at the spot where the body had lain. Beau stared into the hollow where the winter reeds remained bent and flattened. He hadn't known Jessica Warner, but he sensed a hard life that, given the chance, might have been turned into something decent. Her killer had robbed her of that chance, stealing not only her life but also her future.

Dropping to a crouch, he used a stick to probe the soggy reeds. No sign of blood. The girl had almost certainly been dumped here. But why? If she'd been killed in Blanco, there were plenty of closer places to leave a body. Had the killer wanted her to be discovered on the ranch?

"Find anything, Beau?" The deep voice was friendly in tone, but it startled Beau enough to make him turn and grab for his pistol. His nerves unclenched as he recognized Hoyt Axelrod.

"My deputies have been over this place with a fine-tooth comb. But if fresh eyes can find something, I'd say knock yourself out." Axelrod nodded. "How's your brother doing after that snakebite?"

"Will's mending, thanks. But I've got my hands full, trying to run things without him. Especially now."

Axelrod scowled down at the crushed reeds. "Damned shame. She was a sweet little thing, even if she was a whore. This is just between us, but she had a packet of cocaine on her, tucked in her bra, when they brought her in. You're with the DEA, aren't you?"

He nodded. "So you're thinking this thing could be drug-related?"

"Makes as much sense as anything else. We dusted the packet, but it was clean. Didn't even have the girl's prints on it. And if she'd had recent sex, consensual or otherwise, there wasn't enough DNA for a decent sample. If you're nosing around on your own, I hope you'll let us know what you find. She was somebody's lost daughter, and she deserves justice."

"I agree. And the fact that she was dumped on Rimrock land makes this personal. I'll keep you posted if you'll do the same for me."

"Consider it done. And give my best to your brother." With a departing handshake, the sheriff wandered back to where he'd parked his tan Jeep Cherokee in the cedars. Minutes later, Beau heard the growl of the engine and the crunch of underbrush as he drove away. Had Axelrod been waiting for the killer to return to the scene of the crime? Had someone watching the ranch radioed him that a rider was getting close? Was *he* under suspicion now?

Walking with his eyes on the ground, he made a slow circle around the bog. In his work as a DEA agent, Beau had learned not to make assumptions. At this point in the investigation, everyone was a suspect and nothing could be ruled out.

Beau didn't expect to find much here. The ground was trampled all the way around the bog, all visible evidence collected. But the walk did give him a chance to think.

The little packet of cocaine on the girl had to be a plant. She wouldn't have put it in her bra without leaving prints on it. But was it a distraction? A frame-up of some kind? A warning?

And the motive? Had the girl known too many secrets? Had she blackmailed some client with too much to lose? Had jealousy driven someone to kill her?

The answers weren't here, on this malodorous patch of ground. He needed to check out the place where she'd worked and the people who'd known her. That would mean paying a visit to the Blue Coyote. But that could wait till evening. For now, he would ride up the canyon to the pasture where Sky and the men were rounding up cattle. They could use another hand, and he could use some good, hard physical work.

Tori filled two tall glasses with iced tea, carried them to the kitchen table, and sat down across from her friend. She'd known for years that Natalie's marriage was unhappy, but she'd never seen her so agitated.

"What do you want to do about Slade?" she asked gently. "Divorce him?"

Natalie's face was ashen, but her eyes were tearless. "You know I've never believed in divorce. But I never expected anything like this to happen. I want to do the right thing, Tori, but I don't know what that is anymore. That's why I'm here. You're not just my best friend. You're also my lawyer."

"You're sure he's been cheating on you?"

"He didn't deny it. And he went crazy when I accused him. If that woman hadn't walked in when she did, I don't know what he'd have done to me." She took a sip of the tea, struggling to keep her composure. "It all makes sense—the late nights, the way he smelled when he came in, things that I was too deep in denial to notice. Are you suggesting I need evidence?"

"If you go through with the divorce, it might help. You and Slade built your house and the clinic together. I'm guessing his name's on everything you own."

Natalie wilted, her shoulders sagging. "I hadn't thought of that. Slade inherited his trucking business before we were married. That's his. But the house is in both our names, and my clinic's attached. He could force me to sell it out of sheer spite and take half the money."

Setting the glass on the table, she shook her head in quiet despair. "I can't believe I'm even talking about this, Tori. You went through a divorce. And with a child. How on earth did you manage?"

The memory flickered in Tori's mind. She blocked it. Will's settlement had been more than fair, but still, the breakup of their marriage had been the most heart-wrenching experience of her life.

"Every divorce is different," Tori said. "But no divorce is easy. I'll help you any way I can, but before you go ahead with this, you need to look at what you're facing and be sure it's what you want."

Natalie stared down at the dissolving ice cubes in her tea. "You're right. I do need to be sure. Today I'm still in shock. A decision like this one needs to be made with a cool head."

Tori nodded. "Talk to me before you do anything rash. And don't push any boundaries with Slade while you're alone with him. I know he's got a temper."

"I'll be all right. Slade can get pretty loud when he's mad, but he always cools down, and he's never hit me."

"You said he came close."

"Don't worry, I know Slade. I can handle him."

"What about Beau?"

Natalie's head came up. Color flamed in her pale cheeks. "Beau has nothing to do with this."

"Evidently that's not what Slade thinks. Be careful, Natalie. Don't give Slade any reason to think there's something going on between you two."

"You think I don't know that?" Natalie shook her head vehemently. "Beau can't be a part of this. Not even if Slade and I separate. Slade threatened to kill him if he comes near me. Not that he would, but I can't take that chance. I don't want Beau hurt."

"Do you still love Beau, Natalie?"

She stiffened in her chair, her chin squared. "When Beau joined the army, he asked me to wait for him. Like a fool, I did. I waited years, but he never came back. Never called. Never wrote."

Natalie's voice broke on the last few words. Looking flustered, she glanced at her watch and pushed away from the table. "I have a man bringing in a mare with hoof thrush at three. I've got to go."

Tori rose with her, giving her friend a quick hug. "Be careful. If you feel threatened in any way, leave the house and call me. Or just come to my house. Day or night."

Tori stood at the window and watched her friend drive away. Love was a bitch, she thought. Once you gave your heart, you never quite got it all the way back. She'd seen the tears in Natalie's eyes as she walked down the church aisle to marry Slade. And she knew who'd put them there.

As for herself, she'd had plenty of men to choose from since her divorce from Will, including Congressman Garn Prescott. But Will was the father of her child, and somehow he towered above them all.

At least she had Erin, Tori reminded herself. Her daughter had been worth the pain a hundred times over. But Natalie had no children. She was miserable with Slade, and now, suddenly Beau had shown up again. As she turned away from the window, a dark premonition crept over her. Something bad was going to happen. And she couldn't make that feeling go away.

CHAPTER 7

It was 8:35 p.m. when Beau ambled into the Blue Coyote and slid into an empty booth. Not wanting to stand out, he hadn't taken the time to clean up after the roundup. His boots were scuffed, his jaw stubbled, his clothes caked with sweat and dust. He looked like any one of the two dozen or so cowboys who'd wandered in for a cold beer after a long day's work. But he wasn't fooling himself. Anybody who'd spent much time in the county would know the Tylers. And despite the layer of grit, they'd be aware of who he was.

The bar had been here for as long as Beau could remember. But the new owner had spruced it up some. Call it a woman's touch. The autographed photos and retro country music memorabilia on the walls lent atmosphere, if not class. And for a weeknight, business looked pretty good. The bar stools were all occupied and the *clickety-clack* of pool balls blended with the blaring country music.

Jasper had filled Beau in on the woman who'd paid cash for the place two years ago. So Beau was prepared when she sauntered up to his table.

"I like getting to know my customers, cowboy." She looked to be in her early forties, her voluptuous body stuffed into a denim blouse trimmed with rhinestones and a skirt short enough to show off shapely legs clad in red cowgirl boots. Her wavy auburn hair was too bright to be natural, her makeup laid on with a too-heavy hand. Still, she wasn't a bad-looking woman. The most attractive thing about her was her voice, husky-rich like a New Orleans blues singer's.

"Beau Tyler." Beau gave her a gentlemanly nod. "And I take it you're Stella."

"That's right. And I knew who you were as soon as you walked in." She flashed him an overtly sexy grin. Was it an invitation or just practicing good business? "I'd sit down and join you, but I'm doing double duty as hostess and waitress tonight. You know about poor little Jess, of course."

"Heard anything new about the case?"

"No more than you. But I hope they catch the bastard who did it. I'd like to take a few whacks at him myself. She was a sweet kid." Her green eyes narrowed. "I heard tell you're DEA?"

"I'm on a leave of absence."

"So you're not here chasing drug dealers?" Her tone was playful, but Beau sensed something behind the questions. He remembered what the sheriff had told him about the cocaine.

"My brother's in the hospital, so I'm playing rancher in his absence, chasing cows instead of drugs. Today I've worked up a powerful thirst. What've you got that's wet and cold?"

"I can bring you a Corona. Free to first-time customers, especially handsome ones—that is, if you promise to come back."

"You've got my promise." Beau gave her a wink, taking in the sway of her full rump as she moved off.

Pretending to study the photos on the wall, he watched her sashay around the bar and whisper something to the bartender. The man glanced toward him, frowning. Now there was another type. Tattooed arms, shaved head. Nigel, somebody had called him. Despite the name, he looked more Eastern European than British. Not that Beau believed for a minute the name was real. If he could sneak a photo with his cell phone, he could ask a friend at the DEA to run a background check. But something told him the man wouldn't just stand still and pose. Getting a picture would take some careful moves.

Stella came back with the cold beer. Beau was just beginning to turn on the charm when the door burst open and flew back against the inside wall with a bang. Striding across the threshold with poison in his eye was Slade Haskell.

He headed straight for Beau's table. "I thought that was your truck I saw outside, Tyler!" he growled. "What do you think you're doing in here?"

Beau took a moment to size him up. Natalie's husband was dressed in his work clothes. He smelled of alcohol, as if he'd had a few drinks wherever he'd come from.

"Hello, Slade," Beau said with studied cordiality. "I was just having a cold one after a long, hard day. Care to sit down and join me?"

"I'd drink with the devil before I'd drink with you."

"Suit yourself." With a shrug, Beau popped the cap on his Corona and, ignoring the mug Stella had left on the table, took a swig from the bottle. Stella stood to one side, taking in the drama like a cat watching a pair of roosters.

"What're you doing back in town?" Slade demanded. "If you've been fooling around with my wife again—"

Beau looked up at him, one hand balancing the beer bottle. "Get this through your thick head, Slade. I'm not fooling around with your wife. The last time I saw Natalie, she was with you. Maybe you ought to go home to her instead of hanging around here."

If Beau had expected his words to mollify the man, he couldn't have been more mistaken. Slade's florid color deepened. His chest, shoulders, and belly seemed to swell. "You stay away from her, you son of a bitch, hear?" he snapped. "If I find out she's been with you, I'll punch her black and blue, and then I'll come looking for you with a gun!"

Beau had been threatened before, and he could handle it. But Slade's threat to hurt Natalie hit home and hit deep. Everything went hard and cold inside him. Setting his beer on the table, he rose, seized the big man by the front of his shirt, and yanked him so close that their faces were almost touching.

"So help me," he rasped, "if you lay a finger on that woman, I'll hunt you down and tear you apart with my bare hands!"

For an instant Slade was too startled to respond. But as Beau shoved him away, he regained his bravado. Shoulders hunched, he doubled his fists and danced like a boxer. "Why not now, Tyler? Put your money where your mouth is, you yellow coward. Let's duke it out right here."

Beau shuddered inwardly, thinking what he could do to Natalie's husband if he let himself go. But self-control was at the core of his training. To misuse the skills he'd been taught in the military would be beyond reckless. It would be criminal.

"Sorry," he said. "I don't fight drunks."

The only sound in the bar was the throbbing beat of an old Patsy Cline song. Surrounded by shocked silence, with the music ringing in his ears, Beau turned away and walked out the door. By the time his boots touched the asphalt, he could hear Slade screaming, "Come back, you coward! Come back and fight!"

Ignoring the man, he climbed into his truck, switched on the headlights, and headed for the highway. He'd seen some interesting dynamics tonight. He'd bet money that Stella and her skinhead bartender were up to their armpits in some kind of dirty business. But whether they had any connection to the girl's murder was anybody's guess. He'd missed the chance to sneak a photo of the man, but some of those tattoos, although camouflaged with quality work, had the look of a prison job.

As for Slade, he appeared to be little more than a jealous loudmouth. But the idea that he might hurt Natalie worried Beau. And he couldn't interfere without making matters worse. Maybe he should alert Tori. If he couldn't be there for Natalie, at least someone else should be aware of the danger.

Willing his clenched nerves to relax, Beau switched on the radio and watched the lights of the town fade away in his rearview mirror.

After Beau's call, Tori sat at the kitchen table, staring at the phone and thinking. She shared his concern about Natalie, but there hadn't been much she could tell him. Most of what she knew about her friend's marriage was covered by lawyer-client privilege. But maybe that was just as well. Could Beau keep his distance if he knew that Slade had been unfaithful, that he'd come close to hitting his wife, and that Natalie was actually talking divorce?

Her advice to Natalie had been sound. There was no way Beau could be involved.

Rising, she busied herself with loading the dishwasher and wiping off the kitchen counters. From the bathroom she could hear the shower running as Erin got ready for bed. A few minutes later her daughter appeared in the kitchen, fresh and rosy in her pink robe and pajamas.

"Homework's done," she said. "Is it okay if I watch my TV show?"

"As long as you go straight to bed when it's over. You've got school tomorrow."

Erin started toward the den, then paused. "Have you heard how Daddy's doing?"

"I just talked with your uncle Beau. Your dad's doing a lot better. He should be home in a couple days. But he'll need to rest for a while."

"Can I still go to the ranch this weekend? I want to see Tesoro."

Tori hesitated. Will had said it would be fine for Erin to spend the weekend as usual. But that was before that poor murdered woman had been found in the bog. With the killer still at large, Tori didn't want her daughter out of her sight.

"We'll see," she said. "Maybe I can get you there long enough to spend a little time with your foal."

Tori's heart contracted as she watched her child scamper off to watch TV. Erin was on the brink of becoming a lovely young woman. Tori's dreams for her included college, but for now Erin was anchored to the ranch. She had blossomed there, happiest among the cattle and horses. And Will, despite his issues with Tori, was a good father.

A good father.

Was that why she'd canceled her appointments and rushed off to the hospital the minute she'd heard he was there? Because he was Erin's father?

Lute had hitched a ride into town with Ralph. He dreaded walking into the Blue Coyote and not seeing Jess there, but he wanted to pick up the fifty dollars that Slade had promised him. This time he'd earned every penny, calling in about the roundup, Will Tyler's snakebite, and especially the murder investigation. Maybe this time Slade would be pleased enough to give him a bonus.

Slade wasn't in the bar, but Stella gave Lute a wave and a friendly wink, a sure sign that she had the money for him. Playing it cool this time, he sat down at the bar, ordered a beer, and waited for her to come to him. There was a new waitress on duty tonight, prettily plump with lots of makeup and short black hair that looked dyed. He guessed she'd probably moved into Jess's old room, but she wasn't anything like Jess. Looking her over, Lute decided to pass on asking her out.

Stella came by a few minutes later. Instead of slipping him the envelope, she whispered in his ear. "Wander on back to the office, Lute. I'd like a word with you, private like."

The office was down a back hallway past the restrooms. Following Stella's suggestion to "wander," Lute took a moment at the urinal, then came out and sauntered the rest of the way down the hall.

There wasn't much to the office except a locked army-surplus desk with an old desktop computer on it, a spindle of receipts, a couple of wooden chairs, and a dozen cardboard cases of beer and liquor stacked against one wall. Lute was standing with his hands in his pockets, wondering if Stella might be coming on to him, when she walked in, closing the door behind her. "Have a seat," she said in a voice that was all business.

Fishing a key out of her shirt, she opened a locked drawer and handed Lute the envelope he'd been expecting. "Nothing I say leaves this room. If it does, I know how to make you very sorry. Understand?"

Lute nodded, fingering the edges of the three bills inside the envelope. His pulse skittered as he waited for her to speak. Was he in some kind of trouble? Did it have something to do with Jess?

"I know what you do for Slade to earn this," she said. "How would you like to earn more? Say, an extra hundred?"

"A hundred a week?" He gasped. Combined with fifty from Slade, it sounded like a small fortune. "What would I have to do?"

"Pretty much what you've been doing. Only you'd be doing it for me." Stella inspected a small chip in her bloodred nail polish. "Slade and I have a few business deals going. I want to make sure he's playing straight. You'd go on working for Slade and collecting your fifty dollars. But everything you report to him, you'd report to me, too, and you'd also keep me up on whatever Slade's doing."

Lute's hopes sagged. "Fine. Trouble is, I don't see that much of Slade. I only talk to him once in a while on the phone. And except for the trucks, I don't even know what kind of business he's in."

Stella's laugh sounded flat and metallic in the small space. "I'd say that's about to change. Slade's been telling me what a sharp lad you are. I know he's planning more jobs for you. So if you keep your eyes and ears open, you could find yourself sittin' right pretty."

Stella rose and held out her hand. "Well, Lute, do we have a deal?"

Still taking it all in, Lute gave her his handshake.

"I'll give you a phone number to call," she said. "You can use the phone you use for Slade. Just make sure you keep the numbers straight in your head, and don't say anything till you hear my voice. All right?"

Lute nodded. This was the break he'd been waiting for. In no time at all, he'd have money for a decent car, nice clothes, and all the girls he wanted. And all for being a spy—almost like James Bond.

Will had been home for ten days, but his swollen leg still pained him. Unable to put weight on it, he clumped around the house on crutches and relied on the Kubota mini tractor to get him around the ranch yard. Bed rest or the use of his father's old wheelchair might have speeded his recovery, but Will would have none of either.

Pain and frustration hadn't helped his disposition. The attendant hired to look after him had thrown up his hands and quit four days ago, with Will insisting he could take care of himself. As Bernice had muttered at the end of one especially trying day, "Glory be, it's like having Bull Tyler back among the living!"

He rode his brother mercilessly about the management of the ranch. Beau tried to bear it with patience, reminding himself that Will had endured years of the same treatment from their father, but there were times when he was tempted to call the DEA in Washington and tell them he no longer required the leave of absence he had requested. It was only the awareness of how much he was needed at the ranch that kept him from turning his back and flying to D.C.

With Sky off scouting for colts to train and Will unable to mount a horse or sit comfortably in a vehicle, Beau had his hands full. The roundup was over, but there was plenty of other work to be done. In addition to the usual daily chores, the calving season was under way in the lower pasture. On the empty land there were fences to be mended and clumps of mesquite to be chained. Up on the Caprock, the windmills and pipelines that fed the watering tanks had to be kept in good repair, the cattle checked and guarded by the men in the line shack. And there was the endless, vital record-keeping to be done for the ranch, which Beau had taken over when he'd agreed to stay. Now, in addition to the busy days, he was spending his evening hours at the computer. Sometimes until long after midnight.

His most notable accomplishment so far was upgrading the ranch's security. He'd attached small signaling devices to the ranch vehicles, trailers, and other equipment and installed a tracking program on the computer. Will had grumbled about the expense, declaring that nothing had ever been stolen from Rimrock, but in this, at least, Beau had overruled him.

For now the murder investigation had gone cold. The lawmen had collected their evidence and moved on to matters more pressing than the killing of a prostitute.

Running hard day and night, Beau had found his one refuge of calm and wisdom in Jasper. The old man had seen the ranch through good times and bad, and his long-range view gave Beau the perspective he needed to keep up his spirits. Even more valuable was Jasper's in-depth knowledge of the ranch and the day-to-day things that needed to be done.

Tonight the two of them sat on the porch, listening to the crickets and watching the sunset fade into twilight. Supper was over, and Will had fallen asleep in one of the big parlor chairs with his leg resting on a footstool. For Beau, it was a rare, quiet moment in his hectic day, a chance to breathe easy while he and Jasper planned the next day's work.

"If you want to start chaining brush tomorrow, get Ralph and Packer to do the job," Jasper was saying. "They did it last year, and did fine. But make sure they check the oil in the tractors first. You don't want to burn out the engines."

"Thanks, I'll make a note on that." Beau had come to rely on Jasper's experience, and he made sure Jasper knew it. Bathed in the glow of appreciation, the old foreman stood a little straighter these days and even walked with a bit of spring to his step.

Weighing on Beau's mind tonight was another matter—a minor incident that had happened that afternoon. He'd walked into the stallion barn to find Lute sprawled on a pile of clean straw, fast asleep with an empty beer can next to his foot. When

Beau had dressed him down for sleeping and drinking on the job, the young slacker had responded with a smart-mouthed remark that would have gotten any other employee fired on the spot.

Beau would have sent him packing, but Lute was Sky's relative, and Sky was gone. Knowing how Sky wanted to help the boy, Beau was reluctant to fire him without Sky's involvement. At the time, he had settled for tearing a verbal strip off Lute's hide and threatening him with worse if he didn't straighten up. Lute had muttered an excuse, picked up his shovel, and resumed his work.

That should have been the end of it, but as he was walking out of the stable, Beau had glanced back over his shoulder. He'd caught Lute staring at him with a look of such intense hatred that it made his blood run cold. Beau had chosen to keep walking. Now he wondered if he should have taken action then and there. The boy was trouble.

Beau was about to ask Jasper's advice when a pair of headlights appeared around the distant bend. Coming up the long drive, fast enough to leave a plume of dust in its wake, was a big, low, white car. As it came closer, still visible in the twilight, Beau recognized it as a vintage high-end Cadillac.

"Oh, hell." Jasper stood. "If that's who I think it is, I don't want to be here." He hobbled off the porch, pausing before he headed around the corner of the house. "Bull always said to look out for snakes and Prescotts—especially if they show up at your door. Damned good advice if you ask me."

By the time the mafioso-sized car pulled up to the entrance, the old man was out of sight. Beau rose, waiting at the top of the steps as both front doors of the Cadillac swung open. Congressman Garn Prescott, wearing tan slacks and a plaid Western shirt with a bolo tie, stepped out of the passenger side. His driver was slower to exit. Beau glimpsed high-heeled boots extending beyond the door, then long, slim, denim-clad legs.

Behind Beau, the porch light clicked on. Its glow revealed a long-limbed beauty with a model's figure and a wild mane of auburn hair. Clad in a simple ballet-style black tee and weathered jeans, she looked like a young Julia Roberts—very young, Beau realized as the light struck her face. Probably not much over twenty. Had the congressman found himself a hot new girlfriend? In a place like D.C., stranger things had been known to happen.

"Congressman." Beau came down the steps, hand extended, to welcome the visitor. Garn Prescott wasn't his favorite person, but Texas hospitality was an honored tradition.

"Good to see you, Beau." Prescott's handshake was a politician's, firm and hearty. "How's Will? I was on the way home from picking up my daughter at the airport and thought I might drop by for a minute and check on him. Is he up to having visitors?"

Beau glanced at the girl, who was hanging back, as if she found her father's manner embarrassing. Prescott's daughter. Now that was a surprise.

"Will's doing better. He still needs rest, but you're welcome to come in and visit. You, too, Miss Prescott." Beau glanced back at the girl. "It is Miss Prescott, isn't it?"

"Yes. Lauren." The girl spoke with quiet confidence, but seemed ill at ease. Until now, Beau hadn't even known Prescott had a daughter. This one struck him as a princess type, especially given what he recognized as $800 boots on her elegantly narrow feet.

"Lauren's my daughter by my first wife," Prescott explained. "She grew up with her mother, but now that she's finished college, and since she's my only child and likely to inherit my share of the ranch, I've talked her into spending some time here."

"Really, Daddy, why should Mr. Tyler care about all that?" Lauren demanded.

"I want people to know who you are and how you fit into the family, Lauren," Prescott said. "It's important."

Beau mulled over what he'd heard as he ushered the pair through the entry. Prescott's longtime wife, Evelyn, had died of a sudden stroke two years ago. Until now, Beau hadn't known that the congressman had been married before Evelyn or that he had a child.

The sound of voices had awakened Will. He was sitting up, looking tired but alert as Prescott strode into the parlor.

"Please don't get up, Will." He hurried across the room to shake Will's hand. "I heard about your mishap, and I've been concerned about you. How are you doing?"

"Better than the damned snake, thanks. Have a chair, Garn. I couldn't help overhearing that this young lady's your daughter. Please have a seat, too, Miss Prescott. Beau, would you mind rustling up something for these folks to drink? I'll have the same. What'll it be?"

"Bourbon if you've got it." Prescott settled into an armchair that was angled toward Will.

"Nothing for me, thank you." Lauren perched on the arm of the sofa like a bird about to take flight. Beau sensed that she was here under some duress and wanted nothing more than to get this visit over with. Sitting there with her long legs crossed in front of her as if to show off her hand-tooled designer boots, she made a fetching sight. When word got out that she was an heiress, her father would be fighting off suitors.

Prescott glanced toward his daughter as Beau handed him his drink. "Honey, I've got a bit of business to discuss with Will," he said. "You'll probably be bored. Maybe we could prevail on Beau to take you outside and show you around. I know you like horses. The Tylers have some of the finest animals in the state."

He turned back to Will, as if assuming his wish would be carried out. Lauren shrugged, rose, and glanced expectantly at Beau.

Beau was curious about what the congressman had to discuss. He would have chosen to stay and listen. But escorting a pretty girl around the moonlit yard was hardly the most onerous job in the world. Putting on a smile, he offered her his arm and led her toward the front door.

"Enjoy." As Prescott shot them a sly grin, Beau was struck by a thought.

Good Lord, could the old weasel be matchmaking?

Will studied Garn Prescott over the rim of his glass. The memory of his father's hatred for old Ferg Prescott went as deep as Texas soil. Will had no love, let alone trust, for Ferg's son—especially after seeing Garn drooling over Tori at the funeral. But these were new times, and in a changing world, cooperation was the only hope of gaining that canyon land back.

"So what can I do for you, Garn?" he asked.

"It's like you to get right to the point, Will." Prescott was beginning to show his age. His silvery hair was thinning on top and his skin was speckled with sunspots. How old was he? Fifty-four? Fifty-five? Too old for Tori, that was for damned sure, Will thought.

Prescott took a sip of his bourbon and licked his lips. "As you know, I'm running for reelection."

"I'm aware of that," Will said. "And I'm aware that you've won the past eight elections by a landslide. Is there any reason to worry this time around?"

Prescott stretched his legs in front of himself. His cowboy boots were immaculate—definitely not the boots of a working rancher. "It's not so much about the election as the nomination," he said. "The conservative wing of the party's growing. There's talk of squeezing me out in favor of a candidate who'll voice their views. You know I've always stood up for the ranchers, Will."

"I know. That's why I've voted for you." Will could guess where this was leading.

"This time around I'm going to need more than your vote."

"Want to be more specific?"

"The Tylers have a lot of prestige in this district. A public endorsement could make a big difference. So could a cash contribution if you can spare it."

Will's fingers stroked the surface of the cut glass. "And what's in it for me, besides having a friend in Congress?"

"Isn't that enough?" Prescott looked surprised. As usual, he'd expected something for nothing.

Will shook his head. "You can have my support, Garn, but in return, I want you to right an old wrong. Thirty years ago, my father was forced to sell your father a piece of ranch property—that little canyon with the spring. Do you know the place I mean?"

"Yes. The one with the Spanish gold."

"Which your father never found. I want to buy it back—for a fair price that you can keep as my contribution to your campaign. Sell it to me, and you'll get my public endorsement as well."

Prescott downed the rest of his bourbon. "Sorry, Will, but I can't do that. The syndicate—"

"No excuses. I checked the records. The land is yours, not the syndicate's. It's too steep for cattle. You don't need the water, and we both know the gold was nothing but a tall tale. So why not let me buy it back? That way we both get what we want."

The congressman sighed in regret. "It's not that simple. On his deathbed my father made me promise that I would keep that land in the family. That's why the syndicate doesn't own it."

Will suppressed the urge to swear out loud. He should have expected something like this. Either Ferg Prescott had locked down that land to spite the Tylers or he'd still believed the Spanish gold was there, maybe both.

The two men sat in silence for a moment, both of them pondering. "There has to be some way around this," Will said.

"What does it matter?" Prescott demanded. "If the land's as worthless as you say it is, why in blazes do you want to buy it?"

"To get it back in the family. It's the only piece of the ranch that's ever been sold."

"So it's the principle of the thing?"

"More or less. But if you can't—or won't—budge on it, you and I have nothing more to say to each other. You'll get my vote as usual, and that's it."

Prescott appeared to be studying his manicured nails. "I'd sell it to you in a minute, Will, but my hands are tied. You do have access to a legal expert. Maybe I could ask Tori—"

"Leave Tori out of this!" Will snapped.

"All right." Prescott exhaled slowly. "There might be another way, if you'd be willing to make a long-range bet."

"On what?" Will was instantly suspicious.

Prescott glanced toward the front door, where Beau and Lauren had exited earlier. "Your brother's a bachelor with half interest in your ranch. And I have a beautiful, spirited daughter with a great deal to offer a man. What would you say to giving me your support in exchange for my promise that, when Lauren marries, I give her that little canyon as a wedding gift?"

CHAPTER 8

Freed from her father's stifling influence, Lauren Prescott had turned out to be a pleasant surprise. She was smart, spunky, and opinionated, with a razor-edged wit. Beau, who'd had mixed feelings about entertaining the congressman's daughter, found himself actually enjoying her.

"Will you be staying long?" he asked as they strolled across the yard toward the barn.

"That depends." She sidestepped around some horse droppings. "I have a brand-new business and accounting degree from the University of Maryland, and I'm anxious to put it to use. The trouble is, the places where I've applied all want experience."

"Can't the congressman help you out, maybe pull a few strings?"

"Oh, please!" She shot him a disgusted glance. "It's not that he hasn't offered. But I want to make it on my own, not because I'm Garn Prescott's baby girl. It was my idea to come here and work in the ranch's main office for a few months, just to have something to put on my résumé."

"I'm guessing that was fine with your father."

"Oh, Daddy was glad to have me come. But now that I'm here, he wants to put me on display and auction me off to the highest bidder."

"Since slavery was outlawed after the Civil War, I take it you're talking about an advantageous marriage. Yes?"

She tossed her coppery hair. "Yes—advantageous for him, at least. Why do you think he brought me here tonight—and pushed you into taking me for a stroll? He's got two rich, handsome, unmarried ranchers right here—one of whom might even help him get reelected! Bang the gavel! Who wants to start the bidding?"

Beau studied the stubborn set of her jaw. What she was suggesting was outrageous. But Garn Prescott was a man who used people at every turn. Why should he stop at using his own daughter?

He masked his dismay with a laugh. "Lauren Prescott, you're terrible!"

"No, just honest."

He steered her toward the barn where the mares and foals were kept. "For what it's worth, I think you're safe here. Will's almost old enough to be your father, and I'm not that far behind. As for being rich, our wealth is in the land, not in the bank. Like most of the family ranchers in these parts, we're struggling to hang on to what we've got." He paused as a sudden thought struck him. "But I do have a proposition for you, if you'll hear me out."

"A proposition?" She threw him a hoydenish look. "Now that sounds interesting!"

"Not *that* interesting, I'm afraid. But if you'd like to add another line to your résumé, I could use your part-time help setting up an online spreadsheet for our ranch."

She made a little musing sound. "Tell me more."

Beau dramatized a groan. "Where do I begin? The records were a mess when I took them over from Will. I've done my best to get them caught up on the computer, but I need some kind of system to make the job easier going forward. Trouble is, with Will recovering and Sky off scouting new colts—"

"Sky?" She stopped, as if the name had caught her off guard.

"Our resident horse whisperer. You'll meet him if you spend any time here."

"He sounds interesting. Maybe he can teach me a thing or two about horses."

"Maybe. Are you a rider?"

"Not Western. Growing up in Maryland, I competed in dressage and jumping."

They were walking once more, their shadows long across the moonlit yard. A nightjar zigzagged low in its search for insects, its wings slicing the darkness.

"So what about my offer?" Beau asked.

"How soon would you need me?"

"Yesterday, if possible. But I've managed to blunder along so far. It can wait if you need time to settle in to your real job."

"I'll give it some thought," she said. "For the first couple of weeks, I'll need to focus on the work at our ranch. But after that, if I have time and need a break—"

"You will need a break, I'm betting. And when you do, the welcome mat will be out." Beau opened the stable door. "Come meet the ranch's new little superstar."

Switching on the low light, he ushered her down the row of roomy stalls toward the one that housed Lupita and Tesoro. The barn had been cleaned, but not well. Wisps of dirty straw littered the floor, and the air smelled of stale manure. Beau swore silently. Lute again. He was going to have to come down hard on him or even kick his lazy butt off the ranch.

Lauren gasped with delight as the stall door opened. Tesoro stood in a shaft of light, gleaming like a newly minted gold coin. The foal was growing fast. Thanks to Erin's loving attention, he was as friendly as a puppy and more than a little spoiled. When Lauren knelt in the straw, he scampered over and butted her with his head, demanding to be petted.

"Oh, he's precious!" She stroked the plush baby coat. "Would you consider selling him? I'll bet I could talk Daddy into buying him for me."

"Tesoro's not for sale at any price," Beau said. "He belongs to Will's daughter, and she wouldn't take a million dollars for him."

"Lucky girl! I don't blame her!" Lauren continued to fondle

the foal, cooing and murmuring little endearments. Only then did Beau happen to glance back and notice the mare.

Lupita was huddled against the rear of the stall, her head down, her sides and belly distended as if they'd been pumped full of air. Beau could hear the rumbling in her gut and smell the explosive passing of gas. He was no expert, but having grown up on the ranch, he recognized colic when he saw it. The sick mare was in life-threatening danger.

Lauren was staring at him, her eyes wide with worry. Evidently she understood enough to know what was wrong. "Run back to the house," Beau told her. "Tell Will to call the vet. He'll have her number."

As Lauren raced out of the barn, Beau found a halter, slipped it over the mare's head, and attached a lead. Taking care to keep clear of Tesoro, he led her out of the stall and closed the gate. The foal would be distressed without his mother, but for now that couldn't be helped.

Natalie's business card, with her phone number, was thumbtacked to the gate of the stall. Beau had his cell and could have called her himself, but the last thing she needed was to have Slade hear his voice on the phone. Better that Will make the call.

Gripping the halter, he urged Lupita forward, walking her along the row of stalls toward the far end of the barn. Keep her moving. Until Natalie could get here, that was the only way to ease the miserable bloat and help her pass gas. The ranch couldn't lose this young mare.

Growing up, Beau had seen two horses die from colic, and several others recover after getting their stomachs pumped. The ailment was most often caused by food fermenting in the digestive tract, creating blockage and copious amounts of gas that could rupture the intestine. The best chance of saving a horse was to catch the problem early.

Sky, who had a sixth sense about such things, would have noticed the mare's distress at once. Beau was lucky to have caught it at all. Lupita would have died before morning. She could still die if Natalie didn't get here soon.

As he was turning the mare at the end of the barn, Lauren rushed in to tell him that Will had reached the vet and she was on her way. "Daddy wants to leave now," she said. "He's in a black mood. I'm guessing he and your brother had words. Sorry I can't stay and help."

"You've helped already." Beau might have said more, but the congressman was honking the horn outside. For an elected official, the man had the manners of a jackass.

With an apologetic roll of her eyes, Lauren fled, leaving Beau alone. Time crawled as he walked the mare up and down along the row of stalls.

Natalie bailed out of her SUV and raced around the vehicle to get her equipment from the back. Two buckets, a length of surgical tubing, a small siphon pump, and a bottle of mineral oil—she could only hope that nothing else would be needed. Some cases of colic required surgery—a horrific prospect. She'd brought what she needed just in case. But she wouldn't think about that possibility unless she had to.

A thread of light told her the barn door was ajar. Arms full, she shouldered it open and almost stumbled into Beau. He was gripping the mare's halter, his face a study in relief.

A swift glance around the barn confirmed that they were alone. Being here with him was as risky as walking on quicksand. But she had a job to do, and her feelings toward the man who'd broken her heart couldn't be allowed to interfere.

"How's the mare doing?" Natalie forced herself to ignore the rapid flutter of her pulse.

His eyes revealed nothing. Neither did his voice. "I've been walking her, but she's still in trouble."

"And her foal?"

"In the stall. Aside from wanting his mother, he's fine. Thank you for coming, Natalie."

Even the sound of her name on his lips triggered a rush of

emotion. She turned away, avoiding his eyes. "It's my job. Let's get it done."

The stall nearest the door was kept empty for emergencies like this one. To keep the mare in place, Beau used a light rope to cross-tie her halter to steel rings on either side. The smaller of the two buckets was filled with heated water Natalie had brought in an insulated jug from her house.

"Can you hold her by yourself?" she asked Beau.

"She should be fine. She's a calm one."

"Then let's do it." Natalie pulled on a pair of surgical gloves. Intubating a fully conscious horse through the nose was a delicate process, but if done carefully enough, it wasn't painful. Beau stood to one side of the mare's head, holding her steady while Natalie did her work.

"Amazing," he murmured. "I remember when you used to get wobbly at the sight of blood. How many times have you done this?"

"More than I care to count. Now let's see what this lady's been eating . . . Oh, good grief!" She gasped in dismay as the mare's last meal poured out of the tube into the bucket. "Grain! Enough to fill her whole stomach! No wonder she's bloated! Who fed her last?"

A muscle twitched in Beau's cheek. "Somebody who's going to be hauled out and fired first thing tomorrow!"

"Did you check the other mares?"

A muscle along his jaw jumped in anger. "If they've had that much grain, too, we've got a disaster on our hands! I'll check them as soon as you're done with Lupita."

"We could be here all night." Natalie finished flushing Lupita's stomach and gave her a dose of mineral oil to soothe her digestive tract. The mare was already responding. The bloating had lessened, easing her distress. "Good girl," Natalie murmured, her free hand stroking the mare as she pulled out the tube. "Such a good girl."

Beau moved off to check the other mares. Minutes later he was back. "They're fine. Nothing but hay in their feeders."

"So why would this mare have been given grain instead of hay?"

Beau's jaw tightened. "I don't know. But when I find out, there'll be hell to pay."

The foal was pushing against the stall gate, making frantic little whimpering sounds. The mare lifted her head and nickered an urgent reply. "We can take her back now," Natalie said. "But we need to stay and watch her at least until that mineral oil works its magic."

While Beau led the mare back to her stall, Natalie began cleaning up, bagging the used tubing, rinsing the buckets, and stripping off her gloves.

"Does Slade know where you are?" Beau came out of the mare's stall, leaving the gate ajar.

"He's on the road." *And he won't be back till tomorrow night.* She bit back the last words, fearing that Beau might read more into them than she meant.

"He hasn't given you any trouble, has he?"

She made a show of fitting the siphon pump neatly inside one of the rinsed buckets so she wouldn't have to meet the probe of his gaze.

"No, he hasn't. Not that it's any of your business."

His hand gripped her arm, pulling her around to face him. "He made it my business when he warned me to stay away from you and threatened to beat you to a pulp if I didn't." He issued the words in a low growl, all the while his gaze searching for any sign of bruising, old or new.

Shaken a bit by the news, Natalie worked to make sure it didn't show. "Slade tends to talk a lot. And it's usually just that. Talk."

"Usually," he mocked her with her own choice of words.

Rather than meet his gaze, she stared at the front of his shirt, remembering the feel of those broad muscles beneath it. God help her, she wanted to feel them again.

"Why did you have to come back for the funeral?" She hurled the question at him, anger and frustration all mingling together. "Why didn't you leave the next day like you said you would? Why did you have to stay?"

His fingers loosened their grip on her arm but didn't release her entirely. "I know what I told myself at the time," he said quietly. "Now I'm wondering if it wasn't some subconscious desire to see you again. Maybe I wanted to see for myself that you were happily married. You're not."

"Every marriage goes through rough patches." There was no way she was going to admit that hers was more than a rough patch, that divorce seemed inevitable.

"I've seen the way he treats you, Natalie. He's no good for you."

"And you're better, I suppose." Pushed by a surge of bravado, she made the mistake of meeting his gaze.

"You're damned right I am," he murmured, and bent his head, feathering a kiss across her lips.

"Don't." She drew back. "I can't do this again, Beau. You broke my heart once, and that was enough. The worst of it was, I never understood why."

"Maybe I didn't know how to tell you," he said.

"You can tell me now," she challenged him.

He shook his head. "Even now it's not that easy to talk about Iraq. You can't imagine what it was like over there, seeing what I saw, doing what I had to do. I learned not to make friends after seeing so many of them die. And the people I had to kill as a sniper—Lord, so many, and not all of them soldiers. I didn't even try to keep count. By the time my tour was finished, the boy who'd kissed you good-bye was gone. The man who'd replaced him was somebody you wouldn't even want to know. The memories, the nightmares—and the worst of it, having to pretend everything was all right. You deserved a whole man, a clean man, something I would never be again."

She gazed up at him, her eyes tracing the lines of shadow below his eyes. Such kind eyes. And they'd seen so much suffering. "So that's why you didn't write?" Her voice was a whisper of emotion.

"I wanted to. But I didn't know what to say. It was easier to disappear and hope you'd forget me."

"I never forgot you." Her hand slid up his cheek as he bent to brush her mouth with his.

The very tenderness of it evoked a tremor of longing. Her lips parted, seemingly of their own volition, wanting more, inviting more.

When he kissed her again, hard and deep, a moan rose in her throat. Her arms slid around his neck. They were spiraling out of control. They should stop. They had to stop. But the hunger of all those years apart was as powerful as a landslide. He was fully aroused, his erection straining the zipper of his jeans.

His arms caught her close, arching her against him. His hand found its way under the hem of her shirt, sliding up her ribs to cup one small, perfect breast, stroking the nipple through her lace bra. Her fingers raked his hair as she uttered little animal sounds—sounds that triggered a rush of memories. They were nineteen again, and nothing mattered except belonging to each other, body and soul. Now it was the same. So help her, if she burned in hell for it, she didn't want to stop—and neither did he.

But there were other forces at work.

A belching snort from the mare broke them apart. Lupita shuddered and lifted her tail as the mineral oil took full effect. The odor was enough to quell any thought of desire.

"Oh, good grief!" Natalie pulled away from it and stumbled over to stroke the mare's neck. "That's my girl," she murmured, avoiding Beau's eyes. "You're going to be fine now, aren't you, Lupita?"

The moment had turned awkward. Beau darted out of the stall and returned with a shovel to scoop the mess and haul it outside. By the time he came back into the barn, Natalie had gathered her gear and was headed for the door. Her stoically frozen expression was enough to tell him that whatever had passed between them was over.

He stepped into her path. "Thank you," he said. "You saved that mare's life tonight."

"You'll get my bill in the mail." She sounded shaken.

"Will you be all right?"

"Of course." She stood in the light of the single bulb. Her eyes were shadowed with fatigue, as if she'd spent too many sleepless nights. "Beau, what happened back there . . ."

"I know," he said. "Don't worry, it's already forgotten." That was a lie and they both knew it.

"We can't go back to where we once were," she said. "We've come too far over the years. We're different people now."

He gazed down into her dark eyes—so much kindness there, so much truth. A lot of women might be capable of an affair, but Natalie wasn't made that way. "I understand," he muttered. "Sorry things got out of control." He ached to wrap her in his arms and hold her close one last time, but that would only complicate things. "I'll walk you to your vehicle."

She shook her head. "Please don't. I'll be fine."

He let her go then, listening as she loaded her gear and started the engine. As she pulled out of the yard, he stood in the doorway, watching the red dots of her taillights until they vanished around the bend.

Catching the muffled sound of a vehicle's engine starting, Lute slipped from his hiding place in the barn's deep shadows and exited the building through a rear door. Too bad he couldn't reach Slade right now. It would have been quite a sight if Slade had shown up and caught his wife and Beau in that hot embrace. But Slade was on his way back from a run to Mexico and wasn't answering his cell. All Lute could do was leave him the message.

He ought to let Stella know as well. Not that Stella would care, though she might get a good laugh out of the news that Slade's wife was getting it on with her old boyfriend. But that wasn't for him to decide. Stella was paying him to pass on everything he relayed to Slade, so he dutifully made the call.

Maybe this time would make a difference.

Lute was more than ready for his life to change. He was tired of being a shit shoveler for the Tylers, and being chewed out by Beau just for taking a nap was eating at him like a worm in his gut. The more he thought about the man, the more he hated him. He would like nothing better than to watch Slade pound him to a whimpering pulp.

Stella had said that Slade wanted to give him extra jobs. Maybe he'd learn more about that the next time he went into town. Lute wasn't lazy. But cleaning stables didn't fit his kind of ambition. Or put the kind of money in his pocket that he wanted.

The next morning, Beau was up early to head straight to the bunkhouse and catch Lute in bed. He stalked into the small single room. "Gear up!" he barked. "Put your pants on!"

"What'd I do now?" Lute grumbled as he crawled out of the quilts and reached for the jeans that were hanging on the bedpost.

"You damn near killed one of our best mares. Why did you give her all that grain? Any idiot would know better than to do that!"

Lute cast him a whipped dog look. "I didn't mean any harm by it. She was the last one to get fed, and I'd run out of hay. The grain was there, in a sack, and I thought, what'll it hurt this once?"

Beau squelched the urge to grab him and throw him against the wall. "That mare bloated because you were too damned lazy to go to the hay shed and get another bale! She would've died if I hadn't noticed her and called the vet."

The vet.

A sly expression crept over Lute's face, causing Beau to wonder how much the little bastard knew. He always seemed to be slinking around, like he was spying on people.

Lute shrugged. "Then I guess it's taken care of. No harm done. I'll get the hay first thing after breakfast."

"No, you won't. Get your gear together while I find a man to drive you to town. You're fired."

Lute straightened. His lip curled in contempt. "My cousin Sky might have something to say about that."

"Sky works for *me.* And I don't care if he's your blasted twin brother. If he was here, he wouldn't just fire you, he'd beat you till you couldn't piss standing up. The one thing he won't stand for is some idiot mishandling a horse. You're to be outside in fifteen minutes. Somebody will be coming by for you. He'll have your back pay. After that, I never want to see your lazy ass around here again!"

Beau strode downstairs and outside, his step lightened by the sureness that he'd done the right thing. Once he heard the story behind his cousin's dismissal, Sky would be fine with it. The man was slow to anger where most things were concerned, but Will had mentioned seeing him break the jaw of a cowhand he'd caught whipping one of the horses.

Jasper had just finished breakfast in the kitchen with Bernice. The old man would be free to drive Lute into town. Maybe he'd even impart a few words of wisdom into the young fool's ears. But Beau couldn't imagine Lute would listen.

Replacing him would be easy enough. With school letting out, there'd be plenty of husky kids eager to work for the Tylers and earn a little college money. He'd give Jasper a notice to post at Burger Shack when he got into town. Meanwhile, he could get one of the regular hands to do the job.

Before going back to the house, he stopped by the mare barn to check on Lupita. He found her nursing her foal, looking fine. She'd be hungry this morning. He'd get her some hay as soon as he saw Jasper off.

Lute had told the old man to let him off at the Blue Coyote. He climbed to the ground, shouldered his backpack, and watched as the pickup pulled away. The ride to town had taken forever, with the old-timer driving under the speed limit and lecturing him on the virtues of honesty and hard work all the way. Screw that! Lute swore silently. He'd shoveled shit for the last time.

Slade was bound to be sore about the firing. But maybe the news that he'd pretty much caught Slade's wife in the hay with Beau Tyler would make up for that. Lute was counting on Slade to give him more work. Maybe now that he'd proved his worth, he could even get his license and be hired as a driver. He could drive a pickup. How much harder could a big truck be?

The bar wasn't open yet, but peering through the gap between the plastic blind slats, Lute could see somebody moving around inside, cleaning or setting up. Maybe Stella would give him some work, too, or at least help him with a place to sleep. He had to find something. If he had to pay for food and a motel room, the back pay he'd gotten from the ranch wouldn't last him more than a few days. He could be faced with living on the street or hitching his way back to Oklahoma.

Stepping up to the door, he knocked. After a brief silence, it opened a few inches. Lute found himself staring into the sharp, black eyes of Nigel, the bartender.

"We're closed," Nigel growled.

"I . . . I know," Lute stammered, thinking he'd give his right arm to inspire the kind of fear that man did. "I need to talk to Stella."

Looking past Nigel, Lute saw that Stella had come out of the back. He caught her eye. "It's all right," she said. "Let the boy in."

She motioned Lute to a stool at the bar and sat down next to him. She was dressed in a loose tank top that showed her black bra straps at the shoulders. With her face bare of makeup, she looked older than she had the first time he'd seen her, more like somebody's mother. Up close, he could see the graying roots of her hair.

A box of stale doughnuts lay open on the bar. Lute eyed them hungrily.

"Help yourself," she said. "I was just going to throw them out. So tell me why you aren't at work. What happened?"

"Got fired." Lute spoke while cramming his mouth full.

"Damned Tyler blamed a sick horse on me. Wasn't my fault, but anyway, I need work and a place to stay. Is Slade around?"

"He won't be back till tonight. Can't say he'll be too happy about your getting fired. But I'll see that he gives you some kind of work and a back room at the trucking company. For me, it'll be better than having you at the ranch. Now you can really keep an eye on him."

Lute stared at her, puzzled. "Slade's bound to be mad. What makes you so sure he'll hire me?"

"Because I own his business."

"What?" The last of Lute's strawberry doughnut dropped to the floor.

Stella shrugged. "He was having money troubles last year, about to lose the place. I bought him out, and now it's mine. Not many people know that, including that stuck-up little wife of his, so I'd appreciate it if you'd keep it to yourself, even with Slade."

"Sure. But I thought Slade had plenty of money."

"He does—now that I've set him up with some of my business connections. We split whatever he brings in. But lately I've had the feeling he's been holding out on me, making deals on his own. That's why I want you to keep your eyes open. A hundred a week, just like before. Deal?" She held out her hand. Her fake crimson nails were long and sharp.

"Deal." Lute accepted the handshake.

Stella smiled like a satisfied cat. "Now, how's about some coffee to go with those doughnuts, honey?" she said.

Why did so many emergencies have to happen at night? And why two nights in a row? Natalie struggled to keep her eyes open as she drove her SUV homeward over the back roads. Tonight her patient, a yearling stud, had been found tangled in barbed wire. The thrashing colt had to be tranquilized while the wire was clipped away and the deep wounds dressed.

The young horse would be all right, but Natalie was exhausted. All she wanted to do was go home and crawl into bed.

Slade was due home tonight. With luck, he'd be out cold. If she could sneak into the spare bedroom, where she'd been sleeping since the night she'd accused him of cheating, she might be able to get some needed rest.

Stifling a yawn, she sat up straighter behind the wheel.

The house was dark when she pulled into the drive and pressed the garage door opener. Slade's red pickup was there, parked in its usual place. Good, he must be asleep. She'd be less likely to disturb him if she went in through the clinic.

Taking her medical bag and the opener, she closed the garage from the outside and went around to the clinic's front door. Her hand found the lock and inserted the key.

The instant the door swung open, Natalie sensed something was wrong. Heart in her throat, she found the wall switch and turned on the light. Her knees went weak beneath her.

The clinic had been completely trashed, furniture ripped and overturned, glass broken, files scattered across the floor. The computer had been smashed, the instruments and medical supplies crushed as if they'd been stomped by heavy boots. There'd been no animals in the back room, thank heaven, but the cages were toppled and bent as if they'd been kicked across the room.

Everything was ruined.

CHAPTER 9

Natalie stared at the chaos that had been her clinic. From the back of her mind, a warning voice screamed, *Run! Get out of here!* But she was frozen in shock. She stood rooted to the spot, taking in the nightmare. What had happened here—and why?

Then, as Slade appeared in the hallway, she knew.

Even at a distance she could smell the liquor on him. He was dressed in rumpled work clothes, his beard unshaven, his eyes narrow red slits. Natalie willed herself to stand her ground as he lumbered toward her like an enraged bear. Somehow she found her voice.

"Stop right there, Slade Haskell! Have you gone crazy? Why in heaven's name did you do this?"

He paused, close enough to cut her off from the clinic's front door. "Because you been screwin' that bastard Beau Tyler. That's why!"

Natalie's heart slammed. She and Beau had come close to the brink, but what Slade was accusing her of hadn't happened. "That's not true! I was at the Tylers', but I went there to treat a mare with colic!"

He shook his doubled fist at her. "Don't you lie to me, you little whore. I got an eyewitness that seen the two of you in the barn. For all I know, you were there with him again tonight."

"I was working! You can call—"

"Shut up, bitch! You're gonna pay right now! Then I'm goin' after Tyler and shoot his damned balls off!"

He was coming toward her again. Natalie's hand closed on a metal folding chair that was leaning against the wall. If he came at her, she'd need some way to defend herself.

As he lunged for her, she swung the chair with all her strength. The blow glanced off his forehead, leaving a red gash above his eye. He swore, yanked the chair away, and grabbed her arm.

Now she had nothing left. He was twice her weight and as strong as a steer. There was nothing she could do to stop the huge, rock-hard fist that crashed into the side of her face. Pain exploded in her head. Then mercifully, her vision spun into blackness.

She woke alone, in the dark. For the first few seconds, she was aware of nothing but a throbbing, swollen pain from her temple to her chin. As more awareness dawned, she realized she was lying faceup on the cold tile of the clinic floor with bits of shattered glass scattered underneath and around her.

Now the memory came back—Slade cursing her, his fist crashing home, the swirl of pain. And she remembered one more thing.

He said he was going after Beau.

She had to get up. Had to do something. She pushed herself to a sitting position. Her arms seemed fine, but something was tangled around her lower legs, restricting their movement. Reaching down to feel, she discovered her jeans and panties bunched around her ankles and a telltale stickiness between her thighs.

A cold rage flash-flamed inside her. Slade hadn't stopped at punching her and knocking her out. While she was unconscious, her husband had raped her.

She glanced at the wall clock, which, miraculously, was still in place. Only twenty-five minutes had passed since she'd arrived home. Slade could be on his way to the Tylers' right now. No time to weigh her options. Her best chance of stopping him was to call in the law. Fumbling for her cell in her jacket, she found it and punched in 911.

The female dispatcher at the county sheriff's office answered. "Nine-one-one. What is your emergency?"

"This is Dr. Haskell." Natalie's face was so sore she could barely move her jaw. "My husband, Slade Haskell, assaulted me and knocked me out. Right now he could be on his way to the Tyler ranch with a gun. He has to be stopped."

"Do you need an ambulance?" Had the dispatcher heard anything she'd said?

"No!" Natalie would have shouted into the phone if she could. "Just pick him up. He's drunk and probably armed. You can arrest him for DUI—or better yet, domestic violence. Believe me, I intend to press charges. Hurry, before something awful happens!"

Natalie gave the dispatcher a description of the truck and the license plate number. Ending the call, she sank back against an overturned couch. Her head felt like a smashed melon. She needed to warn Beau, but the only number she had on speed dial was for the landline in the ranch office. The phone rang and rang without clicking over to voice mail. Something must be out of order. But even if she could leave a message, how likely was Beau to get it in time?

Using the couch for balance, she dragged herself to her feet and pulled up her jeans. She felt nauseous. If she could make it to the bathroom in the house, she could at least wash up. But what she really needed was to get out of here, to someplace safe.

Maybe she should have asked for an ambulance. But if she had, the whole town would know what had happened by tomorrow. Straining to focus, she speed-dialed the one friend who'd always been there for her.

Tori showed up fifteen minutes later to find Natalie still

slumped on the floor. The first words out of her mouth were, "I'm taking you to the hospital."

Righting the couch, she helped Natalie sit. Then she raced into the house and came back with a bag of ice and a towel. "Hold this on your face," she said. "We can talk on the way. I can't believe that bastard raped you."

"What about Erin?" Natalie managed to ask. "You mustn't leave her alone. If Slade shows up there, looking for me—"

"I took Erin to the neighbors'. She'll be fine, and the house is locked up tight."

Just having her friend here made Natalie feel stronger. She walked to Tori's station wagon on her own and buckled herself into the front seat. "Can you call Beau and warn him?" she asked.

"I don't have his cell number. But there's no need. I called the sheriff's office on my way here. Slade was picked up on a DUI charge. He was weaving all over the road. By the time you called nine-one-one, he was already on his way to jail. We can file domestic assault charges in the morning. You still want to, don't you?"

"It's not that I want to. It's that I *have* to." Natalie fought back waves of nausea. Her head felt like somebody had taken a jackhammer to her skull. She probably had a concussion. And she didn't even want to think about the damage to her face. She could feel the swelling beneath the ice bag Tori had given her.

"This won't be pleasant, so be prepared." Tori had pulled into the street and was headed for the highway. "I'll take some pictures of you in the hospital, as well as some photos of your clinic. The police will need to interview you and collect DNA for the rape kit—"

Natalie groaned. "Is that absolutely necessary?"

"You were unconscious. Slade's lawyer could claim that somebody else happened along—or that you'd been with Beau earlier."

Natalie lay back in the seat as the words sank in. Was spousal rape even a crime in Texas? If it was, and if it could be proven,

Slade could go to prison, maybe for a long time. All she'd really wanted was her freedom.

This was a nightmare. But it was *her* nightmare, and she had to keep it that way.

"Beau had nothing to do with any of this," she said. "Now that he's not in danger, I don't even want him to know what happened. He mustn't be involved."

"You can't keep him in the dark forever," Tori said. "Sooner or later, he's going to find out."

"But not yet. It's for his own good. Promise you won't tell him, Tori."

"Not unless I have to." Tori swung onto the highway and gunned the engine. The needle crept upward to seventy. "Slade's likely to get out on bail. First thing tomorrow, I'll get a restraining order to protect you. Do you want me to file for divorce while I'm at it? We have plenty of grounds for a good settlement now."

"Yes, go ahead." Natalie thought about the destruction of her clinic. The property and equipment were insured. But would the insurance company pay when the co-owner was responsible for the damage?

"Maybe you should stay with me for a few weeks," Tori was saying, "or at least until you're healed. I've got plenty of room and Erin would love having you there. Think about it, at least. You shouldn't be alone at a time like this."

"I'll think about it. Thanks." Natalie closed her eyes and pressed the ice bag against her face. The ice was starting to thaw, leaking down the side of her neck like a trail of melting tears. So many decisions. The list, if she made one, would be as long as her arm. Right now she was too exhausted to deal with the present, let alone the future. And she was in pain—so much pain that only one thing stood out with the clarity of a lightning bolt.

Tonight her life had changed forever.

* * *

Slade had returned to work the next afternoon. Bailed out of the county jail by Stella, he was sore, hungover, and in such a foul temper that Lute couldn't go near him without cringing.

Lute had overheard enough to know that Slade had been charged with DUI and domestic assault and that he'd been served with a restraining order to keep him away from his wife, who was still in the hospital. His trial date was three weeks away.

Slade had come home to find the locks changed on the house and his clothes and other essentials boxed on the front porch. His pickup had been confiscated along with his driver's license. He was sleeping on a cot in his office and dependent on his employees to drive him where he needed to go.

Until this week, Lute had admired Slade to the point of hero worship. But that view had changed. Now what Lute felt was a heady sense of power. It was his simple phone message that had triggered Slade's drunken rampage and brought him down. And it had all been so easy.

Once Lute had aspired to be Slade's right-hand man. Now he had bigger ambitions. Slade would be going to jail, maybe for a long time. Somebody else would be needed to manage the trucking company and do business with Stella's so-called connections. Somebody Stella could trust. Why not him?

The three truckers Slade employed were family men who did local hauling—things like feed, machinery, and livestock. It was Slade, and only Slade, who did the Mexican runs. Whatever was going back and forth on those runs had to involve a lot of money—guns, drugs, maybe illegal immigrants. Lute was no fool. Having grown up in a family of lawbreakers, he knew what kind of things went on across the border. Given the chance, he could handle them just fine.

Plans were spinning in his head. He would shadow Slade for the next three weeks to learn everything he could about the business. Meanwhile, he'd be getting his trucker's license so he could be ready to drive when the time came. And he would curry favor with Stella, letting her know she could trust him to step into Slade's job.

It was all coming together. Soon he would have everything he wanted.

Natalie's stomach clenched as she stared into the hand mirror the nurse had given her. Her left eye was swollen almost shut, and the side of her face was a mass of blue and purple bruises. On the second day after Slade's beating, she looked like a character from a horror movie.

"I guess I should be thankful it wasn't worse," she said, laying the mirror facedown on the hospital bed.

"Yes, you should." The middle-aged nurse, with a manner that suggested she'd seen it all, put the mirror in the nightstand drawer. "At least he didn't crush your nose or break your jaw. You should see some of the women who've come in here."

"I never expected to be one of them." Natalie settled back against the pillows, trying to appear calmer than she felt.

"Nobody does, dear. Not the first time, at least. Your pretty face will look fine in a couple of weeks. But the doctor's still concerned about that concussion. She wants to keep you for another day or two, or at least until the dizziness goes away."

Natalie sighed, reached for the chilled gel pack, and laid it against her face. She had so much to do, so many things to take care of, it was maddening to have to lie here doing nothing. But Tori, who'd been a godsend, securing her house and car and moving Slade's things outside, had insisted that for now, the hospital was the safest place for her. With Slade out on bail, there was no guarantee that any restraining order would keep him from coming after her again.

For that very reason, she'd decided not to stay with Tori and Erin. She didn't want Slade coming anywhere near her friends. If she went back home, she could clean up the clinic and assess the damage while she healed.

Slade's guns were still in her house, locked in his gun safe. The locksmith Tori had hired had changed the combination.

Natalie had always hated guns, but when she got back to the house, she would take one out of the safe, load it, and keep it close for protection. She wasn't sure she could pull the trigger, but at least she could use the gun as a threat.

The nurse had gone. Alone, Natalie turned onto her side and closed her eyes. Tears made stinging salt trails down her cheeks. She knew how to be strong, and she would be. But right now she only felt ravaged, drained, and destroyed.

At the click of a boot heel on the floor, her heart lurched. Her eyes shot open. For the first split second she feared it might be Slade, but as her head came around, she saw that it was Beau. He stood framed in the doorway, looking as if he'd just been kicked.

As his eyes took her in, a slow anger transformed his face. When he spoke, his voice was like cold steel. "How long did you think you could keep me from knowing?"

"Who told you?" Natalie forced herself not to flinch. She knew how awful she looked, but she wouldn't play the victim.

Not with Beau.

"Tori thought it would be a good idea to warn me that Slade was out on bail. I couldn't let her off without hearing the full story."

"She promised—" Natalie broke off as she realized that wasn't true. Tori hadn't promised not to tell Beau. She'd only said she wouldn't tell him unless she had to. Had Tori told him about the divorce, too?

"You can't be here," she said. "You mustn't be involved in this mess."

"Damn it, Natalie . . ." He crossed the floor, cupped her chin in his hands, and gazed down into her battered face. "What the hell happened?"

"Somebody—I don't know who—told Slade I was with you at the ranch. Of course he believed the worst. The next night when I got home late from working, he was there. He'd wrecked the clinic . . ."

Natalie's voice broke. Her face would heal on its own. But

even if the insurance paid, restoring her precious clinic would take time and money she couldn't spare. "I tried to call and warn you about him," she said. "But I couldn't get a message through. Have you been all right, Beau?"

"Me? You're worried about *me*?"

"Slade's gone crazy. He's capable of anything."

"I know." He reached down and captured her hands in his big palms. "That's why, as soon as you're released, I'm taking you to the ranch. You'll be safe there. There'll be no way he can get to you."

"And how do you think that's going to look?" Natalie pulled her hands away and drew herself up in the bed. "You're not in charge of my life, Beau Tyler. I'm going back home to get my clinic running again. If Slade has the nerve to show up, I'll have a gun."

He shook his head, as if he'd expected her reaction. "But can you shoot? I know for a fact you used to hate guns."

"I still do. That doesn't mean I can't point a weapon and pull the trigger."

"But could you shoot your husband—even if he was going to hurt you again? Natalie, you're the gentlest person I've ever known."

"Then maybe you don't know me as well as you think you do!" She thrust out her chin, forcing herself to say the words. "I can take care of myself, Beau. So go away and leave me alone!"

Seething, Beau drove back down the highway toward Blanco Springs. Today Natalie had been like a feisty little wounded kitten, hissing, clawing, and utterly vulnerable. If Slade chose to violate the restraining order, he could murder her—and likely would.

He'd been wise to hold back what he knew, Beau reflected. Tori had told him about the rape, too. And the very thought of Slade ripping down Natalie's jeans, thrusting into her helpless body, and leaving her to lie there was enough to incite a murderous rage. Beau had killed more men than he cared to remember, and he'd done it with the cold efficiency that was part of his job. But he'd never wanted to kill a man as much as he wanted to kill Slade Haskell.

He didn't plan to do it, of course. That would be murder. But he could make certain the man knew what would happen if he didn't leave Natalie alone. At the very least, it might help keep her safe.

When Slade had baited him before, Beau had held in his anger out of respect for Natalie's marriage. But respect was out the window now.

He eased off on the gas pedal as the truck rolled into town. The Blue Coyote would be a good place to start looking. Stella, the owner, seemed a friendly sort. If Slade wasn't there, she might at least know where to find him.

When he pulled into the parking lot, Beau didn't see Slade's red pickup, but Tori had told him it was in impound and that Slade wasn't allowed to drive. If he was here, it made sense that he wouldn't be here alone.

Walking inside, he glanced around the bar. Slade was nowhere to be seen. But Stella spotted him. Dressed in a low-cut black satin cowgirl shirt embroidered with roses, she gave him a wave and a sexy smile. Minutes later she joined him at the bar.

"What can I do for you, cowboy?" She nudged him with one shoulder, causing her ample breasts to jiggle. Beau glanced toward the tattooed bartender, who was wiping a glass and taking no notice. No jealousy there, Beau surmised. But it would be interesting to know more about the relationship between those two. He had yet to snap a photo of the man for his friends at the DEA to run, but he'd have to worry about that later.

Beau ordered a beer on tap, taking his time. "I was hoping Slade Haskell would be here," he said.

"Have you got business with Slade?" One painted eyebrow arched a little higher.

"You might say that." Beau gave her a lopsided grin. He knew how to charm when it suited him. "If you're expecting him anytime soon, I'll hang around. You wouldn't mind that, would you?"

"Not if it means we get to know each other better." She flashed him a wink. "Slade usually comes in about this time, so feel free to wait. Right now I've got my customers to keep happy, but don't you go anywhere, hear?"

She sashayed away, her plump ass doing a little shimmy for his benefit. Hoping he hadn't charmed himself into a sticky situation, Beau sipped his beer and watched the door. Did Stella know what was going on? But why wonder? Beneath that cowgirl-floozy façade, Beau sensed a keen acuity that missed nothing. Underestimating the woman could be a dangerous mistake.

He'd finished his beer and started on another when the door opened and Slade walked in. Beau's instincts sprang to full alert. Slade was flanked by two quiet-looking older men wearing Haskell Trucking shirts. Slade's employees, Beau surmised. They didn't strike him as the sort who'd wade into trouble to save their boss. But there were other men in the bar, tough-looking types who could be Slade's friends. He'd be smart to watch his back.

He could get away with threatening Slade, but if it got physical—and it would—the man would have to come at him first. Beau took his time, sipped his beer, and waited. His training had taught him to fight cold, with emotions detached. He would have to maintain that detachment—otherwise, his anger could push him to kill the man.

Slade had spotted him. His pale eyes narrowed to slits of rage. "Tyler, you wife-stealing bastard!" he bellowed. "Come fight me like a man!"

Beau set down his beer, turned slowly on the bar stool, and stood. "These people deserve to drink in peace, Slade," he said. "Let's take this outside."

"And have you run again?" Slade muttered an obscenity. "I'm gonna beat you till you puke blood! And when I'm done with that pretty-boy face of yours, no woman will ever want you again!"

Customers scattered out of his path, forming a ring of watchers as Slade lowered his head and charged. Beau waited until the last split second, then shifted his position. Slade crashed into the bar stools. Staggering to regain his balance, he was unprepared for the lightning uppercut that Beau knifed into his solar plexus. The breath whooshed out of him. He doubled over. His knees buckled, giving Beau a perfect opening for a sharp-toed boot kick to the groin.

In less than five seconds it was over. Slade lay curled on his side, whimpering in agony. No one else moved or made a sound.

Beau could feel the adrenaline roaring through his body. He pictured Natalie's battered face, her ravaged body. Bloodred fury flashed behind his eyes and he knew he was on the edge of losing control. One more strategic blow could kill the man at his feet or cripple him for life. He couldn't let it happen.

Forcing himself to exhale slowly, he backed away a step. Slade's watery eyes looked up at him.

"Only a coward would beat a woman," Beau rasped. "How much does your wife weigh, Slade? Maybe half as much as you? How did you feel when you punched her in the face? Did you feel like a man?"

Slade muttered something vile, but he was in too much pain to get up.

Crouching, Beau seized his collar and yanked him up to the level of his gaze. There was genuine terror in Slade's eyes. Spit trailed from the corner of his mouth to the stubble on his chin. Sick with rage and disgust, Beau glared at him. He'd reduced this human monster to a quivering hulk, but nothing could touch what the man had done to Natalie.

"Get one thing through your thick head, Slade Haskell," he said. "Don't you ever threaten Natalie again. If you so much as go near her, so help me, the next time I see you I'll kill you."

Shoving Slade back to the floor, he rose, laid a bill on the bar, and walked out.

A pair of unseen eyes had witnessed Slade's humiliation. Lute had come into the Blue Coyote behind Slade and the two truckers. When he'd spotted Beau Tyler and sensed trouble, he'd skirted the crowd, made his way down the hall toward the restroom, and watched from the recessed doorway. Slade had gotten what he deserved. Too bad it had to be at the hands of an arrogant bastard like Beau Tyler.

Now, two mornings later, Lute entered the closed establishment through the back. His weekly cash was due, and Stella had always paid on time. Not finding her at first, he wandered into the bar. The place was silent, the floor swept, the tables cleared and wiped, the glassware polished. Weeks had passed since Jess's murder, but Lute still couldn't walk into the place without picturing her, flitting among the tables in her little pink boots. By now he understood that she'd been a whore. But that didn't mean there hadn't been something special between them—something that, with time, might have become real. He'd fantasized about taking her away from this place, getting a little apartment where he could have her all to himself. But those dreams had ended with the unspeakable discovery in the bog.

Had the cops learned anything about who killed her, he wondered, or had they decided a dead whore wasn't worth their time?

"There you are." Stella came out of the bathroom, wiping her hands on a paper towel. "I've got your money in the office. Come in and sit down. Let's have a talk."

Lute followed her down the hallway. She was dressed and made up for business except for her feet, which sported rubber flip-flops and several corn plasters.

Seated behind her desk, she motioned Lute to a chair and lit a cigarette. "So how are things with Slade?" she asked.

"Pretty bad," Lute said. "All he does is drink and talk about how he's going to put a bullet through Beau Tyler's head. I've been keeping stuff organized, and the drivers have been hauling their loads. But Slade's pretty much useless."

"I see." Stella blew a smoke ring. "So you've been doing Slade's job."

"As much as I can." Lute liked where this exchange seemed to be going. "I can't legally drive the trucks yet, but I'm studying for the test. I should have my license in the next week or so."

"Smart thinking." Stella smiled. "Slade's no use to us anymore. He's got to go. And I'll be needing a good man to take his place."

Lute's pulse had broken into a gallop. It was happening, everything he'd wanted. "I figure Slade's going to jail soon," he said. "After what he did to his wife, he could be there a spell."

Stella's expression hardened. She took a drag on her cigarette and blew another smoke ring. "You're a smart boy, Lute. Look at the big picture. You know Slade can't go to trial, and you know why."

Lute stared through the haze of smoke as her words sank in. Facing prison, Slade would take a plea deal—his freedom in exchange for all he knew about Stella's operation.

Opening a drawer, Stella took out a sealed white envelope and slid it across the desk. When Lute picked it up, he felt the substantial thickness of what it contained. There was a lot more money here than the five $20 bills she usually paid him. The hair prickled on the back of his neck.

"Prove to me that you can do Slade's job. Do that, and the job's yours." Stella sucked on her cigarette and exhaled a cloud of smoke. "As long as you're here, let me share a little secret. Just between you and me, I know you were sweet on Jess, and I know how much it hurt you when she died." She tamped the cigarette in a china ashtray before she met Lute's eyes. "The one who killed her and dumped her body in that bog was Slade."

By the time Natalie was released from the hospital, she was impatient to get home. When Tori came to pick her up, she almost bolted out the door.

"How's your head?" Tori asked as she drove out of the parking lot. "I still wish you would stay with me for a few days so I can keep an eye on you."

"My head's fine. They could've sent me home two days ago."

"At least you're looking better." Tori gave her an appraising glance. "Your bruises are fading fast. A little makeup and nobody will notice them at all."

"Good." But Natalie wasn't concerned about appearance. "Is my house all right?"

"It's fine. I checked on my way here. I even put some leftover lasagna in the fridge for you to warm up."

"What would I do without you?" Natalie reached over and squeezed her friend's shoulder. It felt good to be going home. But home would be a different place now. And she'd be dealing with a mountain of complications—her clinic, the insurance, the money, the divorce . . . Her mood darkened. "I guess I'd better ask what's happening with Slade," she said.

"Nobody's seen him since he had that fight with Beau in the bar. Rumor has it he's holed up at his trucking company, most likely drinking."

"I told Beau to stay out of this, but no, he had to go and make everything worse! Why can't the man leave well enough alone?"

"Beau was worried about you. He wanted to let Slade know you had a protector."

"Don't you dare defend him, Tori! Beau was way out of line! Anyway, I don't need a protector. I've got new locks and a restraining order. And I'll have a gun with me."

"A gun you don't know how to shoot. Maybe you ought to get a dog—something big and scary like a rottweiler."

"Stop worrying, I'll be fine. And I'll be too busy to take care of a dog, especially while I'm getting the clinic operational again. That's going to be a big job . . . and expensive. I just hope I can get enough house calls in the interim to pay for it."

Tori didn't answer. Her eyes were fixed on the road. Was something going on?

They made small talk, mostly about Erin, until they drove

into town. Natalie could feel her tension rising as they pulled up to the house. From the outside, everything looked fine, almost normal except that the lawn needed mowing.

"You'll need new keys for the locks." Tori fished in her purse as they climbed out of the car. "Here you go. The square one's for the front door. There are spares inside."

Natalie found the key on the ring Tori had given her. Her hand trembled as she thrust it into the dead bolt. How many times had she come home to this house wondering which version of Slade would be waiting for her inside—the sociable, good-humored man she'd married or the demanding, suspicious tyrant who'd follow her from room to room, railing at her and criticizing every move she made?

Now the house would be empty. But the memories would rush at her every time she opened the door. It would be a long time before she felt safe here.

The key turned in the lock and the door swung open to silence. The living room had been straightened, Slade's clutter of newspapers, gun magazines, and empty beer cans thrown out. A vase of fresh bluebonnets and daisies sat on the freshly polished coffee table.

"Thank you so much!" Turning, Natalie hugged her friend. "Not just for this but for everything! How am I ever going to pay you back?"

"You already have." Tori returned the hug. "Now let me check the place out so you can relax, knowing you're safe. Then I'll have to run along. Erin will be getting home from school, and I've got clients coming."

Tori gave each room a brief inspection, as if she expected Slade to lunge out of a closet or reach out from under the bed. She even checked the garage and tiptoed down the hall to open the door of the clinic and glance in. Natalie sensed that Tori was doing it for show, but she waited in the living room until her friend came back to report.

"All clear," Tori announced. "Now get some rest. There's a quart of your favorite double fudge ice cream in the freezer.

Find a big spoon, put your feet up, and forget about that hospital food you had to eat. That's an order!" She strode toward the door. "Lock yourself in. That's an order, too."

Natalie sighed as her best friend drove away. Tori had been an angel, but she really could take care of herself. Was it her petite size that made people want to mother her? Or did she really appear that helpless?

The ice cream could wait. After three days of forced inactivity, she was ready to get some things done. She could start by cleaning up the mess in her clinic and making a list of what needed to be repaired or replaced.

Seizing a broom and a dustpan from the kitchen closet, she marched down the hall that connected the clinic with the rest of the house. A chill passed through her body as she reached for the doorknob. Natalie willed herself to ignore it. Tori had checked the clinic and pronounced it safe. And the sooner she entered the crime scene and owned it, the sooner she could heal and move ahead with her life.

Squaring her shoulders, she turned the knob, opened the door, and stepped into the familiar space. She gasped. The broom and dustpan clattered to the floor.

Her clinic was in perfect condition, as if nothing had happened.

CHAPTER 10

Natalie stared at the gleaming floor and counters, the furniture, equipment, and supplies. Was her head injury causing her to hallucinate? She'd left the place in ruins.

Only when a tall figure rose from the couch did everything fall into place.

"Welcome home, Natalie," Beau said.

She gripped the door frame, blasted by a tempest of emotions—gratitude, yes, but surprisingly, the most overpowering of all was outrage. Why hadn't anyone understood that she needed to do this job herself, to work through the wreckage Slade had left behind, to prove that she could manage on her own?

Beau had taken that healing task away from her. Tori must have had a hand in it, too. He couldn't have done it without her cooperation.

Beau was watching her with a concerned expression. She realized she was shaking.

"How . . . could . . . you?" Each word was forced from her tight throat.

A wounded look flashed across his face. Then, as if the truth had dawned, he strode across the room and caught her close.

Natalie went rigid, her fists balling against his hard chest. She fought his strength, but his arms only tightened around her, confining her, confining the storm as he'd learned to do years ago when she was upset. Slowly the resistance ebbed. Still reluctant, she sagged against him, breathing in little broken gasps. She didn't want to take refuge in his arms. She didn't want to need him. But, heaven help her, she did.

His embrace had gentled. "Would you like me to wreck the place again so you can clean it up yourself?" he murmured against her hair.

"You could have asked me first," she said.

"You would have said no."

"I'll pay you back every cent this cost you."

"It wasn't that much. By the time we picked everything up off the floor, there were only a few odds and ends that needed to be replaced."

"Rimrock will get free vet care for the rest of my life."

He moved his hands to her shoulders, shifting her away from him so he could look into her bruised face. "Let it go, Natalie. You've been through a hell of a time. Let the people who love you have the pleasure of helping."

Had Beau just said he loved her?

But no, he hadn't meant it—not that way. And even if he had, how could she welcome his love when he would only break her heart again?

"You shouldn't be here," she said.

"And you shouldn't be here alone," he countered. "Do you have any idea how many women have been hurt or killed by men with restraining orders against them? I'm staying here tonight. And tomorrow I'm giving you a shooting lesson."

She shook her head. "You're a target, too. If Slade comes snooping around and sees us together, it could push him over the edge. Go home. I'll be fine."

His jaw tightened. "The only way I'm going home is if you come with me. Otherwise I'm staying. Your choice."

"You don't own me, Beau. You have no right to just step in and take over my life."

His hands tightened on her shoulders, almost hurting.

"Damn it, woman, can't you get this through your stubborn

little head? I'm not trying to take over your life! I'm trying to save it!"

He stood like a hickory tree, rooted to the ground.

Natalie had seen this side of him in the past. Beau had made up his mind. He wasn't going to budge.

She sighed in defeat. "All right. There's a spare bed in the guest room. Where's your vehicle?"

"Locked in the garage with yours." He released her and stepped away. Only then did she notice the heavy revolver holstered at his hip. "But I'll pass on the guest room," he said. "It's too far out of the way. The living room sofa will work better. And I'll most likely stay awake. If Slade comes snooping around, I'll want him to know that I'm here and that I have a gun. Believe me, I'd rather scare him away than have him break in and be forced to shoot him."

Natalie shivered at his words. Slade had done some awful things, but she didn't want him shot. She didn't want anybody shot, especially Beau. Why hadn't Beau stayed out of this mess? Why couldn't he have just walked away and left her to face her problems on her own?

Sighing in resignation, she turned back toward the hallway. "As long as you're staying, we might as well have some dinner," she said. "I'll warm up Tori's lasagna and make a salad. There might even be a bottle of Pinot Noir in the cupboard. How does that sound to you?"

Beau sat on the sofa, leafing through the newspaper and listening to Natalie rummaging in the kitchen. He'd offered to help her, but she'd shooed him into the living room. She probably needed some time to herself.

He could get used to this—the sharing of intimate space with a beautiful, intelligent, courageous woman who dazzled him every time he looked at her. Even with the bruises shadowing the side of her face, she took his breath away, triggering the kind of domestic fantasies he'd never had with any other woman. If this were an ordinary evening, they might enjoy a pleasant dinner, clear away the meal, and maybe curl up on the sofa to snuggle and watch the news. When it was time, he would scoop her into his arms, carry her into the bedroom, and make tender, passionate love to her until they drifted off in each other's arms.

But this was no ordinary evening. Natalie had been brutalized, and she was still in danger. He was here to keep her safe. The last thing on her mind tonight would be romance.

Was there any chance of a future for them?

At the very least, she would need time to heal. And he would need a wellspring of patience. Rushing her into the kind of intense relationship he wanted could worsen the damage she'd already suffered.

Natalie raised her head to see the digital clock on the nightstand. Two-nineteen, and she'd been tossing most of the night. Maybe she'd gotten too much rest in the hospital. Or maybe she was just too tired to fall asleep.

Beau had insisted she go to bed early. At the last minute she'd decided to sleep in the guest room. The king-sized bed she'd shared with Slade held too many ghosts. Tomorrow she'd call some local charity to have the monstrosity picked up and hauled away.

So many changes. So many plans to make. Rolling onto her back, she stared at the darkened ceiling. It wasn't the idea of being on her own that troubled her. It was the ugliness of it all that gnawed at the pit of her stomach. And that ugliness was far from over.

The dark fog of sleep began to close around her. Her limbs grew heavy. Like an exhausted swimmer, Natalie sank into slumber.

What had she heard? The crunch of gravel? The shifting of a window screen? Instantly alert, she raised her head, catching a faint movement through the blinds. A hand sliding over the sill. A too-familiar face . . .

She screamed.

"Natalie! What is it?" Beau was there in an instant, his pistol drawn. Natalie blinked herself fully awake. Had it been real?

"The window. Someone was coming in. I saw his hand . . ." She was beginning to feel foolish.

Beau checked the window. "It's locked tight," he said. "No one could've opened it without breaking the glass. I'll go outside and look around, just to be sure."

"Please don't." The last thing she wanted was for him to go out and expose himself to an ambush. "I'm sorry. I must've had a bad dream. Did I wake you?"

"No way. I learned to stay awake on watch and on drug stakeouts." Turning on the bedside lamp, he scowled at her. "You're as pale as a ghost. Are you all right?"

"I'll be fine. But I don't know if I can go back to sleep."

"Then come and keep me company." Without asking permission, he bundled her in the quilt, lifted her in his arms, and carried her to the living room sofa. "How about some hot cocoa? I saw some packets of the instant stuff in your kitchen—the kind with marshmallows."

"Actually that sounds wonderful." She snuggled into the quilt. "There's a kettle on the stove. Clean cups in the dishwasher."

"Coming up." She heard him running water and rattling dishes. Minutes later he walked into the living room with two steaming mugs. "Remember how Bernice used to fix this for us when we were kids?"

"I remember. But I believe Bernice made it from scratch. And the marshmallows were the big puffy kind that would fill your whole mouth."

She took one of the mugs, cradling it to warm her hands. The cocoa was hot, but not too hot to sip. They sat in comfortable silence, savoring the shared memory. The light from the kitchen filtered into the room, softening its darkness.

"How long before you have to go back to D.C.?" As soon as she asked, Natalie wished she hadn't.

"When I asked for an extended leave, I made it open-ended,

so however long it takes for Will to get back to where he can run things."

"You must be missing life in the city," she guessed, remembering it was all he'd known for the last several years.

"Not really." His mouth crooked in a lazy smile. "D.C. is all about appearances. As long as you shine on the surface, it doesn't matter how rotten you are underneath. That gets old after a while."

"And Texas?" Natalie smiled back.

"It's the real deal here. If you're a badass in Texas, everybody knows it."

Natalie laughed, reacting as much to the twinkle in his eyes as to his words. This was the old Beau, the one she remembered.

His smile faded as something serious entered his gaze. "Will has asked me to stay. Actually, it was more like an order than a request," Beau corrected himself in a seeming attempt to make light of his statement. But the attempt couldn't disguise how closely he was watching for her reaction. "He thinks we should run the ranch together."

"And?" She held her breath, hardly daring to hope that Beau might be here for good.

"Up till now, my answer has always been a flat no. Mostly because I knew I couldn't stand seeing you with . . . him." A wealth of loathing was shoved into that single word. "Then Tori told me that you'd filed for divorce."

"I have," Natalie admitted. "But not because of you. You just turned out to be the catalyst that brought a lot of other issues to a head."

Privately she wondered whether two such strong personalities as Beau and Will could get along. They were bound to have disagreements. Would Beau walk away in anger again? More importantly, could she handle it if he did?

Almost as if he read her thoughts, Beau said, "I know I haven't given you reason to trust me, but I'd like to find out if there can be an 'us' again. I've lived for too many years with the regret of walking out of your life. Meeting women, measuring them against you, and finding them lacking—"

There was clearly more he intended to say, but she stopped him, placing her fingertips against his lips, moved by the humbleness in his voice. "I'm not a coward, Beau." That was one thing she knew about herself; she had the strength to face tomorrow, whether he stayed or left. "If there's a chance for us—"

This time it was Natalie who was stopped from completing her sentence as he brushed her fingers away and cupped a hand behind her neck to pull her into his arm, his mouth claiming her lips in a devouring kiss.

His mouth tasted deliciously of chocolate and marshmallow. With a yearning whimper, she slid her arms around his neck, pulling his head down to her as the kiss deepened. Her tongue flicked along his lower lip, gliding in and out of his mouth in a teasing pantomime of what she needed. One hand fumbled his shirt buttons. He groaned but didn't try to stop her. She'd been through hell these past few days, and she was tired of holding everything back. She needed to break the dam. She needed Beau to make love to her.

Wiggling free of the quilt, she pushed it aside. She was naked beneath her short, loose-fitting nightshirt—something she made sure he was quick to discover.

"Dammit, Natalie, this isn't the time," he muttered, but his hands had already found their way beneath the thin fabric. His work-roughened palms ranged over her bare skin, awakening a rush of the well-loved sensations she'd all but forgotten. Beau had been the first boy to stroke her breasts, the first to touch between her legs. Now the sweetness of it came back as if time had fallen away. There'd been no shame then. There was no shame now.

All eagerness, she reached down and tugged at his belt buckle. He caught her hand and gently lifted it to his lips. Only then did she remember the loaded revolver holstered at his belt and the real or imagined danger that lurked outside. Beau would not lower his guard. Not even to make love to her.

A murmur of disappointment rose from her throat. Lifting her chin with his thumb, he kissed her. "Take it easy, girl," he whispered. "I've got this."

Easing her back into the support of one arm, he slid his free hand between her thighs to her moisture-slicked folds. His fingertips separated the dripping petals to find the swollen, sensitive nub at their center.

"Oh . . . ," she gasped.

He feathered her with a light stroke that sent heat whorls surging through her body. She arched to meet the delicious pressure, thrusting against his hand as his finger slid into her. He knew her so well, knew exactly how and where to touch her . . . it was as if time had disappeared. It was as if she were young and naive again, as if she loved him with all her soul and nothing could ever, ever happen to keep them apart.

As the wild sensations spiraled through her body, she felt herself spinning, soaring out of control to a shattering climax that left her limp and breathless.

With exquisite tenderness, he bent and kissed her. "To be continued," he whispered.

Without another word, he scooped her up with the quilt, rose, and carried her back to the guest room. Lowering her to the bed, he tucked her in and bent to brush a kiss across her mouth. "Get some sleep," he said. "I'll wake you early."

Natalie settled in with a little purring sound. She was already drifting into peaceful slumber.

At first light, Beau stood, stretched his cramped limbs, and wandered into the kitchen to start the coffeemaker. The night had been quiet, with no sign that Slade had come around. But he wanted to make sure.

While the coffee was brewing, he went out the front door, locked it behind him, and walked the perimeter of the house and clinic. He saw no fresh boot prints, no unfamiliar tire tracks or any other sign that someone had been here in the night.

Satisfied, he went back inside and poured himself a cup of coffee. He would need to wake Natalie soon. He wanted to help her choose a gun and show her how to load and fire it. A 20-gauge double-barrel shotgun would be light enough for her to shoot without too much recoil, simple to aim, and deadly enough at close range to blast any intruder to kingdom come. There was bound to be one in Slade's gun safe.

But would Natalie have the guts to pull the trigger, especially if the target was her estranged husband?

Beau could only hope it wouldn't come to that. If Slade did show up, the sight of the gun and the awareness of what it could do would hopefully be enough to keep him at a distance.

Once he got her set up with the gun, it would be time to leave. He was needed at the ranch, and for appearance's sake, he wanted to be gone before some passing busybody saw him backing out of Natalie's garage.

Setting the coffee cup on the counter, he walked into the guest room to wake her. She lay on her side, so beautiful that she almost stopped his heart.

Last night he'd given her a needed release. But he knew better than to read too much into that. This morning she could wake up and see him in a different light, and the chasm of time and hurt that had separated them would open again.

Either way, what happened next would be up to her.

One bare foot peeked out from under the quilt. Beau reached down and gave her toe a playful tug. She stirred, rolled onto her back, and opened her eyes. "Hello, you," she murmured dreamily.

"Time to get moving, sleepyhead," he said, giving her a grin.

"Not quite yet." She held up her arms, fingers beckoning. "Come here."

Laughing, he bent down to give her a light kiss. As their lips brushed, her arms locked around his neck.

"You said something about 'to be continued.' " Her voice was a kittenish growl. "So continue."

Heart pounding, he deepened the kiss, then pulled away. "You're sure this is what you—"

"Shut up and get undressed, Beau Tyler."

His erection sprang free as he unzipped his jeans. Peeling off his clothes and boots, he lowered himself to the bed and into her waiting arms. She was all sweetness, all warmth and eagerness, pulling him close, offering him her mouth, her perfect little breasts, and the hungry heat between legs, urging him with little whimpers to take her and ease the throbbing need that drove them both.

As he found the familiar sweet spot and eased his shaft into her moist, welcoming silk, Beau felt a sense of completion, as if he'd come full circle. After a long, dark, and painful journey, he was, at last, home.

Natalie stood at the living room window, watching Beau back the battered ranch pickup out of the driveway. Every inch of her body tingled in the afterglow of his lovemaking. It was as if they'd never been apart, but even more poignant this time because they were both older and wiser, both scarred with their own personal wounds and in desperate need of healing.

Her eyes followed the tailgate as the vehicle grew smaller with distance and disappeared around the corner. Making love with Beau had been as natural as breathing.

Just like that, it was like spinning backward through a time warp. A life with Beau was all she'd ever desired. But could she trust him this time? Could she trust fate not to snatch him away from her again?

If she wanted a life with Beau, she would have no choice except to gamble with her heart a second time. Right now the way looked clear. Given Slade's history of infidelity and abuse, the court was likely to grant her a speedy divorce. Then, after a decent interval, she and Beau would be free to marry.

So why was this dark premonition hanging over her? Why couldn't she shake this irrational fear that, once again, some unforeseen force was lurking in the shadows, waiting to tear them apart?

She glanced back at the double-barreled 20-gauge shotgun that was propped against the end of the couch. Before leaving, she'd opened the gun safe with the new combination Tori had left her. The safe was crammed full of Slade's guns, which he'd collected avidly for years—everything from antique muzzle-loaders to modern military assault rifles, many of them loaded. Beau had been forced to remove most of the guns from the safe before he found a weapon she could use.

After he'd replaced the guns and she'd locked the safe, he'd given her a brief lesson on how to load and fire the lightweight shotgun. Just touching the trigger had made Natalie's skin crawl, but she'd promised Beau she'd keep it with her at all times, in the house and in her vehicle.

She could only pray she would never have to use it.

Sky parked his dusty pickup outside the front office of Haskell Trucking, climbed out of the cab, and closed the door with a barely audible click. A middle-aged driver, outside for a smoke, took one look at him and disappeared around the corner of the prefab building. Sky Fletcher was known to be a quiet man. He was even quieter when he was angry.

Walking in the front door, he saw Slade Haskell sitting behind the counter. The man looked like hell, his clothes rumpled, his eyes bloodshot and rheumy, his jaw sporting a scruffy beard. Looking up, he eyed Sky with a surly glare. Sky had heard his story from Beau. But even he was surprised at Haskell's condition.

"What d' you want, Fletcher?" he grunted.

"I heard Lute was working here."

"Out back. You'll see him."

"Thanks." Sky turned toward the door.

"Fletcher."

Sky paused, glancing back over his shoulder.

Haskell's expression had turned savage. "The next time you see that bastard Beau Tyler, you tell him I'm not done with him. I'm comin' to get him, and when I'm through, he'll never mess with another man's wife again!"

With a curt nod, Sky walked out the door. He would warn

Beau, of course, but Haskell's threat hadn't surprised him. The man was all bluff and bluster, and today he didn't look fit to battle a prairie dog.

Walking around the building, he spotted Lute across the gravel parking lot. He was standing next to an empty cattle truck, a clipboard in his hand, evidently going over some shipping instructions with the driver. A rush of cold anger tightened the grim line of Sky's mouth. The boy appeared to be doing well for himself, but his near-fatal mishandling of the Tylers' prize mare topped Sky's short list of unforgivable sins.

Lute had seen him. Sky remained where he was, watching as the boy wavered between running away and coming over to account for himself. In the end he seemed to decide that running would only make things worse.

"Hullo, Sky." Lute looked down at the clipboard, unable to meet his cousin's accusing eyes.

"When I brought you to the Tylers', I told you your behavior would reflect on me and on our family. It seems you didn't care."

Lute's lower lip jutted out as his anger welled up. "You said I could be a cowboy! But you gave me a job shoveling shit!"

"That wasn't just a job. It was your first lesson. I'd planned on training you to help me work with the new colts."

"Yeah? Well, too bad. I got sick of it. Now I've got a job where people respect me! I don't stink at the end of the day, and I'm even making decent money! See that blue truck over there? It's mine, bought and paid for!"

Sky glanced across the lot to where the employee cars were parked. The light blue truck had some rust spots and a sagging rear bumper, but he knew it was the first vehicle Lute had ever owned. Sky remembered the beat-up Ford Bronco he'd bought himself and driven with such pride. For a young man barely out of his teens, it was power and status. Heady stuff.

"Is owning your own truck worth working for a drunken wreck like Slade Haskell?" he asked Lute.

Lute thrust out his chin. "I won't be workin' for Slade much longer. He's goin' to jail soon. And when he's gone, Stella says—" He broke off as if he'd revealed too much. "I've almost got my trucker's license. Once I get that, I'll have everything I want, and I won't have to lick anybody's stinkin' boots!"

Sky's cold anger still blazed. But it was tempered with a twinge of pity. Lute was in for some hard lessons. But the young fool had blown his chances on the ranch. It was time to cut the strings.

"It sounds like you've made your decision," he said. "I wish you the best, Lute. But you're finished on the ranch. You're never to set foot on Tyler land again, and if I catch you anywhere near my horses, I'll whip you within an inch of your life."

Lute watched his cousin stride back around the building. A moment later the engine of Sky's pickup roared to life and faded down the street. Sky was a fool, he told himself. He'd spent most of his life working for the almighty Tylers, and what did he have to show for it? A lot of big, fat nothing. He'd made their horses prized all over Texas, but the family still treated him like the fatherless half-breed Comanche bastard he was.

Not that Sky was his concern. Right now he had weightier issues on his mind. Slade's trial date was getting closer. Lute had spent the cash from Stella to buy the truck. But he still needed to do what she'd paid him for.

Slade's fight with Beau Tyler had left Lute with the makings of a perfect plan—a way to eliminate not just one man he hated but two. The only trouble was, the plan wasn't coming together fast enough. First he'd needed a weapon—no way was Stella going to give him anything that could be traced back to her, and Slade's guns were locked away. He'd solved that problem a few nights ago by making a night raid on the Tyler place. Jasper kept a loaded Remington 30.30 deer rifle strapped under the seat of the ATV he drove around the ranch. It had been an easy matter to sneak into the shed, unbuckle the gun from its place, and hike back to the truck he'd left down the road.

Stealing a rifle that could be traced to the Tylers had been a stroke of brilliance. But he still needed to get Slade somewhere isolated where he could use it. Lute had never killed a man before, never even come close. But there was a first time for everything. And when he imagined Slade shooting pretty little Jess and dumping her body like so much trash, he knew he was capable of pulling the trigger.

Stella was getting impatient. She hadn't said so in words, but he could tell by the looks she gave him when he came into the bar. Time was running short. If he didn't act soon, he could lose everything he'd worked for.

The idea struck him like a thunderbolt. It was so perfect he had to restrain himself from laughing out loud.

Sky's visit had played right into his hands. The copy machine in the front office was stocked with plain white paper. Lute, thanks in part to his mother's training, was an accomplished forger. Beau Tyler had been the one to sign his payroll checks at the ranch, and Lute, out of long habit, had memorized his signature.

All he had to do was wait for Slade to visit the restroom. Then he could take a few sheets of paper and set his plan in motion. Lute smiled a secret smile. This was going to be freakin' fun.

Lute waited till after lunch before he sidled into the front office, where Slade sat hunched at the desk nursing a Corona. Slade glanced up with a scowl.

"Sorry I was too busy to catch you sooner," Lute apologized. "Sky came by to deliver a message. He wanted me to give this to you." He fished a tightly folded sheet of paper out of his pocket.

Slade's eyes narrowed suspiciously. "Who's it from?"

Lute shrugged and passed the note across the desk. He'd written three different versions before deciding this one would have the most impact. Watching Slade's expression as he unfolded and read it, Lute knew he'd made the right choice:

Slade, you bastard, Natalie is my woman now. I want to make sure you never bother her again. Let's me and you fight it out man to man. Meet me tonight at 10 by the bog where you dumped that dead girl. Come alone. I'll be waiting. If you don't show, I'll know you're nothing but a filthy, stinking coward.

Beau Tyler

Most of the note was hand printed, but it was signed in Beau's unmistakable scrawl. Lute, who'd dropped out of school in his junior year, had never been much of a writer. But, as he'd expected, Slade was too mad to notice any minor grammatical mistakes or crude language. And the hint that Beau knew what he'd done to Jess would give Slade one more reason to want to kill him.

True, Slade had lost his truck and his driver's license. But he had access to vehicles at work. At night on back roads, who was going to catch him? He wasn't supposed to carry a gun, either, but he'd have no trouble getting his hands on one.

Lute watched Slade crush the note and stuff it into his shirt pocket. There was no way Slade would miss tonight's rendezvous. But the man waiting for him wouldn't be Beau Tyler. Lute would see to that.

CHAPTER 11

That night was one of those rare evenings when everything seemed right with the world. The setting sun had streaked the clouds with crimson and gold, casting a glow that deepened to violet and indigo as dusk crept across Rimrock land. Swallows darted through the twilight. The blooming honeysuckle that framed the porch steps perfumed every breath of air.

Sitting on the porch with Will, Jasper, and the dog, Beau experienced a rare sense of satisfaction. The swelling was down in Will's leg, and despite some lingering pain, he was chafing to be back in the saddle. His recovery, along with Sky's return, would leave Beau with more time to concentrate on the business and record-keeping facets of the ranch. He couldn't claim to enjoy the job. But in the years since Bull's injury, everything from ledgers to tax records to studbooks had deteriorated. As the only person on the ranch who'd ever held an actual desk job, the task of straightening out the mess had fallen to him. Knowing that the ranch's long-term survival depended on good management, Beau had resolved to grin and forge ahead, maybe even call Lauren Prescott over to help.

Everyone seemed in a celebratory mood tonight. Maybe that was because Erin had arrived to spend the summer on the ranch. Today the whole ranch family had joined in the welcome. Bernice had made Erin's favorite chocolate cake. Sky had supervised an hour of training with her foal, and Will had challenged her to a round of chess—a game she'd last played with her grandfather.

After lunch, Beau and Jasper had driven her out on the range to take turns plinking at tin cans with Bull's boyhood .22. The pop of gunfire still awakened memories of Iraq, but Beau had entered into the fun, laughing when Erin teased him for missing a target.

Jasper had reached under the seat of his ATV, meaning to show her the 30.30 that Bull had given him years ago. To the old man's distress, the rifle was missing. "It was there last week, and I haven't touched it," he said. "That gun means a lot to me. Bull even had my name engraved on the stock."

"I'll put the word out," Beau had promised him. "It's bound to turn up." Puzzled, he'd written a notice to post in the bunkhouse and passed the message on to Sky. A theft on the ranch was cause for instant dismissal. It was hard to believe any of the hands would steal the old man's prized rifle, especially a gun that could so easily be traced. It was the one shadow that had darkened an otherwise happy day.

Erin had begged to sleep in the barn with Tesoro, but Will had drawn the line at that. Tonight she was in the house, texting her friends and rearranging her old bedroom.

Beau had never spent much time around children. Struck by how much he'd enjoyed Will's daughter today, he found himself wondering what it would be like to raise children of his own.

Beau was still lost in thought when Will dropped a bombshell.

"I got a call from Dad's lawyer in Lubbock. He'll be coming here tomorrow to read the will."

"Dad left a will?" The announcement had startled Beau. "How long have you known about this?"

"A while." Will leaned back in his rocker. "I'd have mentioned it sooner, but I didn't want to cause a stir till it was time."

That was like Will, keeping a firm hand on everybody's

strings, Beau thought. "And why some lawyer in Lubbock?" he asked. "Tori's a lawyer. Why not just use her?"

"Would you hire your son's ex-wife to make out your will? Dad liked to keep things private, even from me. Evidently the lawyer's an old school friend. Dad called him and asked him out to the ranch a couple of weeks before he died. He must've sensed what was coming."

"So you haven't seen the will yourself?"

"Not a word of it."

Beau scowled into the twilight. He'd never been fond of surprises, and he sensed there might be a few in store. "One more question. Why now? Why not sooner?"

"The lawyer wanted to wait till Sky was back. Evidently he's to be included."

"Interesting." Beau glanced at Jasper, who hadn't said a word. *The old man knows more than he's telling,* he thought. He might have questioned him, but at that moment Jasper rose to his feet and stretched.

"Well it's been a long day. Guess I'll turn in. See you boys in the morning. Maybe that rifle will turn up tomorrow." With that he hobbled off the porch and headed for his quarters, the Border collie tagging along after him.

Will rose, too. "Maybe I'll catch the evening news," he said. "Coming, Beau?"

Seized by a sudden restlessness, Beau shook his head. "Maybe I'll drive into town."

"Suit yourself. Just make sure you're here tomorrow for the lawyer." Will vanished inside. Beau hadn't told him about his new relationship with Natalie, but it seemed his brother had figured things out on his own.

Beau found the truck keys and backed the vehicle out of the shed, deciding it wouldn't hurt to swing by Natalie's house, just to make sure she was safe. Switching on the radio, he swung the truck around and headed toward the highway.

* * *

Behind the wheel of the company flatbed, Slade was sweating bullets. If the cops caught him driving, especially with a loaded gun in the vehicle, he'd be right back in jail. But he couldn't pass up the chance to meet that bastard Beau Tyler and blow him to kingdom come.

He'd learned the hard way that he couldn't beat Beau in a fistfight. But he could sure as hell get the jump on him with the Smith & Wesson .38 he'd kept stashed in his desk—a gun the police had missed. After the way he'd moved in on Natalie, Beau Tyler didn't deserve to live.

Slade had grown up in this country, and he knew all the back roads, including the ones on the Tyler place. He hadn't killed Jess, but when Stella had given him orders to dump her body, he'd known better than to ask questions. The bog had been his choice—a gesture, like leaving a dead cat on the Tylers' doorstep. It worried him that Beau had guessed what he'd done. Maybe the bastard was just taking stabs in the dark. In any case, unless he'd told others, whatever Beau believed wouldn't be a problem much longer.

As he swung onto a narrow dirt road, Beau's note crackled in his shirt pocket. Slade planned to be at the bog well ahead of his enemy. He was a crack shot. If he was already lying in wait when Beau appeared, all he'd have to do was aim and pull the trigger. He'd weighed that plan against the satisfaction of calling Beau out first. But the safer strategy had won out. Beau was a trained combat veteran. If he'd brought a weapon, too, things could go the wrong way.

The heavy pistol on the seat beside him was one he'd bought in Piedras Negras. It was unregistered in the U.S. and couldn't be traced to him. After the shooting, he'd wipe it clean of prints and toss it in some ditch. No one could connect him to the crime, except maybe that little worm Lute. But Lute hated Beau, too, and even if he had proof, the kid would know enough to keep his mouth shut.

He slowed down as he neared the bog. The swampy area

covered more than an acre, but the plan was to meet Beau where he'd dumped Jess's body.

The moon was full tonight, casting a clear light over the rank cattails. Frogs croaked an eerie chorus in the shallows. Clouds of gnats hovered above the murk. Parking the truck out of sight in the tall mesquite, he picked up the pistol and stepped down from the high cab. Maybe when this was done, he should just take the truck and hightail it to Mexico. Good idea, except that he was going to need cash. If he could get to his secret bank account in Lubbock, maybe he could—

Slade's last thought ended in blackness as a high-caliber bullet slammed into his skull.

It was 9:22 p.m. when Beau pulled up to the Blue Coyote. The parking lot was almost full. The sounds of the NBA basketball game on the big-screen TV blared from the high, open windows. Inside, there was no place to sit. Standing in the doorway, Beau surveyed the crowd. The harried young waitress was rushing between tables, balancing trays of drinks. Stella, looking frazzled, was tending bar. If she noticed Beau, she gave no sign of it. There was no sign of Nigel.

Thinking he might be in the restroom, Beau waited a few minutes. When the man didn't show, he gave up and left. He would have to snap the photo another time.

His visit to Natalie's place proved equally fruitless. The only response to the doorbell was the rapid-fire bark of a dog from the back of the clinic. A peek in the garage's side window revealed that her SUV was gone. She was probably tending to a four-legged patient or spending some needed girl time with Tori.

She'd given him a spare key, but there was no reason to use it tonight. He sent her a brief text saying he'd stopped by the house, then climbed into his truck and headed for home. He'd make it an early night and maybe get some office work done before the lawyer showed up tomorrow. To say the least, the reading of Bull Tyler's last will and testament should make for an interesting day.

On the way to the bog, Lute had pulled off the road, leaned out of his truck, and vomited into the barrow pit. He'd told himself he was strong enough to take a man's life. But now, as he faced the moment of truth, he was sick with uncertainty. What if he froze and couldn't pull the trigger? What if he fired and missed? What if Slade got the jump on him first?

Earlier that afternoon, he'd confided his plan to Stella. She'd praised him for his cleverness, but her unspoken message had been clear. If he couldn't deliver the goods, he was finished. He had to do this.

Ahead, in the moonlight, he could see the dead white cottonwood tree reaching out of the bog, its limbs like skeletal fingers. Time to ditch the truck and go the rest of the way on foot. The luminous hands on his cheap watch showed the time as a quarter to ten. With luck, Slade wouldn't be here yet. But he couldn't count on that.

With the loaded rifle in hand, he eased out of the truck, leaving the dome light off and the door open. The night was eerily quiet. As he crept forward, Lute tried to imagine his Comanche ancestors sneaking up on the enemy. He was a warrior, too, he told himself, and this was his battle—the prize, victory over two men he hated, and the future he craved with a hunger that gnawed at his gut.

A buzzing sound, a stone's toss away, sent a jolt of fear through his body. Rattler. He gauged the location and eased to a greater distance. Safe. But his nerves were jumping.

Twenty yards ahead, the lacy outline of the mesquite was broken by a big, blocky shape. Lute recognized the flatbed from the trucking lot. So Slade was already here waiting for Beau Tyler. No doubt Slade had a gun, but where the hell was he? If he heard Lute coming, he could easily shoot him by mistake.

Change of plans, Lute decided. He could call out, identify himself and tell Slade that Beau wasn't coming. When the man lowered his guard and stepped into sight, Lute could pull the trigger.

He was getting dangerously close to the truck. "Slade," he hissed. "It's me, Lute. Where are you?"

No answer.

"Slade, it's all right." He spoke louder this time. "I saw Beau Tyler in town. He's not coming."

No answer. A chill crawled over Lute's skin. Maybe he should've kept quiet. He wasn't even supposed to know Slade was here.

"Where the hell are you, Slade?"

Still no answer. The door of the truck hung open. Lute could see that the cab was empty. As he inched closer, his boot toe stubbed something soft. He looked down.

Slade lay faceup in the brush a few paces from the truck. A single, neat bullet hole was drilled with almost surgical precision through the center of his forehead. The spatters of blood, what few there were, were still wet.

Lute's knees refused to hold him. He sank to the ground next to the body, swearing to bolster his courage. Some bastard had beaten him to the job. It had to be Tyler. He'd been a sniper in Iraq. But how the hell had he known Slade would be here?

Stella seemed to like Beau. Could she have warned him?

No time to think about that, Lute told himself. He needed to salvage the situation to make himself look good. And then he had to get out of here.

He'd stolen the rifle from the ranch to frame Beau Tyler. The plan was to kill Slade with the weapon, then toss it where it could be easily found. The bullets in Slade's body would be a match for the old man's gun, which Beau could have easily taken. The note Slade had stuffed in his pocket, along with the testimony of witnesses who'd seen the fight in the bar, would seal the evidence. Case closed.

He could still make it work, Lute reasoned, especially since he'd be laying a trail to the real killer.

Standing, he laid the rifle's muzzle on the hole in Slade's

forehead, trying to match the angle of the first bullet. With a shaking finger, he pulled the trigger.

The shot cracked like lightning in the darkness.

Lute stared down at the damage. Firing the gun hadn't been such a big deal after all. Better yet, the bullet had made an ugly wound, pretty much obliterating the first one. Giddy with triumph, Lute pumped three more shots into Slade's still-warm body—for Jess, he told himself. *Bang, bang, bang.* So easy. He forced himself to stop before it became fun. He'd done enough.

There were plenty of shoe and tire tracks around the bog, left over from the earlier investigation. Still, to be safe, he found a broken mesquite branch and brushed out his tracks as he backed away from the scene. He hadn't forgotten the rattler. He gave it a wide berth, hoping there weren't more around.

Reaching his truck, he took a moment to wipe the gun with the damp cloth he'd brought along. On the way back to town, he would use the cloth to throw the gun into the long grass that grew along the roadside. No fingerprints. A clean getaway—and a clear conscience.

Stella would be pleased when he told her he'd done his job. But he planned to leave out one detail. Why bother to tell her he'd fired four bullets into a corpse?

The lawyer, J. Bob Tucker, had arrived precisely at 10:00 a.m., driving a black Lincoln Town Car and wearing a charcoal suit with a bolo tie and a Stetson. Tall and thin with a hooked nose and sparse gray hair, he was in his mid-sixties, the same age as Bull had been.

Since Tucker had requested a desk for the reading, Will had carried the dining room chairs into the ranch office, arranged them in a semicircle, and shifted the computer onto a side table. Bernice had offered to do the simple task, but he was through being a damned invalid. That morning, before first light, he'd gone out to the stable, saddled his horse, and ridden down to the lower pasture. His leg still ached, but not so much that he couldn't stand it. Pain or no pain, the old Will Tyler was back. But he would never take his body for granted again.

Now Will glanced down the row of chairs that faced the desk. Just six people were present for the reading of his father's will—Beau, Jasper, Bernice, Sky, Erin, and himself. Will was a trifle disappointed that Tori hadn't been included. But he should have known better. To Bull the three things that counted were blood, land, and loyalty. It was no surprise that, given the divorce, he'd excluded her from the family.

Sky had shown surprise at being asked to attend the reading. As far as Will knew, the man had never aspired to own anything but his truck, his clothes, his saddle, and his guns. His paychecks—and he was fairly paid—went directly to the bank. Unless he had some secret vice, he must have accumulated a tidy sum over the years, but he never spoke of it. Sky was as private as a lone cougar. Today, dressed in faded jeans and a denim work shirt with his dusty Stetson balanced on one knee, he appeared anxious to get this bother out of the way and go back to shoring up the paddock.

Erin edged closer to her father. Will encircled her shoulders with a comforting arm as the lawyer shuffled his papers on the desk. He could have spared his daughter this serious adult business, but she was growing up. It was time she understood her place in the family.

Tucker cleared his throat, adjusted his glasses, and began to read. "I, Virgil Tyler, being of sound mind . . ."

His voice droned on. Will and Beau were to be given equal shares in the ranch as long as both of them were involved in its management. If Beau chose to stay away, his share would be twenty-five percent. Clearly Bull had wanted both his sons on the land. Jasper and Bernice were to be given a modest income for life and a place to live for as long as they wished to stay. A trust fund, set aside for Erin, would pay for her college education. That left only Sky.

The lawyer cleared his throat again and moved on to the second page of the will.

"To Sky Fletcher, in recognition of his service to the ranch, I leave the contents of this envelope, to be opened in private, at his discretion." The lawyer slid a sealed, plain manila envelope across the desk, toward Sky. "Here you are, Mr. Fletcher. The envelope was given to me by Mr. Tyler, in this condition." Tucker scooped a few stray papers into his briefcase and closed it with a click. "Unless you have questions, that concludes my business here."

The envelope was thin, as if it contained no more than a few sheets of paper. Without taking time to inspect it, Sky folded it and slid it into an inner pocket of his vest. He was one of the most self-contained men Will had ever known. If he was surprised, or even curious, he hid it well.

The lawyer stood to leave, and everyone else rose with him. Beau turned to Sky. "I hope you're going to tell us what's in that envelope," he said. "When are you going to open it?"

Sky shook his dark head. "Not just yet. I'll know when the time is right."

Will glanced past him. Jasper had paused in the doorway. His pale eyes appeared to be studying the three men, taking their measure in some secret way. As his gaze met Will's, he raised a grizzled eyebrow. Then he turned away, leaving Will to wonder what the old man had been thinking.

Sky walked back down the slope toward the paddock, where two of the men had been helping him build a new section of fence. His senses were acutely aware of everything around him—the smells of grass and manure, the whinny of a mare to her foal, the echoing ring of two hammers, striking almost in unison. Through the well-worn soles of his boots he could feel every rock and pebble, every rise and fall of ground. The sun beat down on the felted crown of his Stetson, warming his thick, black hair. Everything was much the same as it had been for years, yet not the same. Whatever was inside the mysterious envelope, he sensed it could have the power to change his life.

He remembered the windy November morning when he'd

first wandered onto the ranch, a fifteen-year-old runaway, filthy and shivering in his thin denim jacket, his stomach a gnawing pit of hunger. The name Blanco Springs had been mentioned by his mother, so long ago that he no longer remembered the context, but it had to be a better place than where he'd come from. Maybe she even had folks there. He'd hitched rides from Oklahoma, stopping at farms and ranches on the way to chop wood or shovel out barns in exchange for a meal. The last ride, a truck delivering winter feed, had let him off here, and here he had found a home.

A plump, kind-looking woman had answered his knock at the back door. Too proud to beg, he'd asked for work. She'd taken one look and hauled him into the kitchen. "Go wash up," she'd directed him. "I'll fix you some breakfast. Then you can talk to the boss about earning it."

He'd devoured his way through three platefuls of bacon and eggs, two cups of coffee, and a small mountain of pancakes when a man walked into the kitchen—a terrifying man who looked as big as a barn door, with a bristling mustache and the fiercest, bluest eyes Sky had ever seen.

Sky had possessed the presence of mind to stand.

The man had looked him up and down. "Good. I like a boy with manners," he'd boomed. "Bernice here says you're asking for a job. But you look too scrawny to do a man's work. How old are you, boy?"

"I'm fifteen, sir." Sky had felt his knees shaking as he answered. "I'm stronger than I look. I'll work hard for as long as you'll have me."

"Sit. Finish your breakfast." The man had taken a seat on the opposite side of the table. Even sitting down, he'd loomed like John Wayne on steroids. "The name's Bull Tyler. Mr. Tyler to you. And I'm willing to give you a try at mucking stables—but only a try, mind you. First time I catch you slacking, you're done, hear?"

"Yes, Mr. Tyler. But I'm no slacker. And I get on with horses. You'll see."

"Fine. What's your name, boy?"

"Sky. Sky Fletcher."

The big man's expression had frozen, but only for an instant. "What about your folks? Can I expect them to show up looking for you?"

"No, sir. My mother died when I was three. Her brother's family in Oklahoma raised me. But I . . ." He'd paused, still feeling the sting of the welts on his back. "I don't belong there anymore."

"And your father?"

He'd shrugged. "I never knew him—or anything about him except that he was white and no good."

"Why no good?"

"Because he didn't give a damn about my mother or me. A good man would have taken care of us."

"And what was your mother's name?"

"Marie. Marie Joslyn Fletcher."

He rose. "Bernice, we should have some outgrown clothes from the boys. Get those rags off the lad and burn them. Then get him a bath and a toothbrush. When he's cleaned up, send him out to Jasper." Without another word, he turned away and strode out of the kitchen.

Bernice had cried out when she saw the welts on Sky's back. "One thing I can promise," she'd declared. "Wherever you came from, you're not going back!"

And so he never had, Sky reflected now. He'd stayed in touch with his cousins and even tried to help Lute, as he'd been helped. But he had no desire ever to see his uncle or aunt again.

Bull had been a fair employer over the years, even insisting that Sky take time off to finish high school. But he'd shown Sky no special attention or favoritism, let alone affection. Whatever place Sky held within the ranch family was the place he'd earned.

Which was why any sort of legacy was so unexpected. *In recognition of his service to the ranch . . .*

The thin envelope felt like a leaden weight inside his vest. Whatever it held, Sky hoped it wasn't money. He had money of his own, saved over the years. Not that he had any desire to spend it. Everything he needed was right here on the ranch.

Perhaps he'd be better off not knowing what was in the envelope. Maybe he'd be smart to simply burn it and walk away.

But Sky knew better than to act rashly. Sometimes the wisest course of action was to do nothing. For now he would let the matter rest. The first group of the new colts would be arriving tomorrow. He would have his hands full all summer with their care and training. Whatever was in the envelope had waited this long. It could wait longer.

Glancing back toward the house, Sky saw that Jasper had come out to sit on the porch with the dog. Jasper had spent the past forty years on the ranch. He was as rich in secrets as the silent stone buttes and turrets below the caprock—and he hid those secrets almost as deeply.

He'd shown no curiosity about the contents of the envelope, almost as if he already knew what might be inside.

Checking the impulse to go and talk with him, Sky kept on walking. He would sit with the old man another day. Right now he had more pressing things to do.

The first of Sky's pupils had arrived. Beau stood with Erin and Jasper outside the fence, watching as twenty-two splendid young horses—yearlings and two-year-olds—thundered out of the long trailers and into the freedom of the grassy paddock.

"Look at that black . . . and, oh, that red one . . ." Erin was beside herself with excitement. Sky had given her the task of naming the new horses, and she took her job seriously. She'd brought a clipboard from the office and was already taking notes. Too bad Will wasn't here to share this with her, Beau reflected. But Will had driven up to the summer pasture above the caprock to spend the day checking on the cattle herds. He relished being back in action.

Beau knew enough about horseflesh to appreciate Sky's

choices. All fillies and geldings, they were on the small side, solid, compact, and agile. Their eyes shone with alertness and intelligence. When word got around that Sky was training them, interest would be high among ranchers all over the state. Hopefully, when they came to auction, the bidding would be over the top.

Sky, on horseback, seemed to be everywhere at once. He sat his blue roan gelding as if he were part of the animal, guiding the horse more with his knees than with his hands. Back in the day, the Comanche had been the finest horsemen on the plains. Something in that ancient blood had trickled through the generations to pool richly into Sky Fletcher. There was no more logical explanation for his rare gift.

Leaning on the top rail of the fence, Beau watched the milling of bodies and colors—bay and roan, black, silver, paint, and buckskin, dun and claybank, in a kaleidoscope of grace and motion.

His cell phone rang. Seeing Natalie's name on the display, Beau walked away from the fence to take the call.

"What's up, gorgeous?" He was in high spirits today.

"Beau, are you alone?" She sounded like a terrified child.

"What is it?" he asked, alarmed. "Is it Slade? Has he threatened you again?"

"Yes . . . no . . . Listen to me, Beau! The sheriff and his deputy just left here. Slade's dead. Murdered on your ranch. And they're on their way to question you."

CHAPTER 12

It had to be a mistake.

That was Beau's first thought. Then reality slammed him like a runaway train. Slade Haskell was dead. And it wouldn't take a Sherlock Holmes to name the prime suspect in his murder.

"Are you all right, Natalie?" he asked, needing to be assured of that.

"I will be." Her voice quivered slightly. "It's just the shock of it. You were at the ranch last night, weren't you? Will can verify that."

"Call Tori," he said, ignoring her questions. "Tell her everything the sheriff said."

"Beau, I'm worried."

"Call Tori," he repeated. "Do it now. I have to go."

Beau ended the call. He wanted to assure her everything would be all right, but he couldn't promise that—not until he knew more about what had happened.

He had added the sheriff's number to his phone contacts after Jess Warner's murder. Walking back toward the house, he made the call.

"Axelrod," the deep voice answered.

"Sheriff, this is Beau Tyler. Natalie just called me about Slade. She says you want to talk with me."

"That's right." Beau could hear the crackling sounds of a police radio in the background. "We're on our way to your place. We're about fifteen minutes out. Stay where you are."

"I'd rather meet you." Beau knew he was innocent. But a roomful of witnesses had seen his fight with Slade and heard his threat to kill the man if he hurt Natalie again. Now Slade had been found murdered on ranch property. It didn't look good.

Axelrod paused before he answered. "All right. Drive out and meet us on the road. We'll give you an escort back to town."

Beau ended the call, an uneasiness churning in the pit of his stomach.

He caught Jasper's attention as he walked toward the vehicle shed. "I need to run into town," he said. "I shouldn't be long."

When Beau spotted the squad car, there was a second officer driving the tan Jeep Cherokee with the burly sheriff in the passenger seat. As Beau pulled off the road, the sheriff got out and climbed into Beau's truck. "We can talk on the way in," he said, shifting in the seat to give Beau a view of the holstered pistol at his belt.

Beau started the engine and pulled onto the road, following the sheriff's vehicle. "I can guess what you're thinking, but I didn't kill Slade," he said. "I detested the man, but I'm not a murderer."

"However, you are a trained killer," Axelrod said.

"So are thousands of other combat veterans."

"But you were a specialist. A sniper."

"What's that got to do with anything? Was Haskell shot?"

"Since you're bound to hear it sooner or later, yes. He was shot several times at close range."

"If I had killed him, which I didn't, one shot would have been enough. And it wouldn't have been up close."

"That remains to be seen. We'll be testing your hands for gunshot residue of course."

A curse escaped Beau's lips. "You'll find it. I was target shooting with my niece yesterday. Jasper was there—you can ask him if you have to." Beau was hoping to clear this up without involving anybody else at the ranch, but the way things were looking, that might not be possible. He could sense the wheels turning in Axelrod's mind—how an explainable shooting event could be used to cover a criminal one.

"What can you tell me?" He steered the conversation away from himself. "Where was Slade? Who found him?"

"A Cessna pilot called it in. He spotted Haskell's flatbed by the bog, with the body on the ground."

"Dumped, like the girl?"

"Nope." Axelrod's eyes narrowed. "We found blood and casings at the scene. There's more, but we can cover that in interrogation."

Interrogation. The word sent a chill along Beau's nerves. Axelrod, it appeared, had already zeroed in on the most likely suspect. "Do I need a lawyer?" he asked.

The sheriff shrugged. "You're a smart man and you know the law. Up to you."

Fifteen minutes later, Beau was seated in a room with a two-way mirror on one wall. The sheriff faced him across a narrow table. The process was one Beau had taken part in countless times. But he'd been the one asking the questions, not the one answering them. He willed himself to stay calm. He was innocent, he reminded himself. He had nothing to hide.

"Can you account for your whereabouts two nights ago between nine o'clock and midnight?" Axelrod sounded as if he'd memorized a script.

"I decided to go into town around nine. Stopped at the Blue Coyote for a few minutes, but it was crowded and I didn't stay. There was an NBA game on TV. Lakers, I think. Didn't pay much attention. After that I drove by Dr. Haskell's, but she wasn't there, so I drove home. Got there about ten-fifteen."

"Can anyone verify that?"

"I didn't talk to anybody at the bar, but Will was awake when I came home."

"Are you intimately involved with Natalie Haskell?"

The question jolted Beau. Despite his best intentions, his temper began to rise. He'd wanted to keep Natalie out of this, but that wasn't going to happen. "After Slade beat her up, she filed for divorce. He was set to stand trial for assault and would have most likely gone to jail. She'd have been free to remarry. Why would I want to kill him over Natalie?"

"I'll take that as a yes to my question." Axelrod scratched the corner of his grizzled mustache. "Did you or did you not threaten to kill Slade Haskell if he bothered his wife again?"

"I did." A drop of sweat trickled between Beau's shoulder blades, soaking into the back of his shirt. It was all circumstantial, but the sheriff was building a damned good case against him.

A manila envelope lay on the table. Opening the clasp, Axelrod slid out a sheet of creased, sweat-stained, blood-spattered white paper enclosed in a plastic sleeve. He passed it across the table to Beau. "Do you recognize this?"

Beau stared at the crudely phrased letter. His stomach contracted. He forced himself to speak calmly. "I've never seen it before. Where did you find it?"

"Crumpled inside Slade's shirt pocket. Isn't that your signature?"

"It's a damned good imitation. But I never signed anything like this and I sure as hell didn't write it." As Beau studied the grammar-school printing, the awkward sentences, realization dawned. He was being framed—by a perfect storm of circumstances and an enemy clever enough to take advantage of them.

But who was it? And why?

"Did you dust this letter for fingerprints?" he asked, knowing his own prints couldn't possibly be on it.

"We tried. But the paper was too far gone. This isn't a blasted TV crime show. We do the best we can with what we've got, and sometimes it isn't much." Axelrod slid the letter back into the envelope and fastened the clasp. "Must've been pretty rough over there in Iraq. I hear tell some men who've seen a lot of killing come back messed up in the head. They have spells where they think they're still in combat." He glanced up, meeting Beau's eyes. "You ever have trouble that way?"

"It's called post-traumatic stress, and that's just one way it can manifest. I had a few issues after I left Iraq, but I was lucky enough to get help. Apart from some bad dreams, I've been fine for years." Beau had answered similar questions openly in the past. He had no problem with answering this time . . . until a horrific thought struck him.

"Why would you ask me that question?" Beau kept his tone calm and neutral, but his pulse was surging.

"Just thinking, that's all." Axelrod brushed a stray fly off his wrist. "We haven't had a murder in this county for years. Since you came home a few weeks ago, we've had two, both of them connected to your ranch. In my line of work, I've learned not to believe in coincidences."

In the tense silence, the droning fly sounded as loud as the engine of a helicopter. Beau rose slowly to his feet. He could feel a vein throbbing in his temple, but he kept his voice level. "You've known me most of my life, Sheriff. You've known my family and you know our values. So far, you've given me nothing but conjecture. Unless you can offer solid proof—"

The door opened partway to admit the deputy. "Excuse me, Sheriff, but there's something out here you gotta see."

Axelrod stood, shooting Beau a glare. "Sit down and stay put," he ordered.

Given no choice, Beau sat and waited. This was a nightmare. He'd had nothing to do with Slade's death. But he'd had motive, means, opportunity, and no solid alibi. Anyone in the sheriff's place would've brought him in. Hellfire, he would have done it himself.

The sheriff was back, trailed this time by his deputy. "A road worker brought in a rifle, a thirty-thirty he found lying next to the highway. No prints, and we'll need to wait for the ballistics report, but the caliber matches the casings from the crime scene, as well as the bullets the medical examiner took out of Slade Haskell's body.

"A thirty-thirty?" Beau shook his head. "Anybody who hunts has a gun like that. There must be thousands of them in the county."

"But not many with a serial number registered to Bull Tyler," the sheriff said. "And none that would have Jasper Platt's name engraved on the stock. That rifle came from your ranch."

Beau remembered the theft of Jasper's gun—a gift from Bull. But before he could explain, the door burst open and a tall, blond whirlwind of a woman swept in. "This stops right now!" Tori commanded. "Sheriff, I'm here to represent my client. You're not to question him unless I'm present."

Axelrod rocked back on his heels, looking smug. "Tori, I'd say your timing's about right. Beau, here, is going to need you." He unhooked the handcuffs from his belt. "Beau Tyler, I'm arresting you for the murder of Slade Haskell. You have the right to remain silent . . ."

Three nights later, Tori picked up a pineapple ham pizza and a couple of Diet Cokes from Burger Shack and drove to Natalie's house. It wasn't much of a meal, but she'd been too busy to cook, and she needed to see that her friend ate something. With Slade's body still in the county morgue and Beau charged with his murder, Natalie was barely holding herself together.

Natalie met her at the door dressed in jeans and a light blue T-shirt. Her hair was combed, her face freshly scrubbed, but her haunted eyes had purple-tinged shadows. Tori guessed she had slept little since the news broke.

"How's Beau?" Natalie asked, holding the door open so Tori could carry the pizza into the living room.

"He's been charged and had his bail hearing. Now he's out and looking for ways to prove he was framed. He asks about you. Every time I talk to him, the first thing out of his mouth is 'How's Natalie?' "

"I need to see him." She closed the door and locked it.

"You mustn't. Beau's right about that. If this goes to trial, you could be called as a witness for the prosecution."

Natalie slumped onto the sofa. "They'll twist my words to make Beau look guilty. The worst of it is, there's nothing I can say to help him. I was tending a sick mare the night Slade died. And if I have to tell the truth about our relationship, it'll only make things worse." She shuddered.

"None of this is your fault," Tori said. "And it's not like you to waste time beating yourself up. Do you have any idea who might have killed Slade? Could one of his employees have held a grudge against him?"

"I wouldn't know if they did. Slade never discussed his business with me—or his finances." She pushed her thick hair back from her face. "I suppose that mess has fallen in my lap, too, and heaven knows when I'll have time to deal with it."

Tori weighed the news she'd come to deliver and decided it could wait. "Did Slade have any family left?"

"Not living. His older brother died in a motorcycle wreck before we were married. And his parents have been gone for years. That's how Slade came to have the trucking business. It was his father's—but you'd remember that, growing up."

Tori opened the pizza box and popped the tabs on the chilled soda cans. Lifting a pizza slice, she shoved it toward her friend. "Eat. You're running on empty and you're going to need your strength."

She watched as Natalie nibbled at the melted cheese. Natalie was tougher than she looked, but even Tori didn't know how her friend would take the news she'd been holding back until now. Taking a deep breath, she plunged ahead.

"I spent some time researching in the county recorder's office today. Brace yourself for some disturbing news." She paused to give Natalie a moment, but Natalie surprised her.

"For heaven's sake, Tori, my husband's just been murdered and Beau is under arrest. Whatever you're about to tell me, it can't be any worse than that."

"All right. Here it is. Slade didn't own the trucking business. The property, along with the trucks and equipment, was taken over last year by Stella Rawlins."

Natalie froze. A blob of cheese slid off the pizza and fell unheeded onto her jeans. "Stella Rawlins. That's the woman who owns the Blue Coyote."

"As nearly as I can figure out, she loaned him money on the company, and when he couldn't pay her back, she took it over. But she kept him there to run the business."

"And he never said a word to me." A spark of the old fire flickered in Natalie's dark eyes. "Not about the loan, not about losing the business . . . nothing. I know we were having money troubles for a while, but Slade said everything would be all right, and it was. After that he always seemed to have money for things he wanted, like his new pickup."

"I'm surprised you're not more upset about this," Tori said.

"I figured Slade would get the trucking business in the divorce, so it's no loss. What bothers me more is that he kept it a secret, even from me. Why?" Natalie sighed and shrugged. "I don't suppose I'll ever know, will I?"

Tori studied her friend. Natalie was taking healthy bites of pizza, as if her appetite had returned along with her spunk. For now, it appeared she was going to be all right. But if Beau was convicted of murder, the blow would be a hard one, especially if what Tori had heard from a contact in the district attorney's office was true.

The prosecution wasn't just seeking a conviction for Slade's murder. They were also gathering evidence in the slaying of Jess Warner. If they could pin both crimes on Beau, he would almost certainly be facing the death penalty.

Natalie peered through the closed drapes, watching Tori's station wagon back out of the driveway. She had always assumed she knew everything about her husband. But according to Tori, Slade had built a whole separate life apart from her and their home. The trips to Mexico, the money, the infidelities . . . was there more to this?

Had she been married to a criminal?

Could his secret life have led to his murder?

* * *

Yellow crime scene tape fluttered from the stakes that marked the spot where Slade Haskell had died. The deputies who'd picked over the ground like so many scavengers had long ago taken their gear and left. The body was gone and so was Slade's flatbed truck. There was no one here to stop Beau and Will from crossing the lines to see if anything had been overlooked.

They'd ridden their horses to the bog and left them tethered in the brush. Now, starting at the outer edge of the staked area, they walked the perimeter and slowly worked their way inward, toward the place where Slade's body had fallen.

The ground was a maze of tire tracks and boot prints, obliterating anything useful. But they had to search. Finding some vital bit of evidence was their only hope.

"Poor Jasper's pretty bummed about that rifle," Will said. "He blames himself for leaving it strapped under the seat. Anybody could have broken into the shed and stolen it."

"Anybody who knew exactly where to look, like Lute, maybe," Beau said. "I certainly wouldn't have put it past him. But I can't see Lute actually using it to kill Slade. It takes guts to face a man—and I don't think Lute has them."

In the absence of chalk, the position of the body had been outlined with string. The red earth was still bloodstained and indented where one bullet had blown through Slade's head. The ground had been probed with tongs where the deputies had recovered the bullet, along with the others that had passed through his body. Will frowned as he studied the spot. "Notice anything funny about this?" he muttered.

Beau bent forward, peering over his shoulder. "I'll be damned. If Slade had been standing when he was shot, the bullet would have landed somewhere behind him, maybe even in the truck. But from the look of the ground, it went straight down, like he was flat on his back."

Whipping out his cell phone, he snapped two photos to record the evidence.

"Could've happened that way," Will mused. "Say the first shots dropped him and then the killer went in close to finish him off."

"No, look." Beau pointed to the other holes where the bullets had been removed—all of them directly under the body. In his line of work, he'd seen plenty of shootings, but this one didn't look typical. For one thing, the close-range body shots had gone all the way through, but there was surprisingly little blood in the soil beneath. And there was something else. Beau bent closer.

"These shots were all fired from above. Either the killer forced Slade to lie down before he was shot, or—"

Will's cool blue eyes met Beau's as he finished the sentence. "Or Slade was already dead."

Natalie walked into the Blue Coyote and sat down in an empty booth. It was midafternoon. The place was open, but not yet busy. Two old men sat at the bar nursing their beers. A middle-aged couple at one of the tables appeared to be arguing. A muscular man with black tattoos on his shaved head was polishing glassware behind the bar.

When the waitress, young and jaded, her jeans straining over her plump hips, wandered over, Natalie ordered a Bud Light in a glass and waited. The speakers mounted against the ceiling were blaring Tammy Wynette's "Stand by Your Man." Ironic under the circumstances, Natalie mused as the waitress returned with her beer.

Her eyes were drawn to the bartender. He looked out of place in this small Texas town, and she couldn't help wondering what had brought him here. He had a hard look about him, like a man who'd spent time behind bars—a man who was no stranger to violence. His eyes were like a raven's, dark, sharp, and emotionless. The hair prickled on the back of her neck. Was she looking at Slade's killer?

The thought fled her mind as Stella emerged from the back hallway. In a tight black denim skirt, black cowgirl boots, and a green silk blouse embroidered with horseshoes, she was striking in an overblown way. Her manner exuded confidence as she spotted Natalie and strode straight toward the booth where she sat.

"My condolences, Mrs. Haskell." Up close, Stella showed her age beneath her too-heavy makeup. Even so, she was a handsome woman.

"Please, call me Natalie." A show of graciousness never hurt. "Do you have a moment to talk?"

"Until things get busy." Stella slid into the opposite side of the booth, her expression guarded. "What can I do for you, Natalie?"

"Not much, really. I'm just hoping you can give me some closure. Until my lawyer mentioned it, I didn't know you'd bought Slade's trucking business."

"He didn't tell you?"

"Slade kept a lot of things from me. I'm just discovering some of them now that he's gone."

Stella shrugged. "There's not much to tell. His business was struggling a couple of years ago—the economy, mostly, along with the drought and some bad debts. I offered to help him out if he put his company up as collateral. When he couldn't pay me back, we came to an arrangement. He'd go on running the business and we'd split the profits. It worked out well for both of us." She leaned forward, her ample breasts resting on the edge of the table. "I liked your husband, Natalie. I'm going to miss him. He'll be a hard man to replace." Her eyes narrowed. "Of course, since you were divorcing him, that's no longer your concern, is it?"

Natalie felt the chill. "Since the divorce wasn't final, it's fallen to me to settle his affairs. I just wanted to make sure there were no loose ends to tie up."

"None. The business is mine. Slade and I squared our accounts before he died, so if you're wondering whether I owe you anything—"

"No, of course not." Natalie was liking the woman less and

less, but she wouldn't walk away until she'd learned all she could. "I was wondering if I could get Slade's personal things from his desk at the trucking company. There might be something his friends would like."

Stella glanced restlessly around the bar, clearly eager to end the conversation. "The desk has been cleared out. But if anybody bothered to box his things, you can pick them up. Just tell the man in the office I said it was all right."

"Thank you." Natalie would have risen to go, but just then Sheriff Axelrod walked in the door. Dressed in his uniform, complete with badge and pistol, he strode over to the booth.

"Stella, if you'll excuse us, I'd like a word with this young lady," he said.

"Fine. I've got things to do." Stella rose and stepped away. The sheriff slid into her place, his husky body barely fitting against the table.

"I've been looking for you, Natalie," he said. "Matter of fact, I was on my way to your place when I noticed your vehicle outside. Can't say I figured you for a drinking woman."

Natalie ignored the comment. "What can I do for you, Sheriff?"

"Just wanted to make sure you were all right. You've been through a lot in the past few days, losing your husband and having your boyfriend arrested for his murder."

"I'm fine. And Beau Tyler is innocent."

"Is he?" Axelrod leaned a few inches closer. His breath smelled of the Marlboros he smoked. "I pulled a few strings and got a look at his military record. The man did a lot of killing over there in Iraq. I mean, a lot. Something like that could get to be a habit—even an addiction. That's why I need to warn you about him."

"Warn me? That's ridiculous." All Natalie wanted was for the man to go away. But she needed to stand up for Beau. "Slade had more than his share of secrets—things I'm just learning about now. Those secrets could have made him some enemies. Have you looked into other suspects, Sheriff? Maybe you should."

Axelrod shook his head. "I believe this case is what's known as a slam dunk. Did you know Beau was treated for post-traumatic stress disorder? That stuff doesn't just go away. I'd guess he was able to satisfy his killing urge as a DEA agent. But here in this little Texas town, with no Al Qaeda or drug runners to shoot, he's having to look for other victims. I can't prove it yet, but I'm pretty sure he killed that poor girl who was dumped in the bog. Sooner or later, if we don't put him away, he's bound to target somebody else—maybe even you. And that, young lady, would be a dirty shame."

Natalie slid out of the booth and pushed to her feet. She was trembling, but she willed herself not to show it. "Sheriff, you don't know what you're talking about," she declared. "Do your job. And that means checking out everything and everyone. Slade always seemed to have money to spend and I don't think it came from the trucking business. It wouldn't surprise me if he was involved in something illegal. That's where you should look for his killer."

Before he could respond, she turned and strode outside. As she closed the door behind her, she could almost feel Stella's eyes burning into her back.

She made it to her SUV and collapsed, quivering against the wheel. Pulling her emotions together, Natalie backed out of the parking lot and drove across town to the large fenced lot where Haskell Trucking was located. The name on the sign out front hadn't changed. But that was no longer her concern, Natalie reminded herself. She was here to collect Slade's personal belongings and look for anyone, or anything, that might provide a clue to his murder.

She'd been here before over the years, though not often. But she recognized the thin, graying driver in the Haskell uniform who greeted her in the parking lot when she stepped out of her vehicle. He'd started here more than twenty years ago, working for Slade's father.

"Right sorry about your husband, Mrs. Haskell," he said. "Slade was a good boss. Always paid us fair and on time."

"Thank you, Ernie," Natalie said, dismissing the kindly man as unconnected to the murder. "I can see you're still open for business. Who's in charge of the place now? I need to speak to someone about getting Slade's things."

A shadow of displeasure flickered over the time-creased face. "Young squirt in there." He jerked his head toward the prefab building that served as the office. "Don't ask me whose ass he had to kiss to get the job, but—" He broke off with an apologetic shake of his head. "Sorry, ma'am, my sainted mother taught me better than to use that kind of language in front of a lady."

"It's all right, Ernie. Please tell your family hello for me." Giving his arm a light squeeze, she hurried into the building—and stopped as if she'd run into a wall.

Sitting behind the supervisor's desk was Lute Fletcher.

For an instant he looked as startled as she was. His jaw dropped slightly. Then his mouth stretched into a smirk.

"Well, if isn't Mrs. Haskell. I hope you aren't here to lay claim to this place."

Irked by his manner, Natalie squared her shoulders and lifted her chin. "I'm aware that Stella Rawlins owns the business now, if that's what you mean."

"So what are you doing here?" His insolent grin widened.

"I might ask you the same question. After Beau fired you for almost killing the Tylers' mare, I'm surprised anybody would give you a job."

"Your late husband appreciated my talents enough to hire me. So did Stella. She promoted me to his spot. So you might say Beau did me a favor." He flipped a lock of long black hair off his face. "So why *are* you here, Mrs. Haskell? Anything I can do for you?"

Somehow Natalie managed to hold her temper in check. "Stella said I could come by and pick up Slade's things. You can call her if you need to."

"No need. You can't take anything related to the business. But since he lived here a while, you might as well take his dirty laundry home. I'll get it for you."

He disappeared into a back room and came out with a cardboard box. It was piled high with dirty clothes and bedding. With a mischievous grin, Lute shoved it across the desk toward her. "Here you go. It's all yours, lady."

Fighting the urge to fling the laundry in his face, Natalie took the box and walked out to her vehicle. Facing Lute had been a maddening experience, but as she pulled out into the street, she reminded herself that she'd made some important connections. Stella had taken over Slade's business. Slade, who'd hated Beau, had hired Lute, who hated Beau, too.

Now Slade was dead and Lute had taken over his job. There was no way these events could've been random. They had to be connected to Slade's murder.

Since Lute had worked on the ranch, he would have known where Jasper kept the rifle. And he could easily have sneaked into the shed and taken it.

What would the sheriff say to all this when she told him? Natalie wondered.

CHAPTER 13

With Beau's arraignment less than a month away, Tori had arranged to meet both Beau and Will at the ranch instead of her office. Coming to the ranch meant more privacy and no interrupting phone calls, and she could spend time with her daughter once all the legal business was finished

Will studied her from his armchair. She sat curled on the couch, one foot tucked beneath her and her laptop balanced across her knees. Today she was dressed in jeans, sneakers, and a soft cotton shirt with an open collar that framed her creamy throat. Her hair was loosely twisted and pinned to the crown of her head with a silver clip. She looked exactly the way Will had always liked her to look. Not that it made any difference. Even in jeans and sneakers, Tori was all business.

Will had suggested that Beau hire a big-name trial lawyer from someplace like Dallas. But Beau had chosen to stay with Tori. It had been a good idea, Will conceded. Tori was invested heart and soul in saving the man who was her daughter's uncle, her ex-husband's brother, and her own lifelong friend.

"So what did the sheriff say when you told him what we discovered at the crime scene?" Beau was referring to the fact that the shots from Jasper's rifle appeared to have been fired from directly above, most likely into a dead body.

Tori shook her head. "I'm afraid that didn't go as well as I'd hoped. He said it was an interesting idea, but the medical examiner's report was inconclusive. The only way to prove our claim would be to find evidence that Slade had died some other way."

"Evidence we don't have," Beau said. "But that doesn't mean we can't look for it. Right now with Axelrod set on closing his case against me, it may be our only choice."

"Let's get back to that after I go over what Natalie told me." Tori scanned the notes she'd typed in earlier. "Stella Rawlins has evidently been pulling Slade's strings for the past couple years. Last year she bailed him out of serious debt and took over the trucking business when he couldn't pay her back."

Beau leaned forward in his chair. "That trucking business would be an ideal front for smuggling—drugs, guns, illegals, anything."

"That's what I thought, too," Tori said. "One of my contacts ran a background check on Stella. Her record's clean."

"Which could mean she's smart enough to let other people do her dirty work," Will said. "What about the bartender?"

"So far he's a mystery man. Nobody seems to know his real name."

"If we can get a photo of him, I can get my friends at the DEA to run it," Beau said. "Whoever the man is, I'm betting he's no angel. I never got a good look at his tattoos, but even at a distance they looked like prison work. If I had to guess who killed Slade, he'd be at the top of my list."

"There's more here," Tori said. "It seems Slade hired Lute at the trucking company."

"Sky mentioned that," Beau said.

"Did you also know that Stella promoted him to Slade's old job? Lute's running the place now. Natalie told me how he bragged about it."

"Lute?" Will shook his head in disbelief. "That lazy little—"

"Natalie shouldn't be messing with those people," Beau said. "They're dangerous. She needs to stay away, Tori."

"Try telling Natalie that," Tori said. "She's determined to help you any way she can. She read Axelrod the riot act for jumping to conclusions and ignoring other suspects. I talked to the sheriff this morning. He wasn't too happy about her meddling."

"Is he still trying to prove I killed that poor girl, too?"

"I'm afraid so. He even suggested that I use your PTSD as a defense to help you avoid the death penalty. As far as he's concerned, the case is as good as closed."

Beau exhaled raggedly. He'd done his best to stay calm and upbeat, but Will could tell the stress was beginning to wear on his brother.

"Let's look at the big picture," Will said, changing the subject. "Lute was working here on the ranch. Beau fired him. Slade hired him. Slade was killed, Beau was framed for the murder, and Lute stepped into Slade's old job. What's the common denominator here?"

Beau shook his head. "It's Lute. But I can't believe he's got the guts to be a killer. My money's still on the bartender—for both of them."

"You may be right," Will said. "But even if Lute isn't our killer, I'd pick him for stealing Jasper's rifle, and maybe firing those shots into Slade, just to frame you. Either way, he's got to be up to his ears in this mess. If we could get him to tell us half of what he knows . . ."

"He sure as hell won't talk to me," Beau growled. "And not to you either, big brother. Maybe Sky could twist his arm and convince him to come clean."

"I know Sky wants to help. We can ask him what he thinks of the idea." Will was preparing to say more when Erin came bounding in from the entry, eyes sparkling, ponytail flying. At the sight of her, something tightened around Will's heart.

"You've got to come see this!" She skipped over to the couch, seized her mother's hand, and reached for Will's. "Tesoro's learned to follow me! You come, too, Uncle Beau!"

Putting serious matters aside for now, they trailed her outside. Sky and Jasper were waiting by the paddock fence where the mares grazed with their foals. The palomino colt was growing fast, putting on weight and already losing his fuzzy baby look. His coat gleamed like liquid sunlight as he explored the wonders of fresh grass, clover, and new playmates. He was already bold enough to leave his mother's side, but he kept glancing back, as if to make sure she was still close by.

Erin climbed over the fence and walked confidently across the grass. She'd be all right, Will reassured himself. Mares could be protective of their babies, but these mares were used to her.

A dozen yards from the golden foal, she stopped, held out her hand, and gave a low whistle. He raised his head and pricked his ears. "Come, Tesoro," she said softly. "Come here."

The colt nickered and took a step toward her. Murmuring encouragement, she kept her hand out until he came close enough to nuzzle her fingers. "Good boy." She stroked his neck. "Such a good boy. Let's go for a walk."

Turning she took a few steps, then glanced back. The foal scampered after her, following like a puppy.

"I'll be damned," Beau muttered. "How'd she get him to do that, Sky?"

A rare smile lit Sky's chiseled face. "It's the imprinting. That's why Erin needed to handle him right after he was born. Now she's like family to that foal."

Sensing that her baby was getting too far away, the mare whinnied nervously. Tesoro paused, looked around, then wheeled and raced back to his mother. Laughing, Erin trotted back toward the fence.

For the flicker of a moment, Will felt Tori's eyes on him.

Turning away from the others, he beckoned Sky aside. "It looks like we're going to need your help," he said.

Sky was headed into town on two vital errands. The first was to find Lute and lean on him hard enough to get some evidence that might help Beau. Not much chance of that, Sky feared. If Lute was criminally involved in Slade Haskell's murder—either as the killer or as an accessory to the crime—he wasn't likely to fess up. And even if he was innocent, the young fool hated Beau too much to offer any kind of help.

Sky figured the best he could hope for was getting Lute to admit to stealing Jasper's rifle.

When he stopped by Haskell Trucking half an hour before closing, he was informed Lute was on the road, hauling a load of hay to a Mexican ranch. The older man at the front desk was courteous enough to tell Sky that the trip usually took about three days and that he was welcome to come back after that.

Sky thanked him and left. The Blue Coyote would be open by now, so he could tackle his second mission. But he'd be smart to wait until the place was busy enough for him to click a photo of the bartender without being noticed. Meanwhile there was time to kill. He treated himself to a double decker and a shake at Burger Shack, picked up a few needed odds and ends at the hardware store, and paid a visit to a wheelchair-bound man who fashioned hand-tooled custom saddles in his home workshop.

By the time he left, it was dark outside. He drove to the Blue Coyote, thinking he would just snap a picture or two and leave. The parking lot was almost full, but he found an empty spot next to a shiny black Corvette, elegantly small and as sleek as a bullet, with a leather interior. The car wasn't new, but it was a classic, in mint condition. He'd never seen the car before, but the pricey vehicle looked much too fine for anybody in Blanco Springs. Sky couldn't help being curious about the owner.

Inside, the bar was noisy and crowded. The tables were full, but Sky managed to slip into the one vacant booth. A half-empty glass with a lipstick print on the rim sat on the opposite side of the table, but its owner appeared to have left, so it seemed all right to stake his claim.

His eyes scanned the customers—pretty much all locals. No sign of anyone who might be driving a racy black convertible. But the skinhead bartender was working, and that was why he'd come.

The man behind the bar was too busy to notice that he was

being photographed. Within the next few minutes, Sky was able to get three good facial shots with his phone and send them to Beau. Mission accomplished, he was about to get up and leave when he found his feet blocked by a pair of elegantly narrow, hand-tooled Western boots that looked as if they'd never known a speck of Texas dust.

"You're sitting in my booth, cowboy." The husky female voice sounded more upper-class East Coast than down-home Texas.

Sky took his time answering. His gaze traveled upward, taking in the length of her legs and the way the soft designer denim fit every curve. Her white linen blouse, sheer enough to reveal glimpses of the lacy bra underneath, was tucked in at the waist and secured by a silver-studded concha belt that she'd probably bought at some snootified place. The lady was about as far from Blanco Springs as you could get, which made him wonder what the hell she was doing here.

"Sorry, I didn't see your brand on the booth," he said.

"It's right there." She pointed to the glass. Her copper-hued hair fell in thick waves around her shoulders. Her fine features were offset by a ripe, sensual mouth. She was young, he realized, younger than she was acting. "Can't a lady even go to the loo without giving up her seat?" she demanded.

Go to the loo? No, she definitely wasn't from around here.

"There are two seats." Sky gave her a hint of a smile. "Sit down. If you'll forgive me, I'll buy you a refill on that beer."

She slid into the empty side of the booth. Her eyes were the color of a pretty little agate stone that Sky had once found in a streambed, green-gold with sparks of copper. "Better not," she said. "This one's my third, and I have to drive home. In fact, I was about to leave, but that was before you showed up. Here"—she shoved the half-empty glass toward him—"you can finish it for me."

Sky's pulse kicked up a notch. If this beauty was playing a game, he wasn't about to leave until he understood the rules.

"As long as we're here, I guess we might as well introduce ourselves. I'm—"

"No." She cut him off. "No names. It's more fun that way."

A red flag went up in Sky's mind. "Jealous husband?" he asked, noting her ringless finger.

She shook her head. "More like an overprotective father. That's all you need to know. I'm twenty-two and he treats me like I'm fourteen, always blathering on about keeping my reputation spotless so I can find a suitable husband. Tonight we had words about the issue. Things got a bit heated and"—she shrugged, the lace bra shifting beneath the thin white linen shirt—"here I am."

"So, do you plan on going home anytime soon?" Sky took a sip of her beer, placing his mouth over the lipstick print.

Her direct gaze held a seductive twinkle. "Not if I can find something better to do. Ever driven a Corvette?"

"No, but I think I can handle it." And he could handle her, too, if he got the chance.

"Come on." She was on her feet, beckoning him toward the door with a toss of her auburn hair. Sky trailed her outside, staying far enough behind to allow himself a view of her confident stride and taut rump. Whatever the lady had in mind was bound to be interesting.

She led him to the Corvette and tossed him the keys. Sky squeezed his lanky frame into the driver's seat and adjusted it all the way back. She slid in on the passenger side and fastened her seat belt. "Hope you can drive a stick shift," she said.

"I can drive a lot of things." Buckling in, he turned the key and tapped the gas pedal. The engine rumbled to life. "Where to?" he asked.

"Anywhere." She leaned back in the seat and raked a hand through her hair. "Please, just be quiet and drive."

Sky shifted the Corvette into reverse and gunned the engine. The car responded like a well-trained cutting horse, shooting backward at a touch of his boot. He adjusted his reflexes as they roared toward the highway and out of town. He wasn't driving the pickup tonight, he reminded himself, easing back on the gas. This powerful car was as sleek, fast, and elegant as the female sitting next to him.

Who could her father be? Rich, no doubt. Most likely some dude rancher from one of the big, syndicated outfits. And the lady? Clearly not a Texas type. Spoiled, rebellious, and out to break every rule in her daddy's book.

Sky picked a narrow but paved back road that headed across the rolling plain and wound up into the escarpment. He drove in silence. Even if the woman hadn't wanted quiet, the noise of the road and the wind rushing past their ears would have made conversation difficult. Sky sensed that, whatever happened, she didn't want him to know that much about her. This was nothing more than a fleeting adventure with an unknown cowboy, to be savored and forgotten. No messy complications. And that was fine. He preferred things that way himself.

Partway up onto the caprock, he pulled out onto an overlook—a spot he knew and liked. The stars were glorious tonight, with moonlight casting the rugged landscape below into ghostly shadows. Pulling the hand brake, he unbuckled and turned in the seat to face his passenger. Her grin flashed in the darkness as she unfastened her seat belt.

"Kiss me, cowboy," she said.

With a growl of anticipation, he reached over the console and caught her close. Her mouth was like an autumn plum, ripe and sweet and succulent. Hungry for her, he ground his lips onto hers. She tasted of cheap beer and smelled of expensive perfume—a combination that sizzled like lightning through his senses.

His hand pulled the hem of her blouse free of her belt. Beneath the linen fabric, her lace bra was secured by a single front hook that came apart at a touch. His hand slid over one firm, satiny breast so perfectly shaped that it seemed to have been fashioned for the hollow of his palm. She moaned as he thumbed her nipple, her eyes closed, her hips doing a bump and grind against the leather seat. She reached over the gearbox to tug at his belt. Under different conditions, Sky would've been all for it. But in this car? With no protection in his wallet?

"I've got a blanket in the trunk," she whispered, tickling his ear with her breath.

Sky groaned, thinking of the rocky ground and the snakes and scorpions that called this part of the escarpment home. "Lady," he muttered, "I'm afraid this isn't going to—"

The squeal of spinning tires on gravel cut off the rest of the sentence. A battered pickup swerved onto the overlook, braking a dozen feet away. Raucous laughter rang from the cab as an empty beer can flew out the window.

"Buckle up." Sky started the Corvette, slammed it into reverse, and backed onto the road. So much for tonight's romantic adventure. Some things just weren't meant to be.

"Where are we going?" She'd fastened her seat belt and was fumbling to hook the front of her bra.

"Back to town to get you some coffee—hopefully enough to ensure you make it safely home."

She huddled silently in the seat as he drove. She was pouting, he surmised, or maybe thinking she'd picked up the wrong cowboy. But it occurred to him that she could've done a lot worse. He'd be remiss not to warn her. "What you did tonight, picking up a stray, it could be dangerous," he said. "Not that long ago, right around here, a young woman was murdered and dumped in a bog. The killer's never been found. For all you know, it could've been me."

No answer. Hopefully she was rethinking her reckless behavior. Or maybe he was sounding too much like her father.

Sky drove into town and ordered a coffee from the drive-through window at Burger Shack. Thrusting the Styrofoam cup toward her, he swung the Corvette back toward the Blue Coyote. "Finish that and you can have your car back," he said. "But only if you promise to go home."

The look she gave him said, *You're not the boss of me!* But by the time Sky pulled up next to his truck, she'd finished the coffee. "Will you be all right?" he asked as he climbed out of her car and offered her the keys.

"I'll be fine." She snatched them out of his hand. "And don't you dare follow me."

Sky said he wouldn't, but he did trail her at a distance for the first couple of miles to make sure she could keep the car on the road and that she wasn't going back to the bar to try her luck with another cowboy.

Whoever she was, he'd grown strangely protective of the blasted woman.

Once he was satisfied she'd be all right, he slowed the truck, letting the taillights of the Corvette fade into the night. Then he swung the truck off the main road and took a shortcut back to the ranch.

The coffee had been strong enough to jolt Lauren back to full awareness. She drove the lonely road with the headlights on high beam and her eyes wide open. She was headed home, but only because she had no place else to go.

So much for her walk on the wild side.

Tonight's blowup with her father, exacerbated by the fact that it was the one-year anniversary of her fiancé's death, had pushed her over the edge. She'd been fool enough to believe she finally had her life under control after the bouts of drinking and promiscuity that had followed Mike's suicide. But all it had taken was Congressman Garn Prescott, screaming at her and calling her a tramp like her mother, to send her tumbling back into the pit.

She'd driven into town and downed enough beer to lower her inhibitions, but there were no likely prospects among the men in the bar. Deciding to leave, she'd gone to the restroom and returned to find the handsomest cowboy she'd ever seen sitting in her booth—dark as sin, with lean looks and stunning cobalt eyes. It was like the devil had dropped her off an anniversary present.

Things had started out pretty much the way she'd expected, with his kisses pushing all the right buttons. She'd been on fire with the need to lose herself in sexual release. But when everything had fallen apart, the wretched man had turned noble on her—noble being the last thing she'd needed tonight. His rejection had hurt more than she'd let on. Driving away from him, she'd blinked back scalding tears.

But by now the coffee was doing its work, easing her back into reality. Tomorrow was a new day, Lauren reminded herself. She would focus on her accounting job, avoiding any encounters with her father. If things got too uncomfortable at home, maybe Beau Tyler could use her help. He'd offered her work, and he'd have a lot on his mind with that ridiculous murder charge to contend with.

Meanwhile she would steer clear of the Blue Coyote. With luck, if she stuck close to home, that scrumptiously maddening cowboy would remain a memory, and nothing more.

The web of back roads led Sky to the edge of the bog where Slade Haskell's murder had taken place. Beau, Will, and Jasper had kept him up to date on the investigation, but until now, he'd been too busy to visit the place himself.

Stopping the truck, he found a small but powerful LED flashlight in the glove compartment. The waning moon was bright enough to light his way, but he wanted to see details. Maybe a fresh pair of eyes could spot something others had missed.

On the far side of the bog, the dead cottonwood gleamed bone-white against the darkness. As Sky swung out of the cab, the rank odors of decay and stagnation filled his nostrils. He didn't consider himself superstitious, but traces of the old beliefs were bred into his Comanche blood. Even before two bodies were found here, he'd sensed that this was a place of death and evil—a place he wanted nothing to do with.

Remnants of yellow crime scene tape fluttered from the stakes. There'd been no rain since the discovery of Slade Haskell's body, but the wind had done its own work to erase the signs. In the glow of the flashlight, Sky could make out the twisted, half-buried string that had been used to mark the position of the body. He could no longer see where the 30.30 bullets had been collected from the soil, but a patch of dried, stained mud marked the spot where Slade Haskell's head might have lain.

Beau and Will had told him their theory about how the bullets from Jasper's rifle had been fired from straight above the body. Sky wouldn't put it past Lute to fire a few shots into a recent kill in order to frame a man he hated.

But how the devil had Lute known where and when to find Slade's body?

And if Slade had been killed before being shot with Jasper's rifle, where was the fatal bullet?

The local deputies weren't trained crime scene investigators. They could easily have missed it—especially given that the victim had been shot full of holes with a deer rifle. It probably hadn't occurred to them, or even to the local doctor who served as part-time medical examiner, to look for another cause of death.

Stepping back, Sky moved the light beam over the ground. If Slade had taken a single rifle shot through the head while standing, the bullet would have fallen some distance behind him. But Beau and Will had combed the area for it and found nothing. So maybe it was time to consider other possibilities.

If the weapon that killed Slade had been a high-caliber military-type sniper gun, accurate at more than a thousand yards, the bullet could've retained enough force to penetrate the chassis of the truck that had been parked behind him. There'd been no mention of damage to the heavy-duty vehicle, which had been seized as evidence. But there was also a chance the exiting bullet could have passed over the flatbed and traveled another couple hundred yards into the mesquite before losing momentum. Such a bullet would be hard to find, though not impossible with a metal detector. Jasper owned one of those devices. Maybe they could come back with it tomorrow and make a search.

Sky switched off the flashlight and studied the landscape, weighing another idea. What if the shot had been fired from a distance at a downward angle? It might have gone under the truck, into the ground.

Half a mile to the east, a brushy hill, dotted with junipers, rose above the pastureland. From the top of that hill, moonlight could have given the shooter a clear view of this spot, within easy range of a high-powered rifle.

Spurred by a hunch, he climbed back into his truck, shifted into four-wheel drive, and rumbled across the half mile of rough, open ground to the base of the hill. Switching on the flashlight, he picked an easy route and began to climb. His long strides carried him swiftly upward.

The hill was crowned by a flat outcrop of rock. There would be no tracks to find, but from here, even in the waning moonlight, Sky could see all the way to the place where Slade had died. With a good scope and a high-powered rifle, a man with a steady aim would have no difficulty picking off his target from here.

A careful shooter—a professional—would have left no proof behind. But Sky's instincts told him to look anyway.

It took him only a few minutes to find the shiny brass shell casing. It was lying in the open, almost as if the shooter had wanted it to be discovered. Using the flashlight and his cell phone, he snapped several photos of the object in place. Then, using the narrow blade of his pocketknife, he picked it up and studied it. He recognized it as a Browning .50 machine-gun round, the type commonly used by military snipers in semiautomatic assault rifles.

Maybe that skinhead bartender had a military background.

Moving carefully, he carried his prize back to the truck and transferred it to a leftover sandwich bag, which he'd turned inside out. Tomorrow he'd bring Jasper out here with his metal detector and search for the bullet.

CHAPTER 14

As he drove into town, Will felt more hopeful than at any time since Beau's arrest. The sheriff had demanded proof that Slade was dead before he was shot with Jasper's deer rifle. Thanks to Sky's discovery of the brass shell casing on the hilltop, and the next day's successful search for the matching bullet, he was carrying all the proof he needed—maybe proof enough to clear his brother.

On Tori's advice, Beau had remained at the ranch. But Will would be picking up Tori at home on the way to the sheriff's office. As Beau's lawyer, she would be there to represent his interests.

"Don't get your hopes up, Will," she lectured him as he drove. "Axelrod is a stickler for tying up loose ends. As long as there's any basis for suspicion, he'll be keeping Beau at the top of his list."

"Hellfire, what list?" Will stormed. "As far as I know, the sheriff hasn't even looked at anybody else. What about that tattooed bartender in the Blue Coyote? He looks like a hired hit man to me. And what about Lute? He hated Beau. And now he's got Slade's old job. How did the slimy little weasel make that happen?"

Will was still asking himself those questions when they walked into the wing of the county building that housed the sheriff's offices and the jail. Glenda Peterson, whose husband owned the town's only gas station, gave them a breezy smile from her side of the reception desk. "The sheriff's expecting you," she said. "Hang on a minute. I'll let him know you're here." She pressed a button on the phone and spoke a few words into the receiver. "You two can go right in," she said.

Sheriff Hoyt Axelrod rose from behind his desk and extended his hand with a smile. "Good to see you, Tori. Will, I got your message. Have a chair. Let's see what you've found."

Will opened the manila packet he'd brought containing the bullet and casing in plastic bags and the photos of the sites, which Beau had printed from Sky's phone camera. He slid the contents across the desk. "You asked for proof that another shooter killed Slade. Here it is."

Axelrod scratched his thick mustache, scowling as he studied the evidence. "I'll hang on to this," he said. "I've no doubt it's what you say it is. Judging from the ammo, I'm guessing the weapon was most likely a Barrett fifty-caliber BMG semiautomatic. Snipers used those guns in Iraq and Afghanistan. Plenty of those babies available at gun shows. I've even got a couple of them down in the evidence room. As far as that goes, there's no way of determining how long that casing was there. For all I know, you could have planted it."

Will felt a surge of frustration. Why was the sheriff determined to pin this crime on his brother? "Beau doesn't have that kind of gun. Nobody on the ranch owns one either."

The sheriff raised one grizzled eyebrow. "Maybe not. But Slade Haskell had one. He showed it to me last year, right after he bought it at a gun show. And Slade had a wife."

Natalie was buttoning on a fresh white lab coat, preparing to open her clinic, when the front doorbell rang. Two uniformed sheriff's deputies stood on the porch—younger men she'd seen in town but didn't know by name.

"Dr. Haskell?"

"Yes." Her pulse lurched. Had something happened to Beau?

One deputy thrust an official-looking paper into her face. "We have a warrant to search your house and examine your late husband's gun safe for evidence." He made a move as if to enter, but Natalie stood her ground.

"I have nothing to hide," she said. "Can you tell me what this is all about?"

"We have our orders, ma'am. Now please step aside and open the safe."

"The safe's in the den. I'll need to get the combination." Natalie hurried ahead of the two men, willing her legs to support her. Something, she sensed, was terribly wrong. And not knowing what it was only heightened her dread.

Slade's den was the one room she'd closed up and left alone. The new combination to the closet-sized safe, which the locksmith had changed while Natalie was in the hospital, was tucked inside the desk drawer. Natalie had used it only once, when Beau had found the shotgun for her. She hadn't touched the safe since.

One of the deputies dusted the dial for prints and took samples. Both men had donned latex gloves. What was going on? Had her house become a crime scene?

Stepping back, the deputy motioned for Natalie to open the safe. She'd had no trouble before. But now her eyes refused to focus on the tiny numbered lines. She handed the paper to the nearest deputy, who worked the combination on the first try. The heavy door swung open to reveal Slade's guns, stored vertically on supporting racks.

"Here's the Barrett." The taller of the two deputies lifted out an ugly semiautomatic rifle that, to Natalie, looked like nothing more than an assembly of pipes and braces. Slade had taken special pride in owning it.

"Was this your husband's rifle?" the deputy demanded.

"Yes."

"Has it been fired recently?"

"Not unless Slade took it out on the range before he was killed. If you want to take it, feel free."

"We don't need your permission, ma'am. It's evidence." The

deputy produced a large, folded plastic bag from his pocket, unfolded it, and held it open while his partner slid the gun inside. *Why?* Natalie asked herself. The only fingerprints on it would be Slade's—and Beau's, of course, since he'd moved the weapon out of the way to get her the shotgun.

Dear God, was that what they were looking for?

"We're done here, ma'am. Thank you for your cooperation." The deputies walked out as abruptly as they'd come. Natalie stood in silence, staring into the open gun safe. She didn't fully understand what had happened, but she sensed that her shattering world had been dealt a final blow and was about to implode into dust.

The jangle of her cell phone, which she'd slipped into her lab coat, startled her. She snatched it up and glanced at the display name.

"Tori, what is it?" Natalie felt as if she were struggling for air.

"I just spoke with the sheriff. According to him, Slade had a semiautomatic assault rifle, a Barrett." Tori's voice was taut with strain. "It should be in his gun safe. I know Beau had to open the safe to find your shotgun. Think carefully. Did either of you handle that rifle?"

"I didn't, but Beau did." Natalie's throat tightened with each word. "He lifted it out of the safe and put it back."

"Then I've got bad news. Slade was most likely killed with that kind of weapon. Sky found the bullet and casing at the scene. The sheriff's men will be coming by to collect the one you have. Try to stall them until I get there."

"Tori, they just left." Natalie felt her knees giving way. She sank onto the arm of an overstuffed chair. "They took the gun, and it'll have Beau's prints on it."

"There's no way the ballistics will match." Beau gazed around the circle of gloomy faces. Tori, Will, Sky, and Jasper had joined him in the ranch house parlor to discuss the latest development in the murder case. "They'll run the routine tests, compare the bullets, and that will be the end of it."

"But that could take time," Tori said. "The nearest ballistics lab is in Lubbock, and I know for a fact they're backlogged. Meanwhile, the sheriff and the DA will be building their case against you any way they can."

"What the hell kind of case can they build against an innocent man?" Will exploded with frustration. "Why aren't they looking at anybody else? Like that bartender?"

"About that bartender . . ." Beau had heard back from his friends at the DEA that morning. It wasn't great news, but he had to share what he'd learned. "They ran facial recognition on Sky's photos and got a hit. His real name is Nick Tomescu. He's in the database for some petty crimes like shoplifting and possession but no violence involved. Back in Jersey he was a runner for the Rumanian mob—took a plea deal when he got busted, which may be part of why he's holed up in the boondocks under an alias."

"But can he shoot?" Jasper demanded.

"Nobody seems to know. He has no military record, and if he's a hit man, he's managed to keep it off the books."

"So he's not a great candidate for our shooter, but we can't rule him out," Sky said.

"At least my friends were thorough," Beau said. "Here's another tidbit they dug up. The man is Stella's younger half brother. They were raised together—same mother, different fathers."

"So it might look as if he's protecting her," Tori mused, "but it could be more like Big Sister is protecting him."

"Let's forget him for now," Will grumbled. "I don't care if the man's a blasted saint! But if you ask me, Slade and that Stella woman were involved in some illegal business with those trucks. What if Slade knew too much, and Lute was given his job as payment for shutting him up?" His fist crumpled the empty beer can he'd left on the coffee table. "And speaking of Lute, he could be the key to this whole mess. Could he be the shooter?"

"I'd pick him as the one who stole Jasper's gun and fired the shots into the body to frame Beau," Sky said. "But Lute never had a steady aim. Even lying down, with a high-powered scope, he'd have been damned lucky to make the shot from that hill. But if he didn't do it, maybe he knows who did."

"So where is the little bastard?" Will demanded.

"Somewhere between here and that ranch in Mexico where he was hauling hay," Sky said. "Leave Lute to me."

The conversation might have continued, but just then Bernice, who'd kept up with all that was happening, came rushing in from the kitchen. "Come look at the TV! Hurry! You're not going to believe this!"

With no time to turn on the big set in the den, they raced after her to crowd around the miniature TV that sat on a shelf above the kitchen countertop. The local newscast was just beginning. On the screen, a gaggle of reporters clustered below a podium erected on the steps of the county building. Looming behind the podium, his uniformed chest glittering with the medals and awards he'd won over the years, stood Sheriff Hoyt Axelrod.

"Thank you for coming, friends." He beamed like a Texas-style Santa Claus as he surveyed his small but enthusiastically cheering audience. "I've invited you here to share this great moment and to say that it's time for our party to replace Garn Prescott, a Washington insider who puts his own interests above those of the people he represents. It's time for a new face in Washington—the face of a man with a proven record, a man who stands for law and order and justice. That is why . . ." The silence implied a drumroll. "That is why I stand before you today as a candidate for the United States Congress from the twenty-fourth district of the great state of Texas!"

Sky sat on the porch of the brick duplex he called home, scowling down at the unopened manila envelope that lay across his knees. On the day the will was read, he'd slid it under his mattress and resolved to ignore it. But try as he might, he couldn't stop its secrets from troubling his mind.

Lifting his head, Sky gazed across the yard toward the sprawling ranch house. The rosy light of sunset lent a glow to its gray river-stone walls. But tonight a shadow had fallen over the Tyler home, and he'd had a hand in casting it.

When he'd searched out the bullet that killed Slade Haskell, he had only meant to help. But in the sheriff's eyes, the discovery had stacked the evidence deeper against Beau.

On top of all that, Sky had failed to find Lute.

Tonight, in his present frame of mind, Bull's mysterious bequest mocked him like a silent rebuke. Maybe he should just light a match to the damned envelope and walk away.

"What's wrong? You look like a thundercloud." Jasper had come out of his front door, letting the screen slam behind him. Dragging his rocker to Sky's side of the porch, he sat down.

"Been watching the news," he said when Sky didn't answer. "More about the sheriff running for Congress. If you ask me, choosing between Axelrod and Garn Prescott's about like choosing between a coyote and a skunk."

Sky gave the old man a quiet smile. He appreciated the humor, but he didn't feel like laughing.

"What's that in your lap?" Jasper frowned at the sealed envelope. "Don't tell me you haven't opened it yet."

"I'm not sure I want to. I once read a story about Pandora's box, how she opened it and let loose a world of trouble. What if I'm holding a Pandora's box?"

Jasper didn't answer. Sky stared at him, the realization breaking like dawn. "You know what's in it, don't you?"

The old man nodded. "I was there when Bull sealed it and gave it to that big-city lawyer. Do you want me to tell you what's inside?"

"I was thinking maybe I should just burn it."

Jasper leaned back in his rocker, his eyes half closed. "You're a strange one, Sky Fletcher. Must be the Comanche in you. They aren't exactly the most cheerful folks God put down on the planet. Not the ones I've known at least. Always wandering around with gloomy faces, expecting the worst."

"This isn't what you'd call a cheerful time," Sky said.

"No, but it'll all come right. Things usually do."

"I wish I had your faith. With the sheriff running for Congress and wanting to look like a hero, he won't give Beau a chance. The last thing he wants is for folks to find out he arrested an innocent man."

"Hoyt Axelrod is a pompous rooster, but he's smart. If we want to beat him, we'll just have to be smarter." Jasper scratched the head of the aging Border collie, who'd plopped down at his feet. "But getting back to that envelope you're too stubborn to open. I promise you it's no Pandora's box. Bull wasn't one for fancy words, but he set quite a store by you—more than he ever let on. What's in there will tell you what you meant to him."

Sky shook his head. "If Bull was here tonight, he just might change his mind. If I'd left well enough alone—if I hadn't brought Lute here and hadn't looked for that bullet, maybe Beau wouldn't be in so much trouble."

"Beau's troubles aren't your fault. And beating yourself up won't change what Bull left you or the fact that he'd want you to have it."

"Then you take this." Sky thrust the envelope toward the old man. "You can give it back to me later."

"And when will that be, you mule-headed young whippersnapper?"

"I'll let you know."

With a mutter of protest, Jasper took the envelope and tucked it under his arm. Restless now, Sky rose, stretched, and walked down the porch steps.

"Where you goin'?" Jasper called after him.

"Just around."

Fishing the keys out of his pocket, Sky headed for the shed where he kept his truck.

CHAPTER 15

The Blue Coyote was humming tonight. Customers crowded the bar, clamoring for drinks and watching the NBA game that blared from the big-screen TV. The plump young waitress, her dyed black hair gelled into spikes, bustled among the tables, her tray balanced shoulder high. Perspiration made a dark streak down the back of her lavender T-shirt.

From the corner booth, Sky nursed his beer and watched the action. He had stopped by Haskell Trucking on his way into town, hoping Lute might be back. But he'd found the place closed. A look through the chain-link fence had revealed no sign of the big rig Lute had supposedly driven to Mexico.

Sky spotted Stella weaving her way among the tables with a foaming glass of beer in one hand. Her striking green eyes were looking directly at him.

"Hello, Blue Eyes. Mind if I join you?"

"I'd be honored." Sky knew how to charm if he needed to.

She slid the full glass toward him. "I've been watching you for the past hour. You haven't drunk enough of that cheap stuff to make it worth your coming in here. This one's on me. Drink up."

"Thanks." Sky took a sip. "Not bad."

She fixed her riveting gaze on him. "You're Lute's cousin, aren't you?"

"That's right. I actually came into town to find him. Since I take it you're his boss now, can you tell me when he'll be back?"

Something flickered in her eyes. "Is that really why you're here? Last time you came in, before you left with that red-headed princess, I saw you taking pictures."

"You don't miss a thing, do you?"

Her gaze narrowed. "Mind telling me what you were up to?"

Sometimes, when backed into a corner, the truth was the simplest way out. "I was taking a photo of your bartender. Beau wanted to have the DEA run a facial-recognition scan."

"And did they learn anything?" One painted eyebrow slithered upward.

"They did. Not that there was much to learn, but we did find out he's your brother."

"I'd have told you that if you'd asked me." Stella's crimson-nailed finger traced the damp ring the glass had left on the table. "Nicky's not a bad boy, just a little wild. Since I took him under my wing, he's straightened out fine. He'll do whatever I tell him to—but in case you're wondering, that doesn't include murder. Not Slade's and not that poor girl's. Nicky's not your killer."

"Any idea who is?"

"My money's on Beau Tyler. He had motive, means, and opportunity, all in spades. And if it wasn't Beau, I'd bet on that stuck-up little widow of Slade's—*Doctor* Haskell, as she likes to be called."

"Natalie?" Sky frowned in surprise. "She was on a call the night Slade died. Besides, she hates guns."

"She wouldn't have been working *all* night. And just because she hates guns, or pretends to, doesn't mean she couldn't use one. Think about it. The divorce would've taken time, and the property settlement would've been a fight all the way. She saw a chance to ditch her husband fast, grab everything he owned, and hook up with the rich rancher she'd never gotten over."

"And what about the girl?" Sky's mind refused to process the notion that Natalie could be a murderer.

"Jess?" Stella chuckled. "Oh, that part's easy enough. Slade was humping that girl every chance he got. Jealousy's a right powerful motivator. And it could've made her mad enough to go after Slade, too. Motive, means, and opportunity. That lady had it all, including a safe full of guns right in her house."

"What about Lute?" he asked, changing the subject.

Stella tucked a lock of wine-colored hair behind one ear. "No way. The kid was plain moon-eyed over Jess. And Slade was like a big brother to him. Lute worshipped the man. Even if he'd had the stomach for it, he had no reason to kill either of them."

"Whatever's going on with Lute, I need to talk to him, and I'm getting worried. What if he's in some kind of trouble?"

A beat of silence passed before she spoke. "Relax. I was worried about Lute, too, but he's fine. He called this morning to tell me he's on his way back. Evidently he had a little too much fun at that ranch. Something about a fiesta and a girl." Her laugh was brittle, without humor. Sky sensed she was annoyed with Lute's delay. "I'll tell him you came by," she said. "But I can't promise he'll call you. I get the impression things aren't too cozy between you two."

She glanced around the crowded bar. "Nice talking to you, Blue Eyes, but it's time I was getting back to my customers. Stick around as long as you like."

"Wait." Sky stopped her as she rose and turned to walk away. "The boy is family, and I'm doing my best to deal with him," he said. "Would you answer one question for me?"

"Depends." Her expression had turned cautious. "You can ask. That doesn't mean I have to answer."

"Why Lute? He was a washout at the ranch, so lazy and irresponsible that he got himself fired. Why put a kid with no experience in charge of your trucking business when you've got other employees who could do the job better?"

She looked startled for an instant. Then a slow smile spread across her heavily made-up face. "Maybe because he isn't really the one in charge."

With that she walked away, her ample rump doing a shimmy beneath her tight denim skirt.

Sky lingered another fifteen minutes for appearance's sake,

sipping his beer and mulling over what Stella had told him—or rather, what she *hadn't* told him.

He was on his way to the parking lot when it struck him—the real answer to the question he'd asked her.

Lute hadn't been hired and promoted because he was competent, or even because Stella liked him. There was only one reason he could have been given Slade's old job.

He was expendable.

The AC had gone out on the truck. Sweating buckets in the ninety-five-degree heat, Lute had stripped down to his cutoff denim shorts. The road between that nowhere Mexican ranch and the U.S. border had to be the hottest damned stretch on the planet—dry yellow grass, blistering sun, and molten asphalt that stank in the heat.

At least he had plenty of water to drink. He should have furnished more water for the nineteen Mexicans hiding behind the extra hay bales in the trailer. They'd be even hotter back there than he was in the cab. But never mind, he'd be crossing into the good old USA toward evening. Once he got across the bridge into Eagle Pass, he'd find a quiet spot, crack the rear door, and turn them loose. They could find their own water.

Stella had warned him not to transport illegals. Human cargo was too risky, she'd said. Too many things could go wrong. But Stella wouldn't have to know. He had her usual supply of high-grade heroin and cocaine loaded and sealed in the truck's spare gas tank—the cartel's payment for the guns he'd delivered to the ranch. Lute knew better than to touch the drugs. He would have to account to Stella for every ounce. But when he'd found out how much cash he could make smuggling passengers across the border—all of it his to keep—the temptation had been too much to resist.

Despite the sweltering day, he was in high spirits. What Stella was paying him for this run was a pittance compared to what he could make on the side. A thousand dollars apiece from those Mexicans in the back, paid in advance. The thought of that thick wad of cash hidden inside the dashboard, and what it would buy, was enough to make his head spin.

But that was just the beginning. He'd hit it off pretty well with Don Ignacio, the owner of the cattle ranch. They'd gotten to talking, and Lute had discovered the man was a fancier of fine horses.

When Lute had casually asked what Don Ignacio would pay for a trailer load of first-rate Texas cow ponies, along with one flawless palomino stud colt, the rich man's eyes had lit with interest. The cow ponies would be useful, of course, he'd replied, and he would be willing to pay a good price for them. But owning a magnificent palomino stallion had long been a dream of his. If the colt was truly as splendid as Lute had described, and if Lute could get it to the ranch in good condition, Don Ignacio had quoted a figure that made Lute stifle a gasp, inflating his dreams of wealth like a hot-air balloon.

The risk of loading a trailer with Tyler ponies and trying to get them across the border might be too great. But the palomino would be well worth the trouble. Sedated, the foal would be easy enough to smuggle in a truckload of hay or other cargo, but only if he had the skill, or the luck, to drug the precious little creature without killing it, especially given the heat. Again, risk was a big issue here.

A better plan would be to take the mare along to keep her foal calm and fed. With the right official-looking paperwork, making the transfer look like a legal sale, the pair could be hauled openly, in a comfortable trailer. Too bad he hadn't thought of asking the Mexican rancher about that before he left. Now he'd have to find his own way around the problem.

But the horses could wait. Right now Lute had more pressing concerns. The road marker he'd just passed indicated that the border was 200 kilometers away. According to Lute's math, that translated to roughly 120 miles, or a couple more hours of driving.

It would be dusk by the time he reached the border. All to the good. The guards would be nearing the end of their shifts.

They'd be tired, less alert, and the fading light would make it harder to spot suspicious details. But the most dangerous part of the trip lay ahead. He would have to be prepared.

Getting into Mexico had been easy. The guards on the Mexican side of the border had recognized the Haskell rig that hauled hay south to the remote ranch. They'd glanced at Lute's paperwork, stamped it, and waved him on. But getting back into the U.S., with the border patrol on constant watch for smugglers, was trickier.

Stella's contact had done a good job with the fake U.S. passport he carried. Lute was entitled to a real one, but with no registered copy of his birth certificate available, the red tape was more bother than it was worth. His other documents—his trucker's license, the registration, and the insurance on the rig—were genuine and shouldn't be a problem. Lute had all the paperwork handy, ready to present on demand.

The illegal cargo was a different matter. But Lute would hopefully have a hidden ace. One of the guards, a Texan named Albert Sanchez, was tight with Stella. She passed him a generous tip every time he "inspected" one of her returning trucks. The cash was waiting for him now, folded into a sandwich bag and tucked under the floor mat on the passenger side of the truck.

Stella had assured Lute that Albert would do his job. The only tricky part would be timing the truck's arrival at the border to catch Albert's shift and choosing the line that would take him through Albert's station.

There were two bridges, with border stations, crossing the Rio Grande into Eagle Pass. The larger Camino Real International Bridge had one lane for big commercial trucks and multiple lanes for passenger vehicles. But Albert worked on the other, smaller bridge. The mid-sized Haskell rig was okay to pass here, but, unfortunately, it was more likely to be singled out for inspection.

When Lute had last phoned Stella, the word from Albert had been that he would be working that evening when the truck reached the border. But that had been yesterday. Arranging for his human cargo had taken Lute an extra day. Knowing that the delay would make Stella suspicious, he hadn't called her back.

So now, where the border was concerned, he was pretty much flying blind.

Lute shoved a lock of greasy hair out of his face. His mouth formed a string of obscenities, the sound of them lost in the roar of the engine. There was still a chance he'd find Albert and make it through the crossing. But what if he'd screwed up—*really* screwed up?

Getting caught with a truck full of drugs and illegal immigrants could land him in federal prison for years. Ditching the truck and crossing on foot would at least save his skin. Stella would be pissed about the drugs, but the truck was insured, and anything would be better than getting arrested. He'd have to make up a cover story, but it wouldn't be the first time.

With a backup plan in place, Lute felt better. He drove until he could see the lights of Piedras Negras through the murky dusk. Passing into the town, which he knew well enough, he found a *supermercado* with a big parking lot, less than half a mile from the bridge. He parked at the outer edge, switched off the engine, and yanked his T-shirt back over his head.

Taking the documents for the truck, the roll of bills from under the dashboard, and the cash for Sanchez, he stuffed the papers in his jeans and the cash in his boots. If he walked to the bridge and found Albert working, he would come back and get the truck. Otherwise, he would just keep walking.

As an afterthought, he took the jugs of drinking water he'd brought along and walked around to the back of the trailer. Unlocking the door, he raised it a few inches and tossed the jugs into the darkness. Scrambling sounds and the mutter of voices told him his passengers had survived the long, hot day. Lowering the door, he left it unlocked so it could be raised from the inside. If he didn't come back, they would figure it out. They might even be smart enough to look for the hidden drugs.

Even with his boots stuffed full of money, it didn't take him long to walk to the bridge. The Mexicans waved him through when he flashed his passport. Why should they care who was leaving their country? He hung back as he approached the U.S. entry lanes. He'd seen a photo of Albert Sanchez, but none of the guards on duty looked anything like the man. Some of them even had dogs, burly German shepherds sniffing every vehicle.

Trying to look casual, Lute sauntered up to one of the guards, a husky red-haired man who shot him a questioning glare.

"I'm looking for a friend who works here," he said. "Albert Sanchez. Do you know when he'll be coming in?"

"Sanchez?" The man guffawed. "You won't be seeing him around here. He got his butt fired this morning for taking a *mordida* from some rich tourist. Damned lucky for him he didn't land in jail. If he's a friend of yours, kid, you need to find better amigos."

Muttering his thanks, Lute wandered away, found the line for foot traffic, and checked through on his passport. In a restroom on the U.S. side, he took the papers for the truck, ripped them up, and threw the pieces in the trash, along with the set of keys to the vehicle. He was walking away from this adventure with almost twenty thousand dollars in cash. But Stella was going to be mad as hell about that truck. He'd better have one good story ready to tell her.

Maybe he'd be better off not going back at all.

Beau was standing on the front porch, finishing his coffee, when his cell phone rang. Caller ID flashed Tori's name.

"I just spoke with the sheriff," she said. "He's got the results of the ballistics test back. He wants us in his office as soon as we can get there."

Beau's pulse slammed. There was no way that fatal bullet could be a match to Slade's Barrett. But with Hoyt Axelrod determined to nail him to the wall, anything was possible. He'd been in the law enforcement business long enough to know how evidence could be manipulated by the right people.

"Did the sheriff say how the test came out?" he asked Tori.

"All he'd say was that he wanted to tell us in person."

"I can leave now and meet you at your office."

"Let me come out and pick you up. It'll take longer, but I have a book that I ordered for Erin. I can bring it to her and we can talk on the way back to town."

Beau acquiesced, although he was anxious to get the waiting over with. Even bad news was better than not knowing.

He took the cup back to the kitchen, changed and cleaned up from chores, and was back waiting on the porch when Will came outside.

"So she didn't have any idea what Axelrod wants?" Will had been told that Tori was coming and why.

"All Axelrod wants is me behind bars and his fat ass in Congress. My guess is he'll do whatever it takes to make himself look like a hero."

"Even fake a ballistics test? That's pretty serious."

"Who's going to call him on it? Tori? She can't prove a thing. I'm preparing myself for bad news."

"Beau, there's something I need to say, and there might not be a better time to say it than now." Will's hands braced against the porch railing. "You know I put up a five-hundred-thousand-dollar bond against the ranch to make your bail."

"I know, and I appreciate it more than I can say."

Will cleared his throat. "I've been thinking, if things were to go from bad to worse, the ranch could survive the loss. I could take out a bank loan, sell off some land . . ." He fixed his gaze on Beau. "Anything I had to do would be better than having my brother spend his life behind bars for a crime he didn't commit."

Jolted by Will's words, Beau stared at his brother. "Are you saying what I think you're saying?"

Will nodded. "If it's looking like a conviction, don't hesitate to run. I know you had to surrender your passport, but there are ways around that. You know them better than I do. And you know how to hide. If it comes to that, just go—until we can prove your innocence."

Beau was not an emotional man. But he felt the salty sting of tears. "I don't know what to say," he muttered.

"You don't have to say anything. If Dad were here, he'd do it in a heartbeat."

"But the ranch, the land—"

"This isn't about the ranch, it's the family."

Beau might have replied, but just then Tori's station wagon pulled up to the house. Tori climbed out, dressed in tan slacks, a white silk blouse, and the designer sunglasses she favored. In one hand she carried a brown mailer with the logo of a popular online bookstore on the outside. "Here's the horse book Erin wanted." She thrust the mailer at Will. "See that she gets it, and tell her I'll be back later for a visit."

"We'll plan on you for lunch," Will said.

"We'll see." Her serious demeanor warned Beau she was expecting bad news. "Ready, Beau?"

"Just waiting for you." Beau hurried down the steps and climbed into the passenger seat. Tori slipped into her place and started the engine.

"Call me!" Will shouted as she swung the vehicle around and started down the drive. Tori didn't look back.

CHAPTER 16

The sheriff was waiting alone in the reception area when Beau and Tori arrived. His hair and mustache were freshly trimmed, his uniform crisp, his badge polished to a blinding gleam. He looked ready for a high-profile press conference, Beau thought. It wasn't what you'd call a hopeful sign.

Beside him, Tori was as tense as a greyhound at the starting gate. Beau could tell she felt it, too—the dark sense of impending disaster.

"Come into my office, you two," Axelrod said, stepping aside as if to usher them in the right direction. "We need to talk."

They entered ahead of him. The room was small, much of it taken up by the massive solid oak desk and the two empty chairs that faced it. The walls were decorated with framed citations, awards, and photos of the sheriff with Texas dignitaries, including both the first and second President Bush. The blinds on the glass windows that flanked the door were closed. A prickle of anxiety crawled up the back of Beau's neck as he waited while Tori took her seat, then lowered himself onto the remaining chair. Across the desk, Hoyt Axelrod smiled at them from his throne-sized leather chair. Lord, he'd even had his big horsey teeth whitened.

"Sheriff, shouldn't you have the county prosecutor, or at least one of your deputies, present for this meeting?" Tori asked.

He dismissed her question with a shrug. "The prosecutor's out of town and my deputies are all busy. Anyway, we don't hold much with formalities around here. So let's get right down to business."

He shifted in the chair and cleared his throat. "As I expected, the ballistic test shows conclusively that the bullet found near Slade Haskell's body was fired from Slade's own Barrett fifty-caliber BMG rifle."

"We'd like a copy of the results," Tori said.

"I knew you'd ask, so I had this made for you." The sheriff slid a plain manila folder across the desk. The single page inside, along with some printed data and a photograph of the gun, showed two magnified pictures of the bullets—one from the test firing, the other supposedly from the crime scene. The striation pattern on both bullets was identical.

Beau swore silently. Given the procedures for handling evidence, it wouldn't be easy to switch a bullet fired from Slade's gun with the original, but someone whose authority was beyond question—like the sheriff—could manage it. It was hard to believe that a man with Axelrod's record would stoop to evidence tampering, but what other explanation was there?

"There's more," the sheriff said. "As you know, Beau, we found gunshot residue on your hands and your prints on the murder weapon."

"Both of which have already been explained," Tori said. "Beau moved the rifle and put it back in the safe. And he'd been target shooting with his niece before he was tested."

"So you say." The sheriff dismissed Tori's words with a shrug. "But more evidence has come to light. Beau, your fingerprints weren't found on the dial or anywhere else on the outside of that safe. So you weren't the one who opened it, correct?"

"That's correct. Nat—Dr. Haskell opened the safe for me." Instinct and experience told him the direction this so-called interview was taking. Beau took a tight hold on his temper.

"You and Dr. Haskell were high school sweethearts, yes?"

"Anybody who's lived around here for a while knows that."

"And the two of you have rekindled the old fires since you came back."

Tori spoke up before Beau could respond. "They were old friends. That didn't change until after Natalie had filed for divorce. And that occurred after Slade had assaulted her and wrecked her clinic."

"That's what I was told. Still, there were reasons for Dr. Haskell to want her estranged husband dead." The sheriff's pale eyes went cold. "Not only was he a physical threat to her, but she was also faced with the possibility of losing her clinic in a divorce settlement."

Beau saw that Axelrod was deliberately baiting him. It was a tactic he had used many times himself. And the sheriff was damned good at it. "Why don't you get to the point? Say what you're really getting at," Beau challenged.

"Fine." The sheriff leaned back in his chair with the expression of a man holding all the aces in a poker game. "It appears to me that Natalie Haskell could be as deeply involved in this crime as you are. By opening her husband's gun safe so you could take one of his weapons, at the very least she could be charged as an accessory. Or she could be a coconspirator, plotting with you to do away with her husband. Maybe it was even her idea and she talked you into it."

"That's a damn lie!" Beau exploded, nearly coming out of his chair. "She's the victim in this."

"And she's played the role well, hasn't she?" the sheriff taunted. "It's only her word that she was attacked and raped by her husband. You two could have staged it all."

Tori gripped Beau's arm, holding him in the chair when he wanted to reach over that desk and jerk Axelrod across it by his shirtfront. Retaining the tight hold on his arm, she turned to the sheriff.

"You do realize that everything you're saying is pure conjecture. Even as a circumstantial case, it's weak." Her words were as crisp as her voice. "You don't have a shred of proof against her."

"Not yet," he conceded, never losing his smug look. "But I'm guessing that if we bring her in for questioning, we'll get what we need to charge the lady."

Rigid with contained anger, Beau glared at the man, who continued to watch him the way a well-fed cat watches a cornered bird. This was all part of some carefully laid plan. But what?

Suddenly Beau saw the end game.

"It occurs to me that if this case goes the full distance, the trial could be months away. Which would be too late to make a difference in your campaign for Congress, wouldn't it, Sheriff? The primary is coming up soon. To win, you need all the good exposure you can get. That's why you called us here today, and why there are only three of us in your office."

Beau paused. Beside him, Tori sat frozen in shocked silence, but the smile on Axelrod's face didn't even twitch. "Go on, Beau," he said. "I'm interested in hearing where you're headed with this."

"I think you know," Beau said. "The one thing that will get you a fast conviction, and maybe enough exposure to win the nomination, is my signed confession or a promise to plead guilty at the arraignment. And your only chance of getting that from me is to go after Natalie."

Tori gasped. "That's enough, Beau! Not another word until we've had a chance to talk! Sheriff, this is highly irregular! I strongly object—"

"Be still, Tori." Beau's voice was gentle but firm. "Otherwise I'll have no choice but to fire you."

She made a sputter of protest but otherwise kept quiet.

"So, do you have an offer to make me?" the sheriff asked. "I don't have to remind you that Texas is a death penalty state. If Dr. Haskell is convicted as a coconspirator, you could both be facing the same punishment."

"I know that," Beau acknowledged.

As Beau took in the sheriff's calculating smile, he felt the trap close around him. Hoyt Axelrod was holding all the trumps, and they both knew it.

Beau said, "If I plead guilty to Slade's murder at the arraignment, would you grant Natalie full immunity?"

The sheriff's smile broadened. "Not good enough. Here's the deal. You plead guilty to Slade's murder *and* to the murder of Jessica Warner, and your girlfriend gets a free pass. Do that, and your service record and your history of PTSD should be enough to get the death penalty taken off the table. You might even get probation down the line in, say, twenty years. If you're prepared to sign a confession, we can take care of this right now."

"That's enough, Sheriff!" Tori was on her feet, quivering with fury. "You're in no position to bargain with my client! Any plea deal has to be made with the county prosecutor and cleared with the judge. You should know that." She glanced at Beau. "Both of you should know that. This stops here and now!"

"Aw, now, take it easy, Tori." The sheriff's demeanor had turned warm and folksy. "I was only trying to put things in order for when Clay Drummond gets back from his daughter's wedding on Monday. Once he's here, we can wrap this mess up nice and legal like."

Beau recognized the name of Clay Drummond, Tori's former law partner and now, evidently, county prosecutor. He remembered little else about the man, but he could be sure Drummond would do anything within the law to put him behind bars. That included extending the plea deal the sheriff had offered.

Tori swept the ballistics report into her briefcase. "We'll talk again when Clay is back in town," she said to the sheriff. "Meanwhile, my client is complying with the terms of his bail. If you want this process to go smoothly, you're not to harass him or Dr. Haskell. Anything you have to say to them is to be channeled through me. Do I make myself clear?"

"No need to be so feisty, Tori. We're still friends, aren't we?" The sheriff's smirk didn't waver.

Tori flashed him a disgusted look and opened the office door to stalk out through the reception area. Beau quickened his step to keep up with her determined stride. Only as they reached the parking lot did she speak.

"*Still friends,* he says! For two cents I'd have given the man a black eye! And you!" She turned on Beau with fury. "You didn't do yourself any favors in there, offering to plead guilty! What in heaven's name were you thinking?"

"I'm not letting Natalie get dragged into this."

He opened the car door for her. She slid into the driver's seat and started the engine as he climbed into the passenger side.

"I know you'd do anything to protect her; she said she'd do the same for you, which makes her even more vulnerable. You saw how Axelrod tried to spook you into a confession so he could call his press conference and play the hero. What he did back there was way out of line."

"You're right," Beau conceded. "He had me cornered and all I could think about was Natalie. But my first concern is still keeping her out of this mess. How would the county prosecutor handle a plea?"

"Clay's a by-the-book kind of man. Whatever he does will be up front and according to policy. But make no mistake, he likes to win. And he'll be out to get you."

"So I could make the same deal with him?"

"No question. But Clay would have the power to make it stick, so if you're crazy enough to take the fall, which would kill your brother, at least don't be in a hurry. If you can wait Clay out, he may offer Natalie her own deal—immunity in exchange for her testimony against you."

"You might suggest it to him and make sure she takes the deal. Knowing she's out of harm's way would at least give me a chance to fight this."

Tori paused at the town's only stoplight. "We have to fight this, Beau," she said, swinging left onto the highway. "Listen to me. You mustn't sacrifice yourself on a plea deal, not even to save Natalie. We can win this."

"We can also lose."

"Do you have a better idea?" Tori asked.

"Yes. Find out all we can about the real killer." Beau forced a mental shift, trying to think more like a federal agent again. "It's Friday morning. We have three days until the prosecutor gets back. Right now Lute is the only solid lead we have. We need to find him."

Sky faced Stella across the bar. He'd already stopped by the trucking company and found no sign of Lute or the truck he'd driven. Stella had just confirmed that he was two days overdue.

"And the last you heard from him was four days ago?"

"That's right, Blue Eyes." She leaned against the bar, giving him a glimpse of her ample cleavage. "I phoned the ranch in Mexico yesterday. They said he'd left two days ago, a little late, but he should have gotten in before nightfall. It's an easy day's drive from there to the border. Mexico can be a dangerous place. I hope nothing's happened to him."

Her face looked older in the slanting afternoon light. Was she hiding something? Maybe not this time, his instincts told him. Stella was a good actress, but she seemed genuinely worried—if only about the truck. He decided to tell her what he knew.

"Beau has connections in the border patrol," he said. "According to their records, Lute crossed the bridge from Piedras Negras to Eagle Pass three days ago. But he checked through the border as a pedestrian. He wasn't driving anything."

Stella muttered an unladylike curse under her breath.

"My guess is that something happened to the truck—might have been wrecked or stolen. Which means Lute's out there somewhere, trying to work up the nerve to come in and tell you about it."

"Why, that little—" She broke off, then laughed and shook her head. "The poor kid is probably scared to death. But these things happen. Anyway, the truck had U.S. and Mexican insurance. If you find Lute, tell him it's covered and he can come back to work. No hard feelings. I'll just be happy to know he's safe."

This time Sky recognized the signs. The subtle narrowing of Stella's absinthe eyes and the twitch of a jaw muscle told him she was fuming inside. Wherever Lute was, he was in big trouble.

Where would Lute go to hide out? Sky asked himself. Back to Oklahoma, maybe? If he had money, he could have headed for one of the big cities. But where would he get money unless he'd done something to double-cross Stella?

Stella could be asking herself the same questions. That might explain why she was furious. Sky would bet a month's pay she'd had a lot more to lose than a truck.

What if Lute was close by, keeping out of sight to see what would happen? That sounded more like the sort of thing Lute would do. Hole up in the back country. Finding him wouldn't be easy. Lute was coyote clever. He would know how to lie low and cover his tracks.

Lute felt the hunger gnawing at his gut. The snacks he'd bought on the road were long gone, and the jackrabbit he'd snared, skinned, and roasted yesterday hadn't had enough meat on it to satisfy a cat. It wasn't that he didn't have money. Except for the seven hundred dollars he'd paid for the sputtering Vespa motor scooter in Eagle Pass, plus a few bills for meals, gas, and a cheap pistol he'd bought off the street, most of his cash from the Mexicans was intact. But he was going to need it later. And here in this abandoned line shack, deep in the escarpment on the western boundary of the Tylers' ranch, there was nothing to buy.

No way was he going back to Stella. He knew exactly what she would do. She'd greet him with open arms, tell him all was forgiven; then soon after that, when he was somewhere alone, he would die. The way Slade had died. The way Jess had died. He would die because he knew too much and could no longer be trusted.

Not that Stella would pull the trigger. She was too smart for that. Someone else did her killing, someone with a dead aim and complete loyalty. Given a chance to bet, Lute's money was on the bartender.

Maybe he'd made a mistake, coming back here to Blanco Springs and the ranch. It would've been safer to hit the road, put Texas and all he knew behind him. But the money he had wouldn't last for long. And he had plans—big plans and big dreams.

Everything hinged on his getting the palomino foal to Don Ignacio in Mexico. With the money the rancher had offered him, Lute could live a comfortable life south of the border, get a cozy house in an out-of-the-way town, maybe find a pretty senorita for company. With his dark coloring he could pass for Mexican, and he knew enough Spanish to get by.

But getting the foal to the ranch would be complicated. First, he'd need a truck. His own pickup would do, but he'd left it in the Haskell Trucking lot. If it was still there, he'd have to find a way to get it, or steal another one. And he would need a two-horse trailer for the mare and foal. Then he remembered that the Tylers had several trailers lined up behind the machine shed. All he needed to do was hitch a trailer to the truck, load the mare and foal, and drive away.

Now he needed to figure out a way to get the truck and trailer to the border. If he remembered right, one time, while helping Sky round up some strays, they had crossed a dirt road. It was little more than a double-rut trail through the mesquite. At the time, Sky had mentioned that it was part of a network of old wagon roads that crossed the south boundary of the ranch and cut east across the rolling plains, skirting towns and eventually joining up with the highway to Eagle Pass. Taking that route, Lute knew he could cover a lot of distance without being spotted.

His best bet would be to reach the highway before daylight and mix with the border traffic. Once he crossed the bridge, getting the horses into Mexico shouldn't be a problem. If the Mexican guards gave him any trouble, a few large bills should be enough to grease their palms. He'd be home free.

Around 11:30, Lute rode the Vespa into town. It was Saturday night, and the Blue Coyote was busy. Country music punctuated by raucous laughter drifted out the open windows. All to the good, Lute reasoned as he drove past. Anybody wandering the streets at this hour would likely be too drunk to pay him much attention.

Reaching the far end of Main Street, he parked the Vespa in an alley and walked the rest of the way to Haskell Trucking.

The lot was surrounded by a chain-link fence, but, as usual, the gate had been left unlocked. Slipping through the shadows, Lute had no trouble finding his pickup. He'd been required to leave the keys in the office, in case the vehicle needed to be moved. But the previous owner had left a spare set of keys in one of those little magnetic boxes on the frame under the driver's side. Even in the dark it was easy enough to find.

The starter took some coaxing, but when the engine caught on the third try, Lute began to breathe again. The gas gauge read half a tank. He'd need more to get to the border, but he'd worry about that later.

Getting the trailer and the horses would be his biggest challenge. He knew Beau Tyler had updated the ranch's security system. There could be alarms, even cameras. And if that mare decided to make a fuss, she could wake the whole ranch, or at least set off the dog. He needed to create a distraction—something spectacular.

Pulling out of the gate, he closed it behind him and headed around the block to pick up the Vespa. There was no turning back now. In the morning, when Stella learned his truck was missing, all hell would break loose. If he wasn't long gone by then, Lute knew he was as good as dead.

It was almost one in the morning, but Natalie couldn't sleep. She'd come home late, exhausted after an emergency procedure on an injured gelding. Calmed by a warm shower and a relaxing cup of chamomile tea, she'd expected to drift off as soon as she closed her eyes. But after an hour of trying, she was wide awake, the pillow smashed out of shape and the covers tangled around her legs.

Tori had called on Friday to warn her about the sheriff's ploy with Beau. At first Natalie hadn't been surprised. Hoyt Axelrod would do anything to get his face in the media, and bringing a murderer to justice would cast him as a champion of law and order.

"How can I help him, Tori? There has to be something I can do."

"Just keep a low profile," Tori had advised her. "Don't do anything that will draw attention to yourself. And if Clay Drummond offers you immunity to testify against Beau, for heaven's sake, take it. If Beau knows he doesn't have to protect you, he'll be free to fight this."

"But what can I say against Beau? I know he's innocent."

"You can tell the truth. Nothing that's true can hurt him. Remember, if it comes to that, I'll be cross-examining you for the defense. Meanwhile, don't talk to anybody about this, especially Beau or the sheriff. And if the prosecutor calls you, I want to be there for any offer he makes. Call me if you have any questions."

Trying to sleep was just frustrating her. Natalie rolled out of bed and reached for her robe. The house could use tidying and she had a week's worth of laundry to do. Maybe burning up some nervous energy would leave her relaxed enough to sleep.

The sight of her purse on the dresser reminded Natalie that her phone battery was low. She would get the wash started, then put the phone on the charger for the night.

After dumping the contents of the dirty-clothes hamper into a basket, she carried the load down to the laundry room at the far end of the hall. As she set the basket on the utility table, her foot stubbed something under the table.

Glancing down, she saw a cardboard box—the box of Slade's dirty clothes and bedding from Haskell Trucking. Until that moment, she had forgotten about it.

Natalie pulled the box into the open. The sour male odor of

his body lingered in the sheets and garments, triggering emotions she never wanted to feel again.

Why had she kept these things? She should have tossed them in a Dumpster on her way home. So why not do that now? Just take the clothes outside and stuff them in the trash for tomorrow's pickup.

She was headed for the door with the box when a sudden thought struck her. What if she was holding evidence, maybe even a clue to Slade's murder?

Donning latex gloves to avoid contaminating any potential evidence, she dumped the contents onto the table. First she shook out the sheets and pillowcase—nothing there. The underwear and socks, apart from their smell, held no secrets. But the khaki trousers, jeans, and work shirts had pockets, as did the lightweight baseball jacket.

The shirts and pants yielded six Burger Shack receipts, two candy bar wrappers, $2.74 in loose change, a pen, a movie ticket stub, and a wad of chewing gum. Nothing to make a difference, but finding these small, meaningless items was like opening a grave and letting a flood of memories escape—the good times and bad, the things they'd built together. All gone now.

She picked up the tan fleece-lined canvas jacket with the Haskell Trucking logo on the front. The weather had been warm for weeks, so he wouldn't have worn it recently, probably not since their separation. She imagined it hanging on a hook in his office, forgotten till the next cold season.

Opening it up, she felt a crackle in the zippered inside pocket. Her exploring fingers found a folded slip of paper. It was a bank deposit receipt.

Puzzled, she studied it. The bank wasn't the one where she and Slade had their joint personal account, nor was it the one used by Haskell Trucking. But the Lubbock address beneath the header jogged her memory. She'd driven past the bank once, a small branch office, sharing a building with a real estate company, in an out-of-the-way part of town. Had Slade made the deposit for someone else, or was this account one he'd kept secret from her, as he'd kept other aspects of his life?

She was still puzzled when she noticed the computer-printed figures on the receipt. She gasped. The deposit amount shown was $26,550. The balance in the account was given as $821,633.11. Almost a million dollars.

Natalie's knees went slack. She leaned against the table for support. That kind of cash had to be connected to something illegal.

Her first impulse was to phone Tori. But it was almost 2:00 in the morning. Tori would be asleep and even if she wasn't, there'd be nothing she could do at this hour.

If Slade had been involved in something dirty, there was a good chance that this receipt could prove someone other than Beau had killed him and framed Beau for it.

She wanted this nightmare over—for Beau and for herself. The fastest way to end it would be to find the sheriff, show him there had to be other suspects, and insist that he check them out. If he ignored her, she would go to the local TV station, tell them what she knew, and blast his political dreams to kingdom come.

Today was Sunday, the sheriff's day off. Fortunately she knew where he lived. As soon as the sun rose a respectable distance above the horizon, she vowed to be on his doorstep with a copy of the receipt in hand.

She would make him listen.

CHAPTER 17

An explosive sound yanked Beau out of a deep sleep. His eyes shot open. Through the bedroom window, the sky cast a hellish glow on the walls. The smell of smoke seared his nostrils. Was he back in Iraq or was this one of his nightmares?

Neither, he realized as he shook himself fully awake. This was all too real.

"Fire!" He rolled out of bed and charged down the hallway to Will's room. "Fire!"

Already awake, Will flung open his door. He was still in his shorts, his hair standing on end, but his manner was calm. "It's the machine shed," he said. "I've called nine-one-one, but it'll take the fire department a while to get here. We'll need everybody to keep the blaze from spreading. Ring the bunkhouse. I'll meet you downstairs."

Beau raced back to his room to throw on his clothes. Swearing as he yanked on his boots, he remembered that the machine shed was where spare gas cans were stored. If the flames had gotten to the gasoline, the shed and its contents were already beyond saving.

Fully dressed, he ran down the staircase, where he met Bernice and Erin on the landing. Erin's eyes were huge with fear.

Beau said, "The fire isn't near the house. Both of you stay inside and you'll be fine."

"But what about Tesoro?" Erin was close to tears. "The mares and foals are in the barn. Will they be all right?"

"The barn's not in danger." *At least not yet*, Beau added silently. "He'll be fine," he assured her. "You stay here with Bernice."

Leaving them, Beau sprinted outside. Smoke raked his nose and throat. He could hear the wild metallic clang of the cook's triangle ringing the alarm. Cowboys were stumbling out of the bunkhouse, some of them still pulling on their clothes.

The machine shed was a hundred yards north of the house. The stored gasoline had turned the steel-roofed building into a roaring inferno that poured black smoke and shot balls of flame whenever the fire reached new fuel. There was no way to save the structure or the valuable equipment inside. All the men could do was try to keep the blaze contained. Under Will's supervision, the vehicles were being moved away from the nearby garage, in case it caught fire. The hay shed, too, was within reach of flying sparks.

Beau spotted Sky connecting the end of a long hose to an outside faucet. The narrow stream of water wouldn't be enough to do much good against the fire, but at least it could be used to wet down everything around it.

Jasper had arrived with gunnysacks piled on the back of his ATV. Beau pulled the sacks to the ground and, as the water came on, began drenching them with the hose. Knowing the drill, the cowhands grabbed the wet sacks and beat the flames around the edge of the blaze to stop them from spreading along the ground. When the sacks were gone, Beau turned the hose on the fire.

"Might as well just have everybody piss on it," Jasper said from behind him.

"I know." Beau gave the old man a tired grin. "All we can do is try to corral it here."

"I'd bet my life some bastard lit it," Jasper said. "Dog started barking about twenty minutes ago. I went outside but couldn't see anybody. Figured it was a coyote or something. Reckon I was wrong."

"I'd bet with you," Beau agreed. "All they had to do was light a match, toss it in there, and run like hell. What I'd like to know is why."

By the time the tanker truck arrived from town, there was nothing left of the shed except blackened sections of corrugated roof and charred, misshapen lumps of equipment. Most of the hands had gone back to the bunkhouse to wash up and rest. Beau, Will, Sky, and Jasper stood together watching the volunteer firemen douse the glowing ruins until every last spark was out. It was almost morning. The night was fading to pale gray above the eastern plain.

Will spat on the smoking ground. His eyes were bloodshot, his face and clothes blackened. "At least the damned place was insured," he said.

"And nothing else caught fire," Beau added, aware that he looked as bad as his brother. "When I catch the SOB who started this, there won't be anything left of him to turn over to the law."

"Well, no sense going back to bed," Will said. "Come on, let's get some coffee and start the day."

They were nearing the house when Bernice burst onto the porch and raced toward them, her flannel robe flapping around her legs. "Erin's gone!" she gasped, out of breath. "She told me she was going back to bed, but she's nowhere in the house."

"Take it easy, Bernice," Beau said. "As worried as she was about her foal, she probably went to the barn. The rest of you go on ahead. I'll get her."

Beau loped across the yard to the barn.

Inside, the barn was still dark. The mares were snorting and stamping in their stalls, probably upset by the smell of smoke. Deciding not to turn on the light and startle them further, Beau made his way toward the stall where Lupita and her foal spent the night. Partway there, his boot touched something soft and solid. He glanced down. His heart slammed.

Erin lay facedown in the straw, her white nightgown barely

visible in the darkness. When Beau dropped to his knees and touched her hair, his hand came away wet with blood.

The truck's fuel gauge was dropping fast. Lute cursed as he negotiated the bumpy, rutted road. Was he using more gas than usual because of the trailer, or did he have a leak somewhere? Why the hell hadn't he thought to grab a can of gas out of that shed before he lit the fire?

The fire had been the perfect diversion. With all hands fighting the blaze, hooking up the horse trailer without being seen had been easy. But as he led the mare and foal out of the stall and started for the rear door, the Tyler girl had walked in.

Lute hadn't wanted to hurt the kid. He'd expected her to scream and run away. Instead, she'd grabbed a pitchfork and come at him. Somehow he had managed to pull the pistol out of his belt and club her along the side of the head. Leaving her where she fell, he had loaded the mare and colt, closed up the trailer, and gotten the hell out of Dodge.

The dark was fading into morning. He had hoped to be on the highway by now, but between the rough, winding road and the heavy trailer, he had been lucky to make thirty-five miles an hour. Worse, this godforsaken cow path showed no sign of hooking up with anything.

But maybe his luck was about to change. As light from the rising sun fingered across the land, he made out the shape of something in the distance, right near the sloping hill. It looked like it could be an old barn with a silo next to it. And close by . . . yes, that had to be a house. Gunning the engine, Lute headed for it. His luck was holding. Everything was going to be all right.

Beau breathed a prayer of thanks when Erin moaned and opened her blue eyes.

The first word out of her mouth was "*Tesoro!*"

"Don't try to talk, sweetheart." Will's voice betrayed his emotion. "You've been unconscious. We need to get you to the hospital."

"No!" She struggled to sit up as her father held her back. "Tesoro and Lupita—they've been stolen! We've got to get them back!"

"She's right." Sky had appeared in the doorway. "The mare and foal are gone. I found tire tracks outside the barn, and one of our trailers is missing."

"It was Lute!" Erin fought against Will's restraining grip. "I saw him before he hit me. He was leading them to the trailer. I tried to stop him, but—" She fell back on the pillow with a groan, a hand reaching up to the bandage Bernice had applied to the cut on her head.

Will turned toward Sky and Beau. "Well, I guess we know who started the fire," he said, "and I guess we know why."

Beau was already moving toward the doorway where Sky waited. "We'll find him."

"Go," Will said. "I'll call Tori, then take Erin to the hospital, in case we're dealing with a concussion."

"Lute's probably headed for Mexico," Sky said as the two men strode toward the front hall. "I'm guessing he found a buyer for the horses there. We'd better call the highway patrol and have them keep a lookout for him."

"Good idea, but I have a better one." Beau motioned Sky into the ranch office. "While you were away buying horses, I put tracking devices on our vehicles, including the trailers. The computer should be able to tell us where he is."

"Pull it up," Sky said. "While you're doing that, I'll bring a truck around front with some feed and water. Knowing Lute, those horses won't have much, if any."

"Grab a couple of loaded guns, too. You know where we keep them." Beau turned on the computer and opened the tracking application he'd installed weeks ago. By the time Sky returned with a .38 Smith & Wesson revolver and a 30-06 Winchester hunting rifle, the program had located the stolen trailer.

"Lute took the wagon road." Beau pointed to the map on the screen. "See, he's headed for the old Winslow farm."

Sky nodded. "I've been out that way. The place has been deserted for as long as I can remember."

"The family left years ago after their house burned," Beau said. "Nobody's lived there since. But look, the trailer doesn't appear to be moving past it. Lute must have stopped."

"My goodness, so that's how it works!" Bernice peered over Beau's shoulder. "I can see right where he is!"

"I'll leave this app running for Will and Jasper," Beau said. "Let's go. The trailer will slow Lute down. With luck we can catch him before he gets to the highway."

Bernice followed the two men out onto the porch and watched them climb into the pickup. "I'll phone the sheriff!" she called as they sped away.

Natalie drove along the quiet Sunday morning streets of Blanco Springs. A block away was the sheriff's brick bungalow, where he'd lived his bachelor's existence since his wife had passed away six years ago. Nearing it, Natalie slowed the Land Cruiser and stopped close to the curb of the vacant lot next to the sheriff's house.

His personal Jeep, minus any official insignia, sat in the carport. She scanned the house for some sign of life, but the shades were down. Natalie hesitated, debating whether to wait until she saw some stir of activity inside, but she didn't have the patience for it.

She glanced at the shotgun Beau had insisted she keep with her at all times. She climbed out of the vehicle, leaving the shotgun where it lay on the floorboard of the passenger seat, and automatically locked the doors behind her.

As she approached the house, Natalie listened for the sound of a television or radio, anything that might indicate the sheriff was up and about, but all she could hear was the squabbling of magpies in a blue spruce near the carport.

The side door opening to the carport was closer than the front door, and Natalie instinctively chose the shortest route. The sudden jangle of a telephone came from somewhere close by. She paused, trying to discern whether it came from within the house or someplace else.

When it rang a second time, Natalie felt sure it came from inside. She followed the sound to the back corner of the house. The same moment that she spotted an open window, someone picked up the phone, cutting the sound off in mid-ring.

"Hello?" The sheriff's voice was gruff, as if he'd just been awakened. "Yes, Bernice, what is it?"

Natalie froze. She knew of only one Bernice. She inched around the corner.

There was a moment of silence as Axelrod listened to the voice on the phone. "I hear you," he said. "Thanks for letting me know, Bernice. I'll get right out there." The bedsprings creaked as he swung his ample weight to the floor.

"Who was that, sugar?" The rich, husky female voice was unmistakable. Natalie swallowed a gasp. *Stella! Stella in bed with the sheriff!*

"Tyler's cook," the sheriff replied. "Seems Lute's turned up. He stole a trailer and a couple of horses from the Tylers, and they've followed a tracking signal to the old Winslow place. I have to get out there before they get their hands on him."

"You know what you have to do." Stella's voice had taken on a cold edge.

"Yes, I know. Whatever I have to. Hand me my belt." There were sounds of dressing, a toilet flushing. Natalie hid behind some bushes, knowing she had to get out of there but unsure of when or which way to go. She was shifting to relieve the strain on her cramped legs when she heard the door to the carport opening. Holding her breath, she moved far enough for a glimpse around the corner of the house.

Axelrod had stepped into the carport and was unlocking the Jeep. He was dressed in a camouflage shirt and wearing his pistol belt. In one hand he carried a military assault rifle.

Natalie's heart dropped. It was a Barrett .50 BM, like the one Slade had owned.

The Jeep pulled out of the driveway and headed up the

street. Praying Stella wouldn't see her, Natalie bellied her way around the back of the house and exited on the far side. Ducking around a hedge, she raced back to the white Toyota parked next door. Her purse, with her phone in it, was tucked under the front seat. She needed to call Beau, to warn him that Axelrod was carrying a sniper rifle and likely bent on murder.

But whose murder? The answer came on the heels of the question. Killing Beau wouldn't be in the sheriff's best interest. He was counting on Beau's conviction to win him a congressional seat. But killing Lute would silence the one person who could shed light on Slade's murder and more . . . possibly much more.

Axelrod was going to kill Lute—as he'd likely killed Slade, perhaps as he'd even killed Jess Warner. And if there was a way to blame Lute's murder on Beau as well, he would find it.

Snatching up her purse, she found her cell phone and tried to dial Beau's number. But the phone was dead in her hand. In her excitement at finding the deposit receipt last night, she'd forgotten to recharge the battery.

By the back roads, the old Winslow place was a little less distance from town than from the ranch. But Lute was already there and the Tylers—whoever that included—had a head start. There was no telling who would get there first.

Starting the engine, she swung the vehicle around, floored the gas pedal, and headed out of town after the sheriff's Jeep.

Lute had arrived at the farm to find a deserted ruin. The house was nothing but a roofless, burned-out shell littered with cigarette butts and empty beer cans. The weathered barn was barely standing and, as he learned when he looked inside, the concrete silo was infested with bats.

But the real problem was that the truck was almost out of gas.

He drove the truck and trailer into the barn, knowing that to go on would mean stalling in the open a mile or two down the road, under the hot sun. At least there was shelter here. But there was no water, no food, and no gas. Screaming every filthy word he knew, Lute kicked at the tires.

His theft of the horses and trailer had been as smooth as hot fudge over ice cream. But now he'd fallen victim to his own stupidity. A shed with plenty of gas, and all he had thought of was setting the damned place on fire.

The horses stirred in the trailer, the mare snorting anxiously. He'd brought no water for them, figuring he'd take care of that later. How long could they last in this heat? How long could *he* last? Somehow he had to find a way out of this mess.

There was some gas in the Vespa, but he didn't have a hose to siphon it into the truck. Still, he could ride it down the road. This infernal cow path had to end up somewhere civilized.

Feeling better now that he had a sensible plan, Lute climbed up to unload the Vespa from the back of the pickup. He considered turning the horses loose, but the barn's rickety walls wouldn't hold them for long. They could push their way out and wander off while he was gone. Better to leave them locked in the trailer. If they died there because he couldn't return . . . well, they were just horses. And if he couldn't sell them, they weren't any good to him anyway.

The Vespa wasn't all that heavy, but with the trailer hitched to the back of the truck, getting it down was awkward. Lute was just lowering the scooter off the side of the truck bed when his ears caught a sound that chilled his blood. It was the unmistakable rumble of a big vehicle, maybe a half mile away but coming rapidly closer over the bumpy road.

Lute's hands froze, letting go of the Vespa. It crashed to the ground, landing on its side. Unless the approaching vehicle belonged to a stranger, it would be someone after him—the Tylers most likely.

The Vespa didn't appear damaged, but it wasn't fast. Lute decided that his best chance was to stay out of sight, keep quiet, and if anybody got too close, use his pistol to scare them off.

The pistol was in the truck, under the seat. As the engine noise grew closer, he checked the clip, cocked the gun, and crouched on the floor of the cab to wait.

Sky pulled the truck to a stop fifty yards up the slope from the old barn. Letting the motor idle, he raised the high-powered binoculars to his eyes and peered into the sunlight.

"Think he's in there?" Beau asked.

"He's in there all right," Sky said. "I can see fresh tire tracks in the dust. They lead right into the barn. I can even see his boot prints where he opened and closed the barn door. Want to look?"

"I'll take your word for it," Beau said. "I just hope we can corral the little bastard and get the horses back without anybody getting hurt."

Sky lowered the binoculars. "Let me go down there. Maybe I can talk some sense into him.

Beau nodded. "I'll wait here. But take the pistol and be careful. If Lute has a gun, I wouldn't put it past him to take a shot at you."

"Understood. But the pistol stays here. I don't want Lute to see me as any kind of threat. If you need to step in, I'll let you know."

"You won't have to let me know. I'll be right here covering you." Beau switched off the ignition and stepped out of the truck. Chambering a shell in the rifle, he watched Sky stride downhill toward the barn, unarmed and exposed. A memory from Iraq flashed through his mind—an army buddy, walking toward a hut with his weapon lowered. A gentle young man, he'd glimpsed women and children inside and he hadn't wanted to scare them. A dozen yards from the door, he'd reeled backward and fallen in the dust, his body riddled with a burst of bullets. Beau had risked his life to drag him to safety, but it was too late. His friend was already dead.

Now, watching Sky, he bit back a cry of warning. This wasn't Iraq. Sky was Lute's cousin, and, hopefully, he knew what he was doing. For now Beau would let him call the shots.

Sky was within shouting range of the barn. "Lute!" he called. "It's Sky! I'm unarmed and I'm coming in to talk."

A single bullet kicked up a puff of dirt six feet from Sky's boots. "Don't come any closer, Sky!" Lute bawled. "I won't shoot you, but if you take another step, I'll shoot one of the horses."

Beau figured that would stop Sky, and it did. Sky stayed put, talking to Lute from where he stood. "We don't want to hurt you, Lute. All we want is to get the horses back and find out what happened with Slade. The rest we can work out."

There was no answer. In the silence, Beau felt the hair rise on the back of his neck.

"I mean it," Sky shouted. "Nothing's happened that can't be fixed. Erin's going to be all right. Everything you burned was insured. Walk on out now and come home with us. If you come clean, we'll protect you from whatever else is out there to hurt you."

Again there was no answer. But Beau glimpsed something moving through the gaps in the dilapidated boards of the barn. He was about to work his way around to approach the barn from the back side when he heard a faint metallic *snick* coming from the low hill behind him. It was a sound Beau knew too well. Instinctively he dropped to a crouch and swept his gaze over the brushy slope behind the truck, seeing nothing.

At that instant, all hell broke loose.

With a chattering roar and a crackle of rotten wood, a blue Vespa, with Lute hunched on the seat, exploded through the side of the barn and swung toward the road. The report of a high-powered rifle rang out from the hilltop. The Vespa bucked and went into a crazed spin that ended with the scooter lying on its side, its wheels still spinning. Lute lay sprawled beneath it, blood pooling beneath his lifeless head.

Sky was in motion, racing toward his fallen cousin, when a second shot rang out. Sky reeled and crumpled to the ground, clutching his side.

The firing stopped. Sky was crawling across the farmyard toward the silo, leaving a trail of blood in the dust. Too much blood.

For Beau, the shots had triggered an avalanche of nightmare memories. He forced them from his mind. Right now he had to get to Sky even though that was exactly what the mystery shooter probably wanted. Get them together in the open and finish them off. Was that why he hadn't killed Sky outright?

Sky saw Beau start toward him. "Don't come out here . . ."

he shouted, his teeth clenching between words. "I'll be . . . fine. Go up that hill. Get the bastard!"

But Beau knew he couldn't do that. If he went after the shooter, Sky would likely bleed to death. He climbed back in the truck and started the engine. The cab wouldn't be much protection against a high-powered military rifle. But it was better than nothing. His plan was to race into the open, haul Sky onto the seat, and make a run for the far side of the concrete silo. From there, the shooter would have to change his position to get a bead on them—and maybe expose himself.

Who the hell was up there with the rifle, anyway? Who would have known they'd be out in the middle of nowhere?

I'll phone the sheriff.

Bernice's parting words, which hadn't really registered at the time, burst into his memory. Suddenly he knew.

Axelrod. Lord, it had been Axelrod all along.

Ducking low, Beau stomped the gas pedal, shot out into the open farmyard, and screeched to a halt with the truck between Sky and the shooter. A bullet shattered both side windows, missing him by inches as he bellied across the front seat, opened the passenger door, and dropped to the ground next to Sky, who looked as if he was going into shock.

"Sorry, this'll hurt, buddy." He seized the wounded man under the arms and hauled him upward onto the rear seat. Sky grunted with pain but didn't speak as Beau vaulted back behind the wheel and gunned the truck the last few yards behind the tall concrete barrier of the silo.

Protected for the moment, Beau jumped to the ground and flung open the back door of the truck. Sky lay on the seat, his face ashen, blood soaking his shirt. Beau had seen similar wounds in combat. With luck the large-caliber bullet hadn't hit any vital organs, but it had blasted an ugly hole in Sky's body. Sky was bleeding out fast. Without medical attention, he might not last long.

Stripping off his soot-streaked shirt and wadding it inside out, he pressed it hard against Sky's wound. With his free hand, he dialed 911 on his cell phone, requested Life Flight, and gave directions. It was the best, perhaps the only, chance of saving Sky. The helicopter would take fifteen, maybe twenty minutes to get here. Meanwhile he had to keep Sky alive and deal with the sheriff.

Sky opened his eyes. His mouth worked as he struggled to speak. "Axelrod," he muttered.

"So you figured it out, too."

Sky's bloodless lips spread in a grimace. "Get the bastard," he rasped, and closed his eyes.

Whipping off his leather belt, Beau wrapped it around his friend's middle and buckled it tight to hold the makeshift pressure bandage in place, then retrieved his phone and the Winchester.

The air had gone quiet, even the birds and buzzing insects frozen in silence. From the hillside there was no sound, no sign of motion. Was Axelrod holding his ground, waiting for someone to step into the open, or was he circling around to get a killing shot at his prey? Forcing himself to stay calm, Beau weighed the odds. Should he hunker down with Sky and try to outwait the sheriff until the helicopter came, or take the offensive and try to lure the man out, maybe get a chance to end this once and for all?

Sky's breathing was ragged, his pulse thready, his eyes closed. It was hard to tell whether he was still conscious, but he'd made it clear what he wanted Beau to do.

Get the bastard! he'd said.

Natalie's plan to intercept the sheriff had fallen dismally short. She'd pushed the Toyota to its limits, but it had been too slow to catch up with the late-model Jeep flying at breakneck speed along the twisting dirt road.

With each mile she fell farther behind, until only a faint dust plume told her the way he was headed.

Spotting a shortcut, she had taken it. Now, half a mile from the Winslow place, she had gotten stuck crossing a sand wash.

In the distance she could see the Winslow place—the dilapidated barn, the burned-out house, the silo, and the low hill behind the property.

As she climbed out of the vehicle, she heard the echoing blast of a high-powered rifle. Seconds later, the first shot was followed by another, so loud that, even at a distance, it made her ears ring. That would be Axelrod's weapon.

Grabbing the loaded shotgun from the floorboard, Natalie took off through the brush at a dead run. Now she heard a third shot and the shattering of glass. There was no return fire. Axelrod was shooting at someone—someone who wasn't shooting back.

Natalie stumbled over a rock, caught herself, and plunged ahead, toward the deserted farm.

Beau crouched behind the open driver's side door of the truck. "I know it's you, Axelrod!" he shouted. "You killed Lute and Slade and probably the girl, too. And then you faked the evidence to frame me. But it's over, hear?"

He waited for an answer. None came, which probably meant Axelrod was moving closer and didn't want to give away his position.

"When did you turn dirty, old man?" Beau taunted him. "Was it after your wife died, or had you been that way all along? When did you decide to start killing people who knew too much? Whatever your reasons, you're finished!"

There was a beat of silence. Then a voice spoke from behind Beau, a voice that chilled his blood. "Don't be so sure of that, Beau. Drop that rifle and turn around . . . very slowly."

Still holding the Winchester, Beau turned far enough to look over his shoulder. Hoyt Axelrod was standing next to the truck's open passenger door, a 9 mm Taurus pistol aimed at Sky's head. He must have slipped around the silo and come on the truck from behind.

"Ironic isn't it? After all that time in Iraq, you come back to Texas to die," the sheriff taunted. "Now throw that rifle down or

I'll blow the half-breed's brains out." His voice darkened. "Do it. And don't try anything."

Faced with the hard reality that anything he tried would never be quick enough to save Sky, Beau had only one option left—to make sure Axelrod didn't get away with this. And his weapon would have to be the cell phone in his other hand.

With exaggerated slowness, Beau cast the Winchester aside, making use of the magician's favorite trick to divert Axelrod's attention while Beau hit the video record app on the cell phone. Keeping his hands raised and the cell phone pointed in the sheriff's direction, he turned to face him with the pistol now aimed at his chest. "Your quarrel is with me, not him."

"He's going to be what you military boys call collateral damage." His glance flicked to the phone. "Called Life Flight, did ya? Too bad he isn't going to last that long. I'll make sure of it. When the paramedics arrive, they'll find three dead men. Lute, the half-breed, and you—with the Barrett in your hands. And don't worry. I can fake a crime scene. I've had plenty of experience. Since I'll be here to meet them, my story will be that you shot the other two, and I had to kill you with my pistol. In self-defense, of course. All very believable, don't you agree?"

"Sounds like you thought of everything." Beau caught some vague movement in his side vision, but he didn't want to break eye contact with Axelrod, hoping to catch a half-second warning before the man fired; maybe it would give him enough time to dive sideways and keep that first shot from being fatal, allowing him to live long enough to reach the rifle on the ground.

"You're damned right I have."

"I don't think so, Sheriff." Natalie's voice was accompanied by the ominous and unmistakable double click of a shotgun being racked. "Drop the gun or I'll blow you in half. And I'm too close to miss."

There was a sick look on Axelrod's face even as he blustered, "You won't shoot."

"Why? Because I'm a woman? Are you willing to bet your life

on that?" She stood near the truck's tailgate, cold and determined.

Unwilling to risk it, Axelrod lowered the pistol and held his hands out to the sides in a show of surrender. Beau immediately stepped forward and relieved him of the weapon, then backed up to cover him. For an instant, Natalie sagged against the side of the truck, hands shaking as she lowered the shotgun. Beau motioned her to his side. She stumbled a bit on the first step, then made a wide circle around the sheriff to join him.

"Nothing's changed," the sheriff told them. "I'll still have you for the murder of these two."

"I don't think so." Beau smiled and wagged the phone in his free hand. "I video-recorded your confession."

Natalie released a shaky laugh of relief. "It's really over," she murmured, and leaned against his side.

"All over," Beau confirmed, and brushed his lips over the top of her dark curls. "Better see what you can do for Sky."

"Of course." As she moved away, they both caught the telltale chop of an approaching helicopter.

EPILOGUE

Sky came home to a celebration. Bernice had baked one of her spectacular sheet-sized chocolate cakes, and Cecil, who ran the cookhouse, had pit-barbecued a steer. Will had invited all the hands and their families to come by the house, share a Saturday afternoon picnic, and give Sky their good wishes.

After almost two weeks in the hospital, all Sky had really wanted was to get back to training his horses. But the doctors, whose skill had pulled him back from the brink of death, had insisted that he rest. And, truth be told, he was secretly touched by the warmth of the Tylers' welcome. It was almost like he was family.

Some things had changed in his absence. Spring had deepened into the beginning of a hot, dry summer. Erin's foal was growing into a strong young colt. Beau and Natalie were engaged and planning a fall wedding. Both of them had been cleared of all charges.

The FBI, who'd taken over the investigation after Axelrod's arrest, had interviewed Sky in the hospital. Despite the blood loss and pain after the shooting, Sky had been conscious the whole time and had heard everything. He'd been able to corroborate Beau's and Natalie's stories down to the last detail.

Ironically, Stella Rawlins had been interrogated and released. Despite some suspicious circumstances, no evidence could be found to link her to any illegal activity. Whatever Axelrod knew about her, he was saving it for a likely plea bargain.

By the end of the afternoon, Sky was worn out. It felt good just to sit on his own porch with Jasper and the dog for company and watch the day fade into twilight. Gazing down toward the paddock, he could see Beau and Natalie walking hand in hand along the fence line. They paused to enjoy a lingering kiss. If ever two people deserved a long, love-filled life together, it was those two, Sky thought. They'd earned their right to happiness. "So how are you really feeling?" Jasper asked.

"Not bad, just tired. I wasn't expecting a party."

"I know you weren't. But the family wanted to let you know how glad they were to have you back. You like to think people don't notice you much. But you're appreciated—a helluva lot more than you realize."

Sky shifted in the chair, feeling the ache in his healing wound. He was still on antibiotics and painkillers and had been cautioned not to ride. Might as well tell him not to breathe.

"I still can't believe Will and Beau gave me blood," he said, remembering how Beau had joked afterward about their being blood brothers now.

Jasper's gaze narrowed. "You're lucky they had your blood type, since the hospital was almost out of it. AB isn't all that common." Reaching behind his back, he drew out the manila envelope Sky had given him for safekeeping. "It's time, Sky," he said. "Open it."

Sky's hands shook as he slid a finger under the sealed flap. Jasper pretended to look the other way as he drew out a two-page document. His breath caught.

The first page was a deed to one hundred acres of land. Bull Tyler's signature was at the bottom, notarized by the lawyer who'd read the will. The name at the top, on the line for the new owner of the property, was his own.

The second page was a legal description of the land, with a map showing its location. Sky recognized it at once. It had belonged to a neighboring ranch on the east border of the Rimrock—prime pastureland with a creek, perfect for horses, a few cows, and maybe a modest home. Sky had ridden that way many times and admired it. But never in a lifetime had he dreamed it would be his.

Jasper nudged him. "Didn't I tell you it wasn't a Pandora's box? What have you got to say?"

Sky couldn't answer. His throat was locked tight, swollen with emotion. What had he done to deserve such a gift? And what would he do with it?

Tactfully, Jasper gave him time. Several minutes of silence passed before the old man spoke, changing the subject.

"Well, with Axelrod out of the way, it looks like Garn Prescott's going to be up for another term in Congress."

Sky was relieved that the conversation had shifted.

"Not that I pay much attention to politics, but is Will still trying to make peace with the man?"

"On and off. But you might find this interesting. Prescott's daughter is with him for the summer. The girl's an accountant, and a damned good one from what I hear. Beau's hired her part-time to help him set up a spreadsheet for the ranch."

Sky managed a chuckle. It hurt a little. "Prescott's got a daughter? That's a surprise. Hope she's better-looking than Garn."

Jasper's eyes twinkled. "You can judge for yourself. That's her car coming up the drive now."

Sky followed the old man's gaze. He stifled a groan as he sensed trouble blowing in like a wild summer storm.

The car pulling up to the house was an all-too-familiar sleek black Corvette.